Some Sweet Day

Some Sweet Day

A Novel

Jennie Hansen

Covenant Comunications, Inc.

Cover Design: Mike Johnson

Book Design: Ryan Knowlton

Published by Covenant Communications, Inc.
American Fork, Utah

Printed in the United States of America
First Printing: March 1997

06 05 04 03 02 01 00 99 98 97   10 9 8 7 6 5 4 3 2 1

ISBN 1-57734-089-2

Library of Congress Catalog-in-Publication Data

Hansen, Jennie L., 1943-
     Some Sweet Day / Jennie Hansen.
         p. cm.
     ISBN 1-57734-089-2
     I. Title.
     PS3558.A51293S66   1997
     813' .54--dc21   97-5632
                                                                    CIP

Author's Note

As a child I would lie awake at night listening to the radio in the next room. A song from that time has stayed in my memory through the years, and I still recall the voice, but not the man, who promised the lamb and the lion would lie down together and there would be peace in the valley some day . . . some sweet day.

This book is dedicated to all those who strive to end hatred, violence, and bigotry. Especially it is dedicated to my son "Bobby" Hansen and his fiancee, Esther Vaz, who have enhanced my awareness of the beauty in differences and the ugliness of everyday bigotry. I love you both dearly.

There are others whom I need to thank for their honest criticism, suggestions, and support. My critique group—Kathy Lloyd, Sherry Brown (Lewis), Deloy Barnes, Darrel Gerard, and Heather Horrocks—who were determined I get it right; the Chapman Branch Library staff, who saw me through some difficult times; my son-in-law Earl Rich for his expertise with guns; and always my husband, Boyd, who clears the decks and lets me write. Thanks to all of you. When the day comes that there is no more sorrow and sadness, and peace comes to all the valleys of the world, it will be because of caring people like you.

One

"He's dead, Carly."

"He is."

"What's dead?" Carly picked up a shirt and shook it before pegging it to the line. She'd helped the children bury enough birds and frogs since they came to Steeple Mountain to take such announcements in stride.

"A man." Petra's voice held an anxious note.

"A big bear." Daniel danced with excitement.

"Daniel . . . Petra . . . ," she said in a warning tone as she picked up another shirt, snapped it in the breeze, and took another clothespin from the pouch at her waist.

"Honest, Aunt Carly." Petra's round face turned earnestly toward her. "Me'n Danny were playing by the ice house and Danny said he could beat me to the top of the hill and I said he couldn't."

"We ran all the way. Clear to the crooked pine tree and I beat."

"No, you didn't. It was a tie."

"Was not."

"That's enough. No fighting. Run along to the house and we'll have lunch as soon as I finish hanging up these clothes."

"But you have to come see the bear." Daniel's lip quivered.

Carly shuddered. She hoped the children were playing a game. She'd seen a few bears since she came to this wild, primitive area, but not upclose. She didn't like to think a bear might come near the cabin. "Where did you see it?" she asked cautiously.

"By the man," Petra explained patiently, as though Carly hadn't been paying attention.

The shirt slid from Carly's fingers. Her throat turned dry as she knelt before the children to look them carefully in the eye. "Is this a game, Petra? Is there really a man and a bear out there?" She inclined her head toward the vast wilderness of forested mountains.

Petra bobbed her head solemnly, sending her long yellow braids bouncing.

"Daniel, how do you know they're dead?"

"Petra said the bear might be just pretending to be dead and she wouldn't let me go down there. But we watched for a long time and neither one moved." The anxious blue eyes beneath blond Dutch boy bangs seemed to be asking for reassurance.

What had the children seen? At six and seven they had vivid imaginations. Could there really be a bear close to the cabin? A prickle of fear inched along her spine. And the man? There couldn't really be a dead man out there, could there? Mentally she accounted for those she knew who lived on the mountain. Josh would be coming down the river when he returned and Isaac had said the trappers had moved on. The men from the compound never ventured out alone.

She would have to go see. Perhaps she should wait for Josh. No, if the children's story was true and a man really lay unmoving on the other side of the hill, he might be unconscious rather than dead. Yes, she'd have to go. But what about the children? She didn't want them anywhere near a bear, but only they knew where they'd seen the man.

She felt a moment's irritation with the children. They should have stayed within the area their father had given them free rein to play in. A spurt of anger at her brother nearly choked her. At first the wilderness had been an exciting challenge and a welcome break from the terrors of the city, but lately he'd been leaving her and the children alone too much while he visited the compound. On the other hand, she knew she should have been watching them closer. She glared at the basket of wet laundry at her feet. Over the past few months Josh had changed, and roughing it wasn't fun anymore. After a full year on the mountain, she was tired of learning just how uncompromising the great Northwest could be.

"You two stay here. I'll be right back." Carly sprinted toward the cabin. She emerged seconds later with a rifle under one arm and a backpack containing first aid supplies slung over her shoulder. The children had probably imagined the whole thing, but she couldn't ignore the possibility that they really had seen something. "Okay, show me where you saw the man and the bear." She ushered the children toward the faint trail leading up the grassy slope. Nervously she tucked behind her ear a strand of hair loosened by a spring breeze blowing off the snowcapped mountain.

She hurried to keep pace with the children. "Not too fast," she cautioned.

Her trepidation increased as they approached the twisted pine tree at the top of the hill above where their cabin stood. Daniel reached the top first. He danced with excitement as he pointed down the opposite slope.

"See! There he is!"

Carly caught her breath. Two figures lay unmoving in the little valley where yesterday there had been only mountain lupine and the whisper of ancient pines. From here they certainly looked like a man and a bear. The man was closer. She could get to him without passing the bear.

"Stay here!" she admonished the children as she started forward.

"But Aunt Carly . . ."

"I want to go with you."

Turning about, she searched for an excuse convincing enough to keep the children from venturing any further. "Petra, Daniel, someone has to be the lookout. You have to watch so if the bear wakes up you can warn me."

Carly edged her way down the slope. This side was steeper and she had to clutch branches and rocks to keep from sliding. Large boulders made a straight descent impossible. She didn't like this. Not one bit. Nervously she glanced toward the man, but it was the bear that kept her fingers moving toward the safety catch on the gun. Noting the huge hunched back and the gleam of silver tipping its shaggy fur, she sucked in her breath. Grizzly. Moving toward a grizzly just out of hibernation had to be insane. It looked dead, but it might be injured or sleeping. She'd rather not be taking this kind of chance. But there was the man.

She considered walking a few steps past the man and discharging a couple of shots into the bear to make certain it was dead. But she couldn't see its head clearly and body shots might only arouse it. No, she didn't dare risk moving close enough for a clear head shot. Besides, there were Isaac's men to consider. They investigated every gun shot on the mountain, and she didn't want to alert them before she knew whether or not this man was one of them. If he was one of the compound men, where was his partner? She shuddered at the possibility there might be another dead or injured man out there somewhere. And if he wasn't part of Isaac's army, it would be best to keep quiet about the presence of a stranger.

When she reached the inert man lying face down in the grass, she crouched at his side, resting her weight on the balls of her feet. She didn't want to be caught kneeling if the grizzly suddenly moved toward her. With one eye on the bear, she placed the rifle on the ground between herself and the man.

She checked the pulse point in his neck. His skin felt warm and flexible. The rhythm of life throbbed against her fingers. She breathed a sigh of relief. He was alive. Whoever he might be, he was alive. From what she had heard of grizzly attacks, survival was some kind of miracle. Anxiously her eyes returned to the still form of the bear, then back to the man.

A pool of blood spread out near his left shoulder. The front side of him wouldn't be pretty. But no matter what the bear had done, she'd have to cope. She'd coped with everything else this land had thrown at her in the past year. She'd do what she had to now. First she'd have to turn him over. It wouldn't be easy. He appeared easily six feet tall and sturdily built, but there wasn't anyone else. She was a nurse. She knew what to do. Taking a deep breath and glancing once more across the clearing, she slipped her hands under the unconscious form.

Amazingly the bear had only struck him once. The swipe of a powerful claw had laid open his shoulder. She glimpsed white bone through the congealing blood. His own weight against the grass had kept him from bleeding to death.

"His fingers moved."

Startled, Carly turned her head. Daniel stood beside her, his eyes round and wide.

"I told you to stay put." She looked toward the bear, then glanced around for Petra.

"Petra stayed by the tree. It only takes one person to be lookout. I came to help."

Carly's hands moved automatically, pulling out antiseptic and gauze while she spoke to her nephew. "You should have minded, but since you're here, stay right where you are. Don't take your eyes off that grizzly. If he so much as twitches, yell. I can't watch that bear and patch up this man at the same time."

She worked quickly cleaning and stitching the wound. Each time her needle penetrated the well-muscled flesh beneath her fingers, a quiver rippled across his broad chest. Thank goodness he was unconscious. Being young and in good physical condition were points in his favor. She estimated his age to be around thirty. The deep sun-bronze of his skin indicated he spent much of his time outdoors.

Carly rocked back on her heels to survey her handiwork. It was the best she could do under the circumstances. He needed a doctor, but she knew how little chance he had of ever seeing one. The nearest doctor was a hundred miles away, and though Isaac owned a plane, his suspicion of strangers extended to doctors. His people went without medical care other than the occasional day she spent at the compound infirmary.

She'd have to find a way to get the injured man to the cabin. When Josh came he would know if the man was one of Isaac's. If so, he could put him in a canoe and take him back to his friends. She'd worry later about what to do with him if he turned out to be an outsider. She reached for a bottle of alcohol. A liberal splash now, she thought grimly as she poured the liquid over the wound, might be her last opportunity to ward off infection.

"Sheesh!" The man's body jerked. Carly's eyes darted to the face she hadn't really seen until now. Heavy brows drew together and his eyes were squeezed shut, revealing small lines at the corners. A dark mustache almost covered his upper lip, which twisted in a grimace. His forehead was wide, his chin firm, and his dark hair was cropped short as if to hide its tendency to curl. A few white hairs mingled with the black in his carefully trimmed sideburns. An unfamiliar jolt held her breath suspended, then her lungs let the air burst forth in a rush. For just a moment the stranger hadn't appeared to be a stranger.

Most of the men at the compound sported short haircuts and wore camouflage fatigues, and even jeans, especially when they first arrived, but Carly knew she hadn't seen him at the compound before. Something about him seemed different.

His eyes opened and she found herself staring into their incredibly blue depths. Blue eyes were the norm both at the compound and in her own Scandinavian family, but this was the deep blue of the summer bluebells that bloomed on the slope below the cabin. They held her mesmerized for long seconds.

"Aunt Carly! The bear! It's moving." Daniel's fingers dug into her leg through the thick denim of her pants.

Carly surged to her feet. She shoved the boy behind her with one hand while the other reached for the gun she'd placed in the grass. It was gone. Fear ripped through her. She shot a frantic glance toward the bear then her eyes swept to the injured man. He no longer lay on his back at her feet. He'd rolled to a prone position with the gun snuggled against his shoulder, the barrel resting on a broken tree limb.

"That bear should be dead. What exactly did you see, son?" The man never took his eyes from the mound of fur less than thirty feet away.

"See! It's moving." Daniel pointed.

A gust of wind blew through the clearing. It drove the great bear's fur into peaks, then flattened them like meadow grass. The man slowly lowered his head and leaned it against the butt of the rifle.

Carly released the breath she hadn't been aware she was holding. "You shouldn't have moved, but thank you," she whispered.

"What're you doing—alone out here—with a kid?" The words rasped through pain-clenched teeth.

"Our cabin is just over the hill." She hurried toward him, concerned that he might have reopened his wound. She knelt beside him and gently urged him onto his back so she could examine the bandage for fresh blood. "Are you alone? Was there anyone else?"

"No . . . No one . . . You're not from . . . the compound?"

"No. Don't try to talk. You've lost quite a bit of blood. You need to rest."

"How're we going to get him back to the cabin, Aunt Carly?"

Carly paused to consider. "I don't know," she said with a slight frown. "Maybe you and Petra can walk on one side of him and he can lean on me."

"I'll walk," growled the stranger.

Daniel took his eyes from the bear to give the man a look of disgust. " 'Course you can walk. I meant the bear."

"That bear can stay right where he is until Captain Isaac's men come get him. I certainly don't want him anywhere near the cabin."

"But Aunt Carly—"

"That's enough, Daniel. The bear is staying here, and we're leaving as fast as we can. See that stick over there?" She pointed to a sturdy tree branch lying on the ground. "Give it to the man."

"Name's Wolf."

She turned back to her patient. He'd pulled himself to his feet and stood leaning against a sapling. Rivulets of perspiration ran down his face. His tattered shirt clung to damp skin, and a flush colored his cheekbones.

"Here!" She quickly moved to his side. Her shoulder fit under his arm and she circled his waist. "Daniel, bring that stick!"

The boy thrust the stick at the man. "Wolf is an animal. You're a man."

The name didn't surprise Carly. All the men at the compound had animal names or names from the Bible.

"Okay, take a step," she coached.

"I can walk."

He moved his feet, and the arduous journey began. Every few steps they stopped to rest. Wolf braced himself against rocks or trees for brief respites then moved on. Sweat ran down Carly's back. Before they reached the top of the hill, she found herself supporting more and more of his weight. Rocks and brush became major obstacles threatening to trip them. When they finally reached the crooked pine, she helped him sit down. His head drooped in exhaustion and she wondered if he'd be able to make it the rest of the way. The children stared openly at him. Fatigued, Carly lowered herself to the ground. Every muscle in her body ached, and she was hot and sticky. Through her lashes she saw her patient shiver. Shock. She'd have to get him to the cabin quickly.

She couldn't help seeing the irony. Just that morning she'd argued with Josh about the bachelors from the compound he thought she should get to know. He wanted her and the kids to go with him, and she'd refused.

"There's quite a few eligible men there who'd like to meet you," Josh said gruffly.

"I'm not interested," she told him with a touch of defiance. "I'm ready to return to the city where I can start nursing again. I'd like to see the children in school."

"Isaac offered to let you set up a clinic at the compound," Josh reminded her. "If you weren't so stubborn, you could marry one of Isaac's men, continue your career, and raise a family of your own."

At that, Carly had told him she didn't want anything to do with any man on the mountain, personally or as a patient. And here she was half killing herself to get one of them back to her cabin. But what could she do? She couldn't leave an injured man to fend for himself.

Wolf watched the woman through slitted eyes. She was practical and tough. Yet when she brushed stray wisps of straw-colored hair away from her damp skin with the back of her forearm, he saw a soft vulnerability that didn't seem to fit the woman who'd stitched his hide back together in a no-nonsense manner and who toted a rifle like she meant business. She was younger than he first thought, too. Closer to mid-twenties than the thirties her competency had led him to suspect.

He needed her help, but he'd have to be careful. Even if she didn't belong to the compound, she must have some connection or Isaac would have chased her away. Until he knew what that might be, he couldn't take any chances. The rest of the country considered this Northwest wilderness government property, but Jerome Isaac claimed Steeple Mountain and everything around it as his "kingdom." If anyone else lived here it had to be through his sufferance. A surge of anger washed through Wolf. What was wrong with Isaac to let a woman and two kids wander around alone out here? What if it had been one of them who'd stumbled on that wounded bear?

Wolf's eyes moved slowly back down the hill to the crumpled heap that a few hours ago had been a magnificent king of bears. It had been shot with some kind of automatic weapon. Whoever did it hadn't had the regard of an ordinary poacher to hang around to claim the hide. Of course this hide was worthless, shredded as it was by several rows of bullet holes. The bozo had walked off, leaving the bear to die slowly and rot. Wolf had been so angry over the needless waste he'd gotten careless. He'd walked right up to the dead bear. Only it wasn't dead. Not quite.

"Do you think you can make it a little further?" The woman was on her feet again. With the aid of the heavy stick and her arm about his waist, Wolf pulled himself upright. Little dots danced before his eyes, then slowly his vision cleared. Looking ahead he saw a grassy slope that led down to a log cabin sheltered by a stand of pine. A shed leaned against one end of the cabin and another stood a short distance away. Firewood and chickens. He could barely make out a log frame and door abutting a jagged cliff. He knew a cellar or ice house would be behind the door. No doubt a small stream surfaced in there as well. To one side of the cabin he could see a clothesline with a few clothes flapping in the breeze. They looked too large to belong to Carly or the kids. So she didn't live out here alone. There was a man. That should have made him feel better, but it didn't.

Beyond the cabin he could see the river. A short dock extended from the bank, but he saw no sign of a boat or canoe. A thin wisp of smoke curled from the chimney of the cabin. In early June a fire would still be needed all day inside the thick log walls. Suddenly he found thoughts of a fire appealing. The sun still shone, but he shivered. He took a step. His feet didn't seem to get the message his brain sent. The ground came rushing up to meet him. Falling didn't hurt. Everything was soft and dark. From far away he heard Carly yell for Daniel to get a blanket.

He came to in the cabin. He moved his head slightly and knew he lay on a pillow. Another had been tucked beneath his injured shoulder. A thick quilt cocooned his body and his eyes caught the flicker of a fire. He lay on the floor before a wide stone hearth. He'd roused enough a couple of times on the way down the mountain to know Carly had rolled him in a blanket and dragged him down the slope. He wasn't certain whether the kids had helped or gotten in her way, but he did know he lay on the floor because she lacked the strength to lift him onto a bed.

His eyes drifted shut again, but he didn't sleep. He knew he'd lost a lot of blood and wondered how big a chunk the bear had taken out of him. He had no more strength than a baby. Lucky for him Carly had come along. He knew she'd stitched him up, but he couldn't precisely remember her doing it. There'd been a red haze and a lot of pain, then a clear picture of an angel bending over him. Tendrils of pale hair escaping from the crown on her head fell forward to frame her face as she concentrated on his flaming shoulder. The next thing he knew, liquid fire splashed against him and the kid yelled that the bear was moving.

The quiet sank into his consciousness. He wondered where everyone had gone. An inch at a time, he levered himself up on one elbow to look around. The room was small. It boasted a couple of well-padded pine chairs and cushions covered a matching bench. Blue and white gingham curtains partially obscured a small paned window. A table with a bench on either side of it resembled a picnic table. Pine cupboards filled one corner of the room, and a washstand and stove finished the room's furnishings. He eyed the stove thought-fully. It wasn't the great Aga of frontier fame, but a smaller version with just two lids and an oven that wouldn't hold more than two loaves of bread. He could imagine Carly baking bread—or running a corporation. The woman was a puzzle. Why on earth would she choose to live like her grandmother?

Summer people? He dismissed the idea immediately. Tourists didn't come to Steeple Mountain. A few hardy backpackers might, but Isaac would soon show them the error of their ways. A handful of die-hard hermits, miners, and back-to-nature types made their homes out here. Most of them predated the compound. They tended to cut a wide swath around Isaac, and he mostly ignored them. Mostly.

Gut-wrenching sickness swamped Wolf's stomach. Pictures of

the poachers' camp swam before his eyes. He'd never had any sympathy for poachers, but no man deserved to die like that. He'd never get the picture of those men out of his mind. Especially the half-breed. He clenched his eyes shut in a vain attempt to block out memory. Seconds later he opened them again to search for distraction from his thoughts.

Opposite the fireplace he noticed a closed door. Bedroom, he speculated. Glancing up he found the expected loft. He also found four wide blue eyes staring into his. Broad grins split the children's faces.

"Come on down." He motioned for the children to join him.

"Uh-uh."

"Aunt Carly said she'd nail our hides to the cabin wall if we took one step down the ladder," Daniel informed him solemnly.

"She isn't in a good mood," Petra added.

Wolf hid a smile. He just bet Carly wasn't in a good mood. Probably worn to a frazzle trying to keep up with these two, and then the added chore of dragging him down the mountain.

"We're supposed to take a nap, but we're not sleepy." Petra's round face made clear the injustice of Aunt Carly's order.

"I'm too big for naps." Daniel's voice revealed his indignation.

"I'll bet you are." Wolf tried to smile. When did smiling get to be such an effort? He eased himself flat on the quilt again. His shoulder was on fire. He ached all over and he couldn't remember ever being so weak. His eyelids drooped. Just before his eyes closed, a rifle caught his eye. It rested on two pegs above the fireplace.

His eyes jerked open. Pain receded to the back of his mind. Where was his rifle? It had gone flying from his hands when the bear raised up to make that one last furious sweep. What if Isaac's men came back for the bear? They'd find the rifle and start asking questions. Somehow he had to get up, get that gun, hide it. He struggled to a sitting position. The room tilted crazily. He had to get to his feet. His hand stretched toward a chair for support. He missed by only an inch.

Shadows played across the wall and flickered against the ceiling when Wolf next awoke. Something smelled good. Bread baking. And chocolate cake. He moved his head cautiously. The little girl stood on a low stool by the stove with a wooden spoon in her hand. She stirred something in a large kettle with enthusiasm. He saw no sign of Carly or Daniel. Perhaps he could make it to the door without the kid noticing.

He didn't try to stand. Instead he rolled over, then eased his way to a crawling position. He quickly discovered his injured shoulder wouldn't bear any weight. In a three-point scrabble he edged toward the door. Voices stopped him. He hunkered behind a chair. Through the open door he heard the rumble of a man's voice, then Daniel's.

"Aunt Carly's gone to the ice house. She needed stuff for supper."

"Why didn't you get it for her?"

"She told me to gather the eggs."

"You should have done that a long time ago." The man's voice sounded impatient. "Shouldn't she be back by now?"

"She said she had to get the clothes off the clothesline, too, and she might go up Short Creek for watercress."

Wolf heard what sounded like a boot striking against the front step. He tensed. "Still mad, huh?" the voice asked.

"Yeah. She doesn't want to live here anymore, Dad."

"Come on, Peterson." Another voice sounded from further away.

The closer voice called out a reply then dropped to a conspiratorial whisper. "Look, Daniel. I can't wait around. A couple of Captain Isaac's men shot a big bear this morning a few miles up the river. It got away, but it couldn't have traveled far. We're going to camp tonight where they last sighted it, then as soon as it's light we'll track it. Tell Carly I'll be back sometime tomorrow."

Wolf held his breath. As soon as the kid told his dad about the bear, Isaac's men would be swarming all over the place.

"Aunt Carly's gonna be really mad."

"I know."

"Peterson!"

"Coming! Bye, Daniel. Remind Carly to bar the door tonight."

The sound of disappearing boots grew fainter. Wolf breathed a sigh of relief. He could rest a couple of hours, then sneak out after Carly and the kids settled down for the night, find his rifle, and be miles away by dawn. He made his trembling way back to the pillows and quilts on the floor where he collapsed against their softness. He didn't get it. Why hadn't Daniel told his father about the bear? About him? Come to think of it, why did the fool run off and leave a woman and kids on their own when he knew a wounded grizzly was running amok somewhere nearby?

"Daniel!" Petra shook her spoon at her younger brother. "You didn't tell Daddy supper was ready. He shouldn't go hunting bears without eating first."

Wolf watched Petra's eyes grow round. She opened her mouth, but no words came out. A quick glance at Daniel, who had just entered the cabin, and he saw an identical expression.

"You didn't tell Daddy about the bear." The little girl made a statement, not an accusation. "Daddy and Captain Isaac are looking for that bear."

"He's my bear!"

"They'll find him and take him away."

"No! I found him. He's mine!"

"He's mine, too!"

"We've got to hide him."

"How're we going to hide a grizzly bear?"

"We could put him in a blanket like Aunt Carly did the wolf-man. We could pull him to the river cave."

"He's pretty big."

"I'll get a big blanket."

Wolf made a strangling sound deep in his throat. He'd have to stop them. No way two kids could budge a bear that size; no worry about that. But he couldn't take the chance that the carcass might have company by now. Just the smell of bear would keep most critters away for a while, but sooner or later scavengers would move in. Steeple Mountain was no place for two little kids in the daylight. And at night . . . He shuddered.

"Josh?" He hadn't heard Carly's approach. She stood in the doorway, her hands on her hips. Her eyes scanned the room. "Where's your dad? I saw his canoe on the river quite awhile ago."

"He went with Captain Isaac. He said to tell you he'll be back tomorrow."

The cabin door slammed shut with an angry thump. *I wouldn't want to be in Josh's shoes.* Wolf suspected the other man had made a tactical error he'd soon regret. Carly was mad clean through. Her eyes sparked. Her back was ramrod straight and her fists bunched at her side. She muttered something under her breath he didn't hear. She picked up a tray and started toward him. He suspected her pride would be hurt if she knew he'd been watching her. Also he might learn more if he pretended to be asleep. Quickly he closed his eyes.

He willed himself not to flinch when she touched his shoulder. Her touch was surprisingly gentle as she removed his bandage in spite of her anger. Strong fingers smoothed some kind of ointment along the line of stitches. A thick pad followed, which she taped in place. Was it his imagination or did her fingers linger a moment against his cheek? He opened his eyes a crack to watch her walk away and rejoin the children on the other side of the room.

"Daniel didn't tell Daddy we found somebody," Petra reported importantly.

"He'd say I was making up stories if I told him we found a wolf and a bear," Daniel defended himself.

Carly didn't respond to the children's comments, but appeared distracted. She made short work of feeding them and hustling them off to get ready for bed. She refused to listen to their protests. Inside Wolf could feel a slow grin try to break free. She reminded him of his mother, who could get four rambunctious boys off to bed in no time. Ma never took any sass either.

"You can sleep in your dad's bed tonight, Petra, so Daniel won't be alone in the loft." Carly tapped their pajama-clad bottoms and sent them up the ladder. She gave Petra permission to read one story aloud to Daniel. "Make it short, Petra," she cautioned. "I don't know when we'll be able to get more batteries for your lantern. And don't forget to say your prayers."

From his bed on the floor, Wolf noticed flames leap against the chimney of the lantern on the table. Evidently she saved the batteries for the children's light. Carly moved back across the room to the stove. She ladled a generous portion of the mixture in the pot into a bowl, tore off a chunk of warm bread and placed it on a plate. She added a slab of cake and walked toward him.

"Can you feed yourself?"

"Yes." She'd probably known all along he was awake. He braced himself on his right elbow and levered himself to a sitting position. It was easier this time. Carly placed the food on the floor beside him, then without a word returned to the table to eat her own supper.

The food was plain, but he'd never eaten better. When had he eaten last? Sometime yesterday. But that didn't count. He'd lost it all when he found the poachers' camp. He forced his mind away from the blood and the image of the half-breed's body hanging from a tree. Instead he watched the woman. Light from the Coleman lantern bathed her face in a golden glow.

She never glanced his way. He noticed how tired she looked. And troubled. He felt something stir deep inside. *Watch it,* he told himself. *Don't get involved.* He had a job to do.

He'd wait until she and the kids were settled down, then he'd go after his rifle. He'd like to wait until morning, but he wasn't sure he had that much time. He'd lucked out so far. Carly had sewed him up. Josh had been in too much of a hurry to chase bear to set foot in the cabin. And the kids were so possessive of that grizzly that they hadn't told their father about it. But if he didn't get to his rifle before Isaac did, his luck was going to run out. He'd have to listen for the kids, too. He had a hunch they had their own plan to sneak out after Carly went to bed. He'd wait until after they made their attempt, squelch it, then go after his gun. Once he had the gun, he'd just keep going.

"Would you like a cup of coffee?"

He'd been so wrapped up in his own thoughts, her movement toward him with the steaming cup took him by surprise.

"Sure." He reached for the cup. Gratefully he took a deep swallow. "Thank you, ma'am. That was a fine meal." She sank to the floor beside him and smiled encouragingly as he drained the cup. He found his hand unsteady as he handed it back to her.

"You should sleep well now." She smiled at him. "I added something to your coffee to block the pain and help you sleep."

Panic struck his heart. He had to tell her what the kids

planned, but the warning tangled in his throat. A deep, soft blackness rushed toward him and he couldn't get the words past his thick tongue. Ma stood over him shaking her head. She didn't approve of drinking coffee, said it was bad for him. He wished he'd listened.

Two

Carly stared into the darkness. She was so tired her arms and legs were like lead weights, but she couldn't go to sleep. A painful ache lay deep in her chest, just under her breastbone. It wasn't so much a physical pain as fear and regret. More and more she suspected she'd made a mistake leaving Los Angeles to come to this mountain. Something was terribly wrong here.

She'd been skeptical when Josh said he had quit his job and bought a remote cabin high in the mountains. He'd made up his mind to take his children far away from inner-city violence and the vicious gangs that plagued the city. He'd wanted Carly to go with them, and she'd let him persuade her. After Anna's death the children had become fearful and withdrawn, afraid of strangers and sudden sounds. Carly had stopped walking the few blocks from work at the hospital to Josh's small apartment where she'd moved to help him with the children. Josh had become bitter and angry, and Carly thought the change of environment might help them heal.

Something bumped against the front door. The hair on the back of her neck became stiff and bristly. She could hear a faint scratching. Had the bear revived? Could it break down the door? Nervously she edged out of bed. She paused as the sound came again. A sort of thump followed by a scraping reached her ears. She straightened her spine. No bear was going to get the children—or her patient.

She reached for the heavy flashlight she kept beside her bed. She'd need it to find her way past her sleeping patient to get the rifle above the fireplace. She moved soundlessly on bare feet. At her touch the bedroom door opened wider, and her flashlight beam centered on the cabin door.

"Aunt Carly!" Standing on a chair, Petra and Daniel looked back at her. Their hands froze on the heavy door bar.

"Get away from that door!" She rushed forward and clasped them both to her. The flashlight slid to the floor, casting eery shadows on the wall. Hugging the children to her, she ran her hands down their backs, as though checking for injuries. Suddenly she tensed. Her hands felt denim, not soft flannel. The children were completely dressed.

She glanced toward the door. Nothing was trying to get in; the children were trying to get out! The big quilt Anna had made for the bed she shared with Josh lay on the floor. Where were the children taking their mother's quilt?

Carly stayed on her knees and tightened her grip on each child's arm.

She turned shocked eyes toward her small niece. "You know you're not allowed outside after dark. What are you doing?"

Petra stared back with a resigned expression, as if Carly should know the answer to such a simple question.

"We have to." Daniel spoke matter-of-factly. "If we don't hide our bear, Captain Isaac will take him."

"Oh, Daniel." She hugged him close. "The bear is dead. Pretty soon he'll smell terrible and other animals will come to eat him. Some of those animals are dangerous. If Isaac wants that old bear, let him have it."

"Couldn't you fix him? You could sew him up like you did the wolf-man." Tears glistened in his eyes.

"I'm afraid not." Carly shook her head.

"Sometimes it's too late." Petra spoke with a painful knowledge beyond her seven years that told Carly the child was thinking of her mother. "Isaac's soldiers shot him, so he's dead, and nothing can make him alive again."

Daniel's shoulder went stiff beneath Carly's arm. "Did Isaac's soldiers shoot my mama?"

"No! Oh, no," she whispered and rocked the small body against her breast. She wished the children didn't know their mother had been shot, but in all the anger and confusion of that nightmare night, too much had been said in their presence. She closed her eyes, remembering the night she and Anna had left the hospital together a little before midnight. She'd planned to stay the night and be there the next day to watch Petra and Daniel while Josh and Anna went house hunting.

Anna had been excited about buying a house, and she'd chattered about plans as they walked. They'd almost reached their apartment building when they suddenly found themselves surrounded by a dozen jeering teenagers. The boys grabbed the women's purses and dumped the contents on the sidewalk searching for money. When they discovered only a few quarters and dimes, they turned their anger toward the women. A heavy arm grabbed Carly from behind, and she felt a sharp point press against the side of her neck. Terror held her nearly catatonic, but her eyes were glued to her sister-in-law who had been shoved to the sidewalk by a huge boy in baggy pants and a black T-shirt with his head shaved except for a shaggy top knot. Anna screamed and twisted as her tormenter ripped her uniform and laughed at her struggle to free herself.

Suddenly Josh was there, yelling and swinging his fists, while a siren screamed in the distance. The boy holding Carly shoved her viciously aside, and she fell to the sidewalk. Several heavy, high-topped shoes slammed into her crumpled body before the gang began to run down the street. Carly watched in horror as Anna's tormentor reached inside his jacket and pulled out a gun. He took deliberate aim, then discharged his gun into Anna's chest before firing a second time toward Josh.

Carly would never be able to shut out the anguish that twisted her brother's face moments later as he held his wife's lifeless body in his arms. No matter what it took, she vowed that night, she would keep her brother's—and Anna's—children safe from the senseless violence that had taken their mother's life.

Carly looked at Daniel and Petra. "We're not strong enough to move that bear," she tried to explain. "We couldn't get him on the blanket, and if we did we couldn't pull it. Besides, I don't think we want to let that old bear get your mama's pretty quilt all dirty. I know your daddy wouldn't like it. He loves that quilt as much as you two love the little ones she made for you."

Petra started to cry. "I'll put it back," she said. Picking up the quilt, she hurried up the ladder and put it on her father's bed. In a few minutes she was back. "Can I sleep with you tonight, Aunt Carly? I don't want to sleep alone." She rubbed a fist against her eyes.

"Did Isaac shoot the wolf-man?" Daniel demanded to know.

"No, of course not, Daniel. The bear clawed him." Carly was appalled. Why did the boy assume Isaac had shot either his mother or the stranger? She knew Daniel didn't like Isaac; she didn't either. Still, she'd been shocked several times in the past week by the depth of the six-year-old's anger toward the compound leader.

"Petra, you can sleep in my bed with me tonight. Daniel can sleep in yours. We'll all be in the same room." She picked up the flashlight.

"Isaac shot Frank."

"What!" Carly nearly dropped the flashlight. "Isaac didn't shoot Frank. Frank and the other trappers just went away. With us and the compound people on the mountain, it was just too crowded for Frank and his friend."

"No, Isaac shot him." Daniel was insistent. "The gun made a big noise, then Frank was bleeding in lots of places. He called Isaac a bad word, then Luther slapped him. They tied him up and made him walk to the boat, but he kept falling down."

"You're making it up!" Petra stopped with her hands on her hips to glare at Daniel. "You were just mad 'cause I wouldn't go to the falls with you that day."

"I'm not making it up!" Daniel stamped his foot. "I saw them. I was going to the falls, but I found a tree the lightning breaked open, so I climbed up to look inside. Lots of branches were in the way and it took a long time. I was sitting in the hole when Frank and Two-Toe Johnny came along with Isaac and Luther behind them. Frank tried to run away so Isaac shot him. They was mean to Two-Toe Johnny, too. They put a rope on his sore foot and pulled him right through the weeds and dirt to the boat."

Carly stared at the boy. "Daniel, did you tell your father about this?" she asked. She wouldn't put such behavior past Isaac or some of his men, since they made no secret of their contempt for the old man who was part Indian, but Daniel did make up stories. Carly had fallen for his wild tales more than once.

"He didn't believe me," Daniel said. "He said if I told anybody else he'd blister my hide. Are you going to tell him I told?"

"No. Go to bed." She felt achingly weary. Mechanically she helped the children undress and sat on the side of the big double bed, where she usually slept alone, and watched to make certain they fell asleep. Once again her mind filled with uncertainty. She wished she could persuade Josh to leave Steeple Mountain. At first the mountain had seemed to help them heal. The children had thrived, becoming strong and confident again. During the summer Josh had gained some kind of comfort from the hard work. The solitude had been welcome then, but during the winter he'd become restless.

Cabin fever hadn't bothered Carly or the children as it did Josh. She'd been proud of their self-sufficiency and enjoyed the new challenges. They'd had a few visits from prospectors and learned that a couple of trappers, old Frank Cohen and Two-Toe Johnny, claimed a cabin a few miles downstream. All winter the trappers had shown up about once a week with venison steaks and a hankering for biscuits. The children loved the attention the men showered on them and were enthralled with the old Indian's many versions of how he lost three toes and became Two-Toe Johnny.

In the late fall Josh told her he'd noticed a large group of men building a fort about five miles upstream where the river widened to form a small lake. It was only partially enclosed when the snows started, but the group stayed and continued to work on it as the snow deepened. Josh visited the compound several times through the winter. He told her their leader was a preacher, and sometimes Josh stayed for church services, but Carly didn't visit the compound until early spring.

At the time she had been excited over the prospect of taking the children to church. In the months they'd been on the mountain she'd found herself thinking about God and finding him in the majestic natural beauty around her. Slowly she'd reached a kind of peace with Anna's memory. She hoped that attending church services would complete the healing process for all of them, but what she saw there made her uneasy. There were at least fifty heavily armed men roaming around the compound, and they spoke of reenforcements arriving shortly.

Josh introduced her to Captain Isaac, a man who made her skin crawl. Isaac smiled and shook her hand, and Carly fought the urge to wipe her hands on the legs of her jeans. She guessed he might be forty-five, possibly a year or two older, with silver hair and chilling blue eyes. She wanted to leave, but Josh insisted they stay to hear him preach.

Isaac came alive as he took his place before the people. His voice started out low and seductive and grew in urgency. The crowd swayed toward him, and Carly felt swept along in their fervor. She knew a rising horror as he whispered of cities taken over by Blacks. His voice rose, decrying the plague of murderers and thieves who invaded the country from the south. He shouted his wrath at the evil Asians swarming across the nation spreading mysterious diseases and displacing rightful heirs to America's riches. Then came the promises. Soon his people would rise in power to destroy the impostors. They would form a pure nation high in the mountains. Others of the superior race would join them until their borders spread to reclaim the promised land.

Carly cringed at the fanatical approval sweeping through the crowd. The peace and closeness to God she'd felt in her little valley didn't exist here. She didn't have to be told to know Isaac reigned with absolute power over these people. Deep within her something resisted the hate and violence disguised by his hypnotic voice as God's will. As if he could feel her resistance, Isaac's eyes fell on her. With one look, he conveyed the message that he expected complete obedience from her as well.

A woman's voice rose in a high, keening wail. Carly turned her head to see a small group of women and children huddled to one side of the crowd. A few looked as strong and militant as their men, while some stood quietly with heads bowed. One woman, hardly more than a teenager, stood out as she swayed and sobbed in praise of Isaac. Carly felt pity tinged with disgust sweep through her.

Making up her mind to find out more about the strange assortment of women and children, Carly tried to befriend them over the next few weeks, but the children mostly stayed out of sight and the women in their plain, long cotton dresses viewed her with contempt, making her feel cheap and brazen in her jeans and oversized sweater.

That day marked the beginning of the arguments between Josh and Carly. Josh reminded her that their parents had taken them to church when they were children. When he insisted it would be good for Petra and Daniel to attend Captain Isaac's sermons, Carly had objected hotly, scorning Isaac's zealous pronouncements.

"The man is evil," she had argued. "He doesn't know a thing about the Jesus we learned about in Sunday School."

"What about you?" Josh had said accusingly. "Isaac's invited you to help out in the infirmary, and you won't even look at it. Doesn't sound like you remember anything you learned about Jesus." At that remark, Carly reluctantly agreed to work in the clinic a couple of times a month.

When she left the clinic she returned immediately to their cabin, and Josh voiced his disappointment that she wouldn't eat dinner with any of the young men who invited her, nor go for walks with them. Gradually she realized he felt guilty and blamed himself because she didn't have a husband and children of her own.

She and Josh had always been close. He'd looked after her when their parents died when she was seventeen and he was just twenty. He'd paid her way through nursing school by working long hours for a demolition company. When he married Anna, he'd begun volunteering for the most dangerous jobs involving explosives to earn higher pay so Carly could remain in school and he could support his own household, too. Now he was behaving like a stranger. He ignored her concerns and spent little time with his children. She gave a sigh. Perhaps things would get better when Anna's brother arrived. He'd written last fall to tell them he was coming to visit this summer.

Carly looked toward the children, seeing Petra asleep, burrowed between the pillows, and Daniel sleeping with his face in the pillow and his rump in the air. He twitched and moved as though he couldn't be still even in his sleep, and Carly felt a tug at her heart. She knew she should be sleeping as well. She was tired enough, but still too keyed up. She glanced toward the partly open door and decided she might as well check on her patient. It would be a while before she could settle down.

On silent feet she moved toward the pallet on the floor. She was surprised to see Wolf lying half off the blanket with one hand grasping a nearby chair leg. She wondered if her altercation with the children had penetrated his drugged slumber. She loosened his grip and made him comfortable again before checking his pulse and touching his bandage to assure herself no blood was seeping through.

Only a few red coals remained of the fire, so she added a small log, then sank down on the floor to watch it catch and the sparks shoot up the chimney. At a sound behind her she turned to look at Wolf. Light from the fire illuminated his face and she could see him grimace and struggle to raise himself.

"Sh-h." Her hand covered his in an attempt to soothe him.

"Ma?"

Carly smiled at the mumbled call. Somehow it both pleased and amused her that this big, strong man called for his mother when he was hurt and helpless.

"Ma . . . gotta stop . . . the kids . . . goin' after . . ."

Something swelled inside her chest. He wasn't calling his mother. He was concerned about Daniel and Petra. She thought of his response when Daniel thought the bear had moved. Her instincts told her that Wolf wasn't like the men at the compound who treated children as nuisances to be swatted out of their way. He cared about them.

"Sh-h, they're safe." She tried to reassure him. "I stopped them. They're back in bed." Whether or not he understood, she didn't know, but he seemed less agitated. She watched his face in the flickering light as it settled into deeper sleep. He had a strong face with no sign of the narrowness and meanness she saw in Isaac's followers. Little lines around his eyes told her he laughed frequently.

Her mind returned to Daniel's words. She didn't want to believe his story, yet the trappers' departure had been abrupt, and no prospectors or backpackers—not even a ranger—had stopped at the cabin this spring as they had last summer. There had been no one—except Wolf. Wolf didn't belong to Isaac's army, and that placed him in danger. Carly had no tangible evidence, yet somehow she knew.

She turned her face back toward the fireplace. She watched a flicker of flame lick its way across the bottom of a log. When it reached a pocket of sap, it sizzled and shot sparks up the chimney. She turned her head toward the man lying on the floor. She watched his chest move rhythmically up and down. She wished she really could hide the bear since Isaac's men would follow its trail right to the cabin and Wolf.

Carly returned to her bed, but hours passed before she drifted into a troubled sleep. When she awoke, a faint grayness filled the room. She glanced around and realized the children were missing. Panic rose in her throat and she lost no time scrambling into her jeans and shoes. She paused only long enough to grab her rifle. The cabin door stood ajar and she bolted through it. They'd head straight for the bear. She knew it.

"Petra! Daniel!" she shouted as she dashed up the hill. Her shoes slipped on the sparse, spiky grass, wet with early morning dew, but she didn't slow her pace. When she reached the top she scanned the other side for the children. There they were! They sat side-by-side on a boulder partway down the hill. Petra had her arm around Daniel's shoulders, and their heads were close together. When Carly slid her way down the steep slope to stand beside them, she noticed their cheeks were wet with tears. Before she could speak, Petra spoke in their defense.

"We didn't go by the bear. We stayed here to say good-by."

"Something was eating my bear." Daniel sounded sad and his voice held an accusatory note.

"I'm sorry, honey, but there's no way we can keep a bear."

"I know. I wanted that animal to eat the bear all up so Isaac couldn't have any, but he got full too soon. Petra thought he was a cub looking for his mama, but I told her he was a great big badger."

Carly gripped the rock for support. A picture of a wolverine formed in her mind. "Oh, please, no," she half-prayed. She'd never seen one, but Frank had told her enough to convince her the animal was vicious and unpredictable, as dangerous as a grizzly.

Daniel went on talking. "Then two dogs came, but they didn't eat much. You scared them with your yelling."

"Look, now birds are coming!" Petra whispered in awe of the black shapes silhouetted against the silver-pink dawn.

Carly felt nauseated. *Josh has to listen to me. We have to get the children away from here.* Bears, wolverines, coyotes! And watching scavengers devour a dead beast almost within sight of their home was too much.

"Isaac will be here pretty soon, won't he?" Daniel asked.

What could she say to the little boy? Especially when she shared his aversion to the man.

Daniel continued, "How come everything is his? He said this whole mountain is his. He took Frank's sack of nuggets and Two-Toe Johnny's necklace. He got my daddy, and he's going to take away my bear."

"Oh, Daniel. He doesn't own everything, certainly not your daddy."

"Daddy goes away with Isaac. He doesn't like me anymore."

"That's not true. Your daddy loves you very much."

"I don't think so. Isaac said I was a squalling brat, and Daddy said to git to the house or he'd kick my pants."

Oh, Josh. What is the matter with you? Can't you see what's happening?

"What's that?" Carly's eyes followed Petra's pointing finger to where something flashed near the dead bear. Rays of bright early morning light reached long fingers into the small meadow, striking a metallic gleam from an object lying in the grass.

"I'll get it!" Daniel jumped to his feet.

"No!" Carly grasped the back of his shirt. "You're not going down there."

"Maybe it belongs to the wolf-man. Do you want Isaac to get it?"

"We don't even know what it is." But Carly knew Daniel was right. If there was a clue to Wolf's identity down there, she'd have to retrieve it before Isaac's party arrived.

"This is crazy," she muttered to herself as she worked her way down the steep incline. "It's probably just a tin can." But she knew it wasn't. This part of the world wasn't cluttered yet with the usual debris of civilization.

The slight breeze stirring leaves on the aspens carried the scent of the bear away from her so she didn't notice the rank odor until she came within a few feet of it. A flock of quarreling magpies fluttered their black and white wings in the air as she approached, then settled back to their feast. Nervousness sent a tremor through her legs even though she had no doubt the beast was dead. She glanced warily toward the bushes, hoping none of the scavengers would return. Her eyes dropped quickly to the ground.

A gleaming rifle lay at her feet. Of course. She should have guessed Wolf carried a rifle. Men didn't wander through these mountains unarmed. She snatched it up and turned to retrace her steps.

"It's a gun. Wow!" Daniel exclaimed with enthusiasm. He began sliding down the hill toward her. "Let me see it!"

"Stay right there. You can see it in a minute." Carly rejoined the children beside the rock. "Careful. You know better than to grab for a rifle." Quickly she checked to confirm the safety was in place before laying it on the rock where the children could see it.

"What does that say?" Daniel's chubby hand almost obscured a small silver plate on the stock.

"Look, don't touch." She pulled Daniel's hand away from the gun.

"I can read it." Petra puffed up with importance. "It's fancy writing like Uncle Dieter writes from Dusseldorf. The top word is *WOLVERTON* and under that *Some Sweet Day*. And there's a little, tiny star down in the corner."

"What does it mean?" Daniel turned puzzled eyes toward Carly.

"I don't know. Maybe Wolf is a nickname for Wolverton." Her head buzzed with questions, and the memory of an old phonograph record of her father's filled her senses, the words echoing in her mind: *I pray no more sorrow and sadness or trouble will be. There'll be peace in the valley for me . . . some sweet day.*

"Carly! Don't come any further!" The shouted warning sounded faintly from the distance.

She jerked around to see half a dozen men emerging from the trees on the far side of the bear. For just a moment she'd forgotten about Josh and Isaac.

"Carly, don't let him get the wolf-man's gun!" Daniel's whisper was a plea.

Petra added a plea of her own. "I found the wolf-man. Don't let

Isaac take him away."

The men stopped to prod the bear. She heard coarse laughter. It was all she needed to make up her mind. Dropping to her knees, she slid the rifle off the rock and into a crevice. She covered the opening with rocks and twigs. While she worked she gave the children careful instructions. "Hurry," she warned and sent them scampering up the hill. When they were out of sight, she turned to face the men who were still absorbed with the bear. "God, forgive me," she murmured under her breath and waited for her brother to approach.

The cabin door crashed against the wall. Wolf jackknifed to a sitting position and rolled to a crouch.

"Good, you're awake." Petra was all business. "You're supposed to get in Aunt Carly's bed."

Daniel tore around the room putting away bandages, rolling up the bedding on the floor, and slamming dishes onto the table.

"Hurry! They're coming." Petra caught his hand and tugged him toward the bedroom. Dazed and groggy, he let her lead him. He stumbled against the bed.

"Put this on." The small tyrant thrust a shirt in his hands. Awkwardly he eased the shirt over the thick pad on his shoulder. "Now get into bed. Remember you just got here and you're really tired." She slammed the door behind her as she dashed from the room. From the other room came the clatter of pots and pans.

Wolf glanced in dismay at the bed, then at the bright light streaming through the window. A very small window, he noted. He groaned. Why did the woman have to drug him? He should be a good fifteen miles away by now. It was too late to go after his gun. If he could make his way to the river, perhaps he could snag a canoe. If not, he'd grab the first deadfall that drifted by. He glanced at the window. No way. He'd have to march right past the children. He took a step and winced. No boots.

He flung open the door and yelled, "Where are my boots?"

"You don't need boots in bed." Petra spoke matter-of-factly.

"I'm not going to bed; I'm getting out of here. Where's your aunt?" He reached for the boots he'd spotted under a chair. He sat on the chair to pull them on. It was harder than he'd expected. Each tug on the leather reverberated through his shoulder, and he clenched his teeth to keep from yelling. Tarnation! That bear had got him good.

"Don't go!"

"You gotta stay."

Daniel's arms wrapped around one leg while Petra clutched at his waist. He tried to pry himself free. He didn't have much time. He had a pretty good idea what would happen if Isaac found him, especially if the cult leader had already seen his rifle.

"I found you. I won't let Captain Isaac take you away."

"You have to do what Aunt Carly says, or Isaac will shoot you and drag you in the dirt."

Wolf froze. Hazy memories of the night before struggled to the surface. He remembered fighting the drug, trying to stay awake, the children's attempt to sneak out, and Carly catching them. The boy was shouting about Isaac shooting somebody. Old Frank. An Indian with a crippled foot. Carly called them trappers, but they were poachers. Sweat trickled between Wolf's shoulder blades. The boy was a witness to murder. He'd have to take the kid with him. If Isaac discovered what Daniel had seen, he wouldn't hesitate to get rid of him.

Wolf struggled to his feet. The room swayed, then righted itself. Pain ground relentlessly through his shoulder. He could barely stand, how was he going to take care of a kid?

Voices! It was too late. They were here. Maybe he could reach Carly's rifle. One of the children tackled his legs and he lost his balance. Desperately he clutched at the chair. He landed on it with a thud. Before he could catch his breath, Petra was on his lap with her little arms wrapped around his neck. Daniel leaned against his uninjured shoulder.

"Who are you?" He heard a voice thunder from the direction of the doorway. He looked up to see a tall, heavy-boned young man striding his way. A thick lock of blond hair almost obscured his glowering eyes. Must be the kids' pa. Blocking the entrance was a slender, silver-haired man Wolf recognized from old photos and numerous descriptions. Jerome Isaac. Wolf's arms moved protectively around the children.

"Dieter!" Carly slipped under Isaac's arm and raced past her brother to stand in front of Wolf. "I expected you to sleep all day. After the trip you had, you should be resting." She turned her back on Wolf to address the giant beside her. "Josh, this is Dieter, Anna's brother. He had a terrible time getting here. His flight from Hamburg was held up a whole day in London because of a strike. He missed his connection in New York, then the pilot he hired to fly him from Seattle refused to bring him all the way. After dumping him off at Twin Lakes, the pilot pointed out Short Creek and told him to follow it to our cabin on the river, then he flew off with his luggage."

"Dieter?" The big man's face worked to control great emotion. "Welcome to my house. Anna dreamed of the day you would come to see our babies." His face broke into a broad grin. "Children, this is your mama's big brother." Huge arms lifted him to his feet and wrapped him in a tremendous bear hug.

Wolf fought to remain conscious. Dieter? Had they all lost their minds?

Three

"Careful, Josh." Carly drew Wolf away from her brother's crushing grip. "Dieter injured his shoulder stumbling around in the dark last night. I think his ankle is sprained too. I'll get him settled in a chair while you and the other men get washed up. Breakfast will be ready in a few minutes."

Dieter! The woman was crazy. How'd she expect to convince Josh he was his brother-in-law? And she was making him sound like a wimp. But he'd have to go along, at least until Isaac and his men went back to their compound.

"Be right back." Josh smiled happily and headed for the door. Wolf held his breath. Was he supposed to say something? Did this Dieter character understand English? The few German words Wolf knew weren't for polite company.

The moment the door closed, Carly rushed to his side. She rapidly checked his wound and taped his perfectly good ankle. While she worked, she talked. "I was right. You aren't one of Isaac's soldiers. I don't have time to explain, but the man who stood in the doorway a few minutes ago is dangerous. Until you're strong enough to travel, you'll have to pretend to be my brother's brother-in-law. Your sister, Anna, died eighteen months ago. She was shot by a street gang in Los Angeles. Dieter Karlis is nine years older than Anna. That makes you thirty-six. You left home in Dusseldorf, Germany, at seventeen to go to school at UCLA. Your mother was American, so no problem with the language. You were in the Antarctic when Josh and Anna got married, from there you went to Australia and then South Africa. You spent the past three years on American oil rigs in the North Atlantic until last fall when you returned to Dusseldorf to be near your father after his first heart attack. He died in January. You've only seen Anna once since she married Josh. She met you for a brief reunion at the L.A. airport when you were on your way to Alaska—"

"Whoa! I'm not going to remember half this. You're out of your mind. I can't pretend to be—"

"They're coming!" Daniel jumped down from the chair where he'd been standing in front of the window. Carly rushed to the stove to help Petra.

Wolf groaned silently. He didn't know when he'd ever felt so helpless. He'd done some traveling, but he couldn't hold a candle to this Dieter fellow. He'd been to Germany with the army and he'd taken an assignment in Alaska once. The worst of it was, if Isaac caught on to him, he'd also know Carly and the kids had covered for him. What he couldn't figure out was why Isaac hadn't already produced his rifle and started asking questions.

Petra swept up a tray and carried it to Wolf as the men trooped into the room. He watched Carly dump huge spoonfuls of thick oatmeal into bowls and rapidly slice a couple of loafs of bread. He looked away when she picked up a big black coffeepot. He just might give up drinking coffee until he got out of this place.

"I'm eating with . . . Uncle Dieter." Daniel pulled up a stool beside Wolf's chair and balanced his bowl in his lap. Wolf noticed how careful Daniel was to keep some distance between himself and Isaac. It was probably a good thing, but the kid's nervousness would trip him up. He'd noticed the hesitation before the boy called him Uncle Dieter, too.

When the men finished eating, Isaac sent them to cut up the bear and dispose of it. They groused about the unfairness of the bear dying before they got another crack at it. When they were gone, Josh and Isaac picked up their cups and joined Wolf and the children in front of the fireplace. Wolf eyed the door. He wondered if he could make it to a canoe before Isaac or Josh could catch him. He looked back at Josh. No, not much chance.

"Well, Dieter, we've waited a long time to meet each other. Anna would be glad you've come. She talked about you often and was excited when your letters came." Josh settled himself comfortably on the padded bench. Isaac remained standing, a crooked elbow resting on the mantle shelf. His eyes were cool and unreadable.

Wolf felt a small arm encircle his leg, silently reminding him that he, the children, and Carly shared a common bond of danger. "Call me Wolf. No one has called me Dieter but Anna and my paycheck for years." He'd have to risk using his own name. Isaac would be suspicious if he had to explain away the name *after* the kid slipped.

Daniel grinned. "I like Wolf better than Dieter."

"Why Wolf?" The question came from Josh, but Wolf didn't miss the attention Isaac gave to his answer.

"A long time ago I worked with a bunch of guys from all over the world. Our boss never could remember our names, so he called all the Swedes, Gus, and the Germans, Wolfgang. The name stuck. I didn't mind; I was just glad I wasn't French. I don't think I'd fancy being called Pierre."

Josh and Daniel laughed. Isaac merely lifted one corner of his lip in a faint smile. They talked in vague generalities until a commotion at the door drew their attention. The men had finished disposing of the bear and were trailing into the cabin in their blood-spattered clothes. Wolf held his breath, waiting for someone to produce his rifle. He couldn't see it and no one said anything. Slowly he exhaled.

He watched Carly turn up her nose, offended by the rank smell the hunters carried with them. Wolf hid a smile. Ma would have pitched a kettle at him if he'd ever traipsed into her kitchen smelling like that. He could tell Carly was tempted.

One big lout with a babyish face and a paunch beginning to sag over his belt edged closer to her. His words didn't carry across the room, but Carly's reaction was easy to read. Her back stiffened and her chin thrust forward. She turned her back and nearly stomped her feet as she walked away. Wolf's hands tightened into fists and he half rose to his feet. Uncle Ulysses had drilled into him that a man didn't stand around and let a woman be insulted. No. He reminded himself to relax. For all their sakes, he couldn't risk a confrontation. Besides he had a hunch Carly could take care of herself.

"Are you staying long?"

Wolf turned his head. It was the first time Isaac had addressed him directly. "A while." He deliberately made his answer ambiguous. He felt Josh's hand settle on his shoulder.

"We plan to keep him as long as we can."

"You and your sister were close?"

Wolf knew what Isaac was really asking. His stomach tightened with the urge to set the bigot straight. Unflinchingly his eyes met Isaac's. "She was my *baby* sister."

Isaac nodded knowingly and walked toward the door, signaling his men with a gesture to follow. They left the door standing open and Wolf didn't take his eyes off Isaac's back until he stepped into a canoe and sent it surging against the current.

After Isaac and his men left, Daniel and Petra coaxed their father to go outside to see where a fox had tried to get into the chicken house.

"You need to rest." Carly moved toward him. "Let me help you into the bedroom."

"I can manage." The moment he stood, the floor tilted. Carly quickly slid her shoulder under his arm until the room righted itself. He had no choice but to let her lead him toward the bedroom where he collapsed onto the bed. Beads of moisture ran down his face. In minutes she had his boots and socks off, and he was only vaguely aware of Carly spreading a quilt over him. His eyes met hers. A spark flashed between them and her arm trembled where his fingers touched her skin. He expected her to hastily leave the room, but she only backed away a few steps.

"Pants." She folded her arms and stood her ground until he wiggled out of his pants and kicked them onto the floor. She wasn't satisfied.

"The shirt, too."

"But I've only had it on a couple of hours," he protested.

"Everything." She held out her hand. "I'll wash them for you while you rest."

He grumbled but did as she ordered. He watched her bundle up his clothes and walk toward the door. "Just because some guy smelling like a rotting bear carcass gets fresh with you, why do my clothes need washed?" he asked.

"Luther has nothing to do with it. Your clothes are filthy."

Two pink spots rode high on her cheeks as she snapped the door shut behind her. For the first time, Wolf saw that pretending to be Dieter for a few days might not be too bad.

Wolf stretched out in the bed. It felt good to lie down. It was a nice bed, big, made from logs, and the mattress was firm. Enough room for a man big as himself to be comfortable. Except that he was as hog-tied as if he had been drugged again. He couldn't prance out of here in his birthday suit!

Carly heaved a sigh of relief when the door closed behind her. Keeping a professional distance from her patients had been drilled into her in four years of nursing school and five years at Central Hospital. She'd cared for many male patients and not one had affected her the way her present patient did. She just hoped he hadn't noticed how much he rattled her. Keeping a professional distance from Wolf might prove difficult. She'd be glad when his shoulder healed and he could move on. Until then she'd have to make sure no one guessed he wasn't really Dieter Karlis.

Picking up two buckets, she trudged to the spring for water. She'd washed the day before, but Wolf needed clean clothes. She'd pick out two or three of Josh's shirts to replace the one the bear had ruined. Wolf was a big man, probably weighed 190 pounds, and he was wide through the shoulders so her brother's shirts would do, but there was no way Wolf could wear Josh's pants. Josh was a good four inches taller and at least fifty pounds heavier.

Back at the cabin she poured the water into a large kettle to heat. While she waited for it to boil, she busied herself mixing a batch of bread. As she pounded and kneaded the dough, she thought of Isaac. Josh found much to admire in the man, but every time she looked at him she remembered that Rita Marquez's last letter had been opened before Carly received it.

Once a week a mail drop was made to Isaac's encampment. The mail for Carly and Josh was no longer dropped separately, but arrived with the compound mail. Her former roommate's letter had been placed in her hand by Isaac himself with a warning there was to be no further communication with a Mexican.

"My friends are none of your business," she'd retorted.

"No one on this mountain is allowed to fraternize with inferior breeds." He'd turned and arrogantly walked away, leaving her to sputter her indignation to Josh.

Josh had refused to intervene. "Who do you think murdered Anna?" he asked coldly.

"It wasn't Rita!" she shouted, but Josh couldn't be moved. It sickened her that Isaac's poison had spread to her brother. He blamed all dark-skinned people for Anna's death, not just the young hoodlum who'd actually pulled the trigger. She couldn't bear the thought that her dear, generous brother was becoming a bigot.

She pinched off enough dough for biscuits, then slapped the remainder from hand to hand, shaping it into loaves. After covering and setting the pans of bread on the table to rise, Carly turned to the clothes she intended to wash. She dropped them in the boiling water, then returned to the spring for rinse water. When she got back she added a strong detergent to the water and churned the clothes vigorously with a wooden paddle.

She'd rather not think about Wolf, but it was hard not to while wringing and twisting his jeans. She couldn't help wondering where he'd come from. Was his name really Wolverton? And was that his first name or his last name? She pegged the wet pants to the line, then lifted her eyes to the hill that hid the little valley where the children had found a bear and a man.

"Oh, Anna," she whispered as a brisk breeze freed a tendril of hair and lashed it across her face. "I know how much you always valued honesty. I never meant to teach your children to lie. I couldn't think of anything else to do. It seemed important to keep Isaac from knowing Wolf is a stranger. I know the children don't like Captain Isaac. They're even a little afraid of him. And so am I."

She hoped no one would doubt her story before Wolf was well enough to hike out. Poor man. She hoped his wound would heal quickly.

When she carried a supper tray into the bedroom, she found him sleeping on his back, with the sheet pulled back to his waist. The white bandage contrasted starkly with his deeply tanned skin and the dark curls that formed a thick matt on his chest. Her eyes moved up the contour of his throat and across his high cheekbones to his mustache and well-shaped lips. Startled by her thoughts, she hurriedly set the tray on a low bedside table and reached to secure a strip of tape that had worked its way loose.

A band of steel circled her wrist and tugged her closer until she fell forward onto the bed, her face just inches above Wolf's. As his lips parted in a wide smile, she saw that dimples flashed in his cheeks.

"Let me go!" she protested, although heaven help her, she really didn't want him to.

"What?" A warm, teasing chuckle rumbled in her ear. "You entice me into your bed, take my clothes, fall all over me, and you want me to let you go?"

"Release me at once." Even to her own ears she sounded breathless, not at all like a no-nonsense nurse. Still, she wasn't frightened. From somewhere deep inside her came the assurance Wolf would never hurt her, not physically anyway. Nonetheless, she struggled to free herself.

"Relax, Carly. You worry too much. Work too much, too, I suspect. Just rest a minute. I won't try anything, I promise." His eyes sparkled with mischief.

"I can't stay here," she gasped. "You're a stranger!"

"Not too strange," he grinned back. "I'm just a guy who grew up chasin' cows with my brothers and sneakin' off to fish when my ma wasn't lookin', just like hundreds of other boys."

Carly quit struggling and grinned. "You called for your mother last night."

Wolf chuckled. He didn't seem embarrassed. "Ma is quite a woman. She spent a lot of years patching up four boys after all the escapades we got into. Doesn't surprise me I yelled for her. You remind me a little bit of her."

"Is she a nurse, too?"

"No, but she gets things done, copes with what life throws her, like you. She grew up on a bone-dry ranch in Oklahoma. When she reached eighteen, she enlisted in the Marines."

"The Marines?!"

"Sure. She figured any outfit that needed a 'few good men' could use a few good women, too."

"What about your father? Is he a military man?"

"Not really. Though he and Ma continued a family tradition by naming all four of us boys after military men. He worked in a silver mine. One day he decided he wanted to see the world, so he enlisted in the Marines. He met Ma and after their hitches were over he went back to the mine. He was killed there a few years later. Uncle Ulysses showed up the next day, packed us all up, and took us to live with him and Aunt Suzy on his ranch in a quiet mountain valley a lot like this one. Some day when I'm old and gray, I'll go back there to retire."

Before Carly could answer, she heard Josh and the kids coming through the outside door. "Enjoy your supper," she said hurriedly as she wiggled out of his arms and slipped back through the door, closing it behind her.

Wolf ate his supper and drifted back to sleep. When he awoke he felt disoriented for a moment. The light through the window told him it was morning. He glanced around warily and listened for any sound that might indicate trouble. On the stand beside the bed he noticed his supper tray gone and a neatly folded stack of clothing sat in its place. He was buttoning his shirt when he heard a tap on his door and Josh walked in. He braced himself for the questions that would blow his cover.

"I fixed you some sticks so you can make your way to the outhouse and around without Carly's coddling." Josh thrust a pair of homemade crutches at him.

"Thanks!" He'd forgotten he was supposed to have a sprained ankle. Carly must have thought that up to explain why he couldn't move around much while his shoulder healed. It wouldn't do for anyone to know he'd tangled with a bear as he'd come over the mountain, supposedly to meet his dead sister's family.

To Wolf's surprise Josh didn't ask questions. He simply accepted Wolf as Dieter. Mostly Josh did the talking, and Wolf discovered he was a gold mine of information. He talked freely of his family's life on the mountain and of Isaac and the men at the compound.

"You say he has more than 300 guns?" The two men sat before the fire long after the children were in bed that night. Carly still puttered around the kitchen and Wolf knew she was listening, though she never spoke.

"You never saw anything like it. He's got all kinds, from little bitty handguns to a .50-cal. M-60 machine gun mounted on a tripod. Plus dozens of fully automatic AK-47 assault rifles with night 'scopes." Josh seemed highly knowledgable concerning the extent of Isaac's arsenal. "M-16s, bazookas, shotguns, dynamite, plastics, the whole works. More than enough ammunition for all of them too."

"That's a lot of fire power." Wolf strove to sound impressed when in reality the knowledge sickened him. He already knew about the M-16s missing from a train derailed in Kansas and the crate of AK-47s that never made it to Fort Lewis. He also knew that some powerful explosives had found their way to Isaac's mountain retreat.

From a corner of his eye, he saw Carly's face grow pale. She lowered her eyes and began tossing cushions and quilts on the floor for a bed with a little too much energy. She clearly didn't like talk about guns. When she finished, she walked into the bedroom and slammed the door behind her.

Wolf sighed. Obviously he was back to sleeping on the floor.

Josh appeared lost in contemplation, his attention riveted to the red coals glowing in the stone fireplace. Finally he spoke, not of Isaac, but of Anna.

"I never expected anyone would love me like she did. I would have died for her. Instead it was Anna who died. She was happy and always doing good things for people, all kinds of people. You know that's why she became a nurse. Then they turned on her. I heard something that night, and I looked out the window to see a dozen or so of them milling around a blur of white. I couldn't see them well, but somehow I knew they were after Anna and Carly. I'll never forgive myself for not getting there in time to save her." When his great shoulders heaved with emotion, Wolf hated himself for usurping Dieter's place. He ached to comfort Josh, and a surge of anger shocked him with its intensity as he imagined the picture Josh described and the terror Carly had endured.

Josh continued slowly. "For a long time I didn't want to see or know anything about guns. Then we came here, and I had to have a rifle for meat and to protect my family if a bear or big cat showed up.

But Isaac helped me see wild animals aren't the real danger. He says there are millions of bloodsuckers in the world who aren't smart enough to build their own civilizations and who are too lazy to work. They leech off of white people, taking everything they can get their greedy hands on. Someday they'll come here, just like they came after Anna. But this time we'll be ready."

Guilt and anger churned in Wolf's stomach. He had no right to listen to Josh bare his soul, but why couldn't the big man see that Isaac was using his pain and grief to recruit him to an army of hate every bit as evil as the gang that took his Anna's life?

Wanting to steer Josh in a better direction, Wolf said softly, "A very wise woman told me once that when a thief robs something precious, too often the victim loses twice; first what he held dear and second his ability to trust. Often he can't do much about the first, but he doesn't have to be a victim forever by giving in to hate and distrust."

Josh stared into the fire, seemingly lost in thought for a long time. When he spoke it was of settling in for the night.

"You sleep in my bed up there." Josh pointed toward the loft. He stood and stretched. "I'll sleep down here tonight, and tomorrow we'll rig up another bed up there for you."

"No, I'll be fine down here." He'd been waiting for hours for everyone to go to bed so he could go after his rifle. He needed to find his gun and put miles between himself and this family. Something told him the longer he stayed, the more difficult it would be to stay emotionally detached.

"Anna would never forgive me if I let her brother sleep on the floor." Josh's voice said there would be no more discussion. Wolf knew further argument was useless. He just hoped he could make it up the ladder without pulling the stitches out of his shoulder.

Josh stayed near the cabin for a couple of days. Wolf recognized a kind of restlessness in the other man and sensed he was nearing an emotional breaking point of some kind. Josh helped Carly plant a small garden in the shallow rocky soil, mended the chicken coop, and dashed from project to project with frenzied energy. He encouraged Wolf to sit in the shade of the cabin and watch.

From a stump rolled against the wall to provide him with a

seat, Wolf's eyes followed Carly. He liked the way she moved and the way she kept Petra and Daniel in line. He looked forward to the times when she changed his bandage because it gave them a chance to talk together privately for a few minutes. He knew those brief interchanges shouldn't matter as much as they did, but he was beginning to care for the woman who had saved his life.

Wolf knew the growing friendship between him and her brother worried her. He'd sidestepped most of her questions about why he was on Steeple Mountain, and his reticence to explain himself irritated her. His wound was healing rapidly, and in a few days he'd become strong enough to leave. Still he stayed. He knew Carly was anxious for him to move on, but what would happen to her and the kids if he did? The more Josh talked, the more sure Wolf became that she and the children were in danger, but Josh wouldn't see it until it was too late.

Or was Wolf endangering them more by staying?

The day came when Josh announced he was going to the compound and invited Wolf to go along.

"No! He's not strong enough." Carly's face looked pinched and worried.

"I want him to stay!" Petra threw her arms around him and Daniel started to cry.

Josh swore. "We'll only be gone a few hours."

"Maybe I ought to stay here this time," Wolf interjected, although he hated turning down a chance to actually get inside the compound. "I already promised Daniel he could teach me to fish today, and I make it a point to keep my promises."

"I'd like you to get to know Isaac, see the town he's building. It's a good place. There's no crime, or jails, or drugs. No gang wars or graffiti. It's a safe place for women night or day."

"Safe? That place is scarier than the streets of Los Angeles!" Carly certainly didn't see the same rosy utopia her brother did. It pleased him to know she hadn't been drawn into Isaac's web.

"Next time. I'll look forward to it." He mentally crossed his fingers hoping Josh would go without him. As much as he'd like to accompany Josh, locating his rifle seemed more important at the moment. No one had said anything about finding it. He couldn't see how they could have failed to, but if it was still out there he had to get to it first. His name was on it and the star Bradley had engraved on the stock was a dead giveaway. It wouldn't take long for Isaac's sources to let him know Deputy Marshal Wolverton had been assigned to this district.

"You're not saying no because of Carly, are you? She's got some bee in her bonnet about Isaac, says she doesn't trust him. The kids have picked up her nonsense. Don't let her fill your head with her rubbish." He picked up his hat and waited for Wolf's answer.

"No. Carly hasn't said anything about this Isaac fellow, except that he's some kind of preacher. If I'd known before I promised Daniel . . ."

"All right. I'll be back before dark." Josh turned to Carly before settling his hat on his head and moving out the door. Wolf watched him stride toward the river. From the doorway he saw Josh step into the canoe, then use an oar to push off from the small dock. A powerful thrust of the paddle sent the small craft shooting forward, hugging the bank and avoiding the swift current that flowed the opposite direction. The river was high with spring runoff. That would be to Wolf's advantage if he had to leave in a hurry. If anything went wrong he could be miles downstream in a short time.

"Are we really going fishing?" Daniel beamed with pleasure.

"I want to go, too." Petra demanded to be included.

He wished he'd thought of a better excuse for not going with Josh, but it was the first thing that had come to mind. He guessed he'd have to go and think of an excuse to cut it short. He might not get another chance to look for his rifle, and the longer he hung around, the greater the risk for himself and the Peterson family.

"Don't catch more than we can eat." Carly smiled and turned back to the stove when Petra and Daniel ran to fetch fishing poles. Wolf suspected she'd be happy if they stayed out all afternoon. Carly was a puzzle. She'd taken tremendous risks to protect him from Isaac, even lied to Josh, yet she obviously didn't fully trust Wolf. He knew she saw through Isaac, so why did she stay?

And why was he spending so much time thinking about her? Women came and went without much thought and that was the way Wolf liked things. Ma always said man wasn't meant to live alone, that God meant for men to marry, but he'd sworn long ago there'd never be any serious relationships, no marriage, and no grieving widow if he got caught by a stray bullet.

Carly leaned over the open oven door exposing her long slender neck to his view. Wolf grinned, wondering what she'd do if he walked right up behind her and kissed that spot on the back of her neck where a few short gold hairs refused to stay slicked into her braids. Something about her brought out an impish streak he thought he'd left behind him years ago at his uncle's ranch in the Bitterroot. Suddenly he remembered sneaking into his aunt's kitchen and tying Ma and Aunt Suzy's apron strings together and howling with laughter when his brothers swiped three pies off the window ledge and took off running while the two ladies stumbled all over each other trying to catch them.

No, guess he'd better not. Ma had warmed his behind with a fly swatter; Carly was holding a cast-iron Dutch oven lid.

It was easier sneaking away from the kids than he'd expected. As soon as Daniel hooked a ten-inch brook trout, neither child would leave the hole. It wasn't a deep hole, no more than a foot, but deep for Short Creek. Two heads nodded and they kept their attention on their lines when he told them he'd like to look for another hole further upstream. Ten yards into the trees he headed for the little valley.

Using a stick to probe the tall grass, he retraced the path he'd followed out of the trees to where he'd encountered the bear. An ugly smear remained in the grass where the bear had fallen. The entire area showed signs of being trampled by heavy boots. Could one of the men have found his rifle and hid it without telling Isaac in order to keep it for his own use? No. From what he knew of the militant preacher, none of his men would risk Isaac's wrath for a single rifle.

Wolf sensed eyes on his back. Isaac? Beads of sweat formed beneath his hairline. Muscles bulged, prepared for fight or flight. It could be the children. They might have followed him. Slowly he turned around. Carly stood on the opposite side of the clearing. Slowly she walked toward him.

"Is this what you're looking for?"

Wolf's eyes widened. His rifle rested in the crook of her arm. "You had it all the time."

"Take it and go." She thrust the rifle and a small packet toward him.

"You know . . ."

"I don't know anything except you're in danger here."

"What about you and the children?"

"We'll be fine once you're gone."

"Daniel knows things he shouldn't."

"Daniel doesn't know anything. Please just go."

"What about Josh? Won't he be suspicious when he comes back and finds me gone?"

"I'll tell him you decided to go for a hike. When you don't return, I'll discover a note saying you hate good-byes so you decided to leave quietly and that you're expected back at work in a few days."

"Sounds pretty cold-blooded to me."

"Don't argue. The important thing is for you to get away."

He tucked the rifle under one arm and pulled her close with the other. "Why are you so sure I'm in danger?"

Frightened blue eyes stared into his. "I don't know." Her voice trembled, but she didn't resist as he pulled her closer. His eyes searched her face, found what he sought, and slowly he lowered his mouth to hers. With a roar like the rushing of wind in tall firs, the kiss rocked him back on his heels.

"Go. Please go." She stepped away.

He nodded mutely, gripped his rifle tighter, and headed for the trees.

Carly watched until he disappeared from sight. He didn't look back. Her fingers strayed to her mouth, and she touched her lips almost reverently as an ache squeezed tightly in her chest. She wasn't sorry he'd kissed her, or that she'd kissed him back, but it would be so much better if it hadn't happened. Oh, she'd been kissed before, not often, and certainly not recently, but no one else had ever kissed her like that. Deep inside she knew no other man ever would.

She took the path along the creek to check on Daniel and Petra on her way back to the cabin. Proudly they showed her three small trout and pleaded to be allowed to stay longer.

"We need two more for supper." Petra explained. Carly decided not to tell them Wolf was gone. There would be time for that later.

Slowly she made her way back to the cabin. She chided herself for the melancholy that drifted over her. Instead of being glad Wolf was safely on his way, she worried he might meet another bear or run into one of the hunting parties from the compound. If he followed the river, by late tomorrow he'd reach the point where two tributaries of the river converged. From there it wouldn't be far to where a small band of Indians set up a fishing camp each spring. He could hitch a ride with them to one of the fishing lodges where the mail plane picked up and dropped off an occasional visitor.

Of course, he might not follow the river. She wished she'd discussed a route with him. Assuming he was an experienced mountain man just because he grew up in the mountains might cost him his life.

"Carly!"

Startled she looked toward the river. Josh was jogging toward her. She read the alarm on his face and rushed toward him.

"What is it?" *Please not Wolf. Don't say Isaac is coming after Wolf.*

"Luther said he spotted a nigger sneaking across Steeple Ridge about four miles above the compound. He got off a shot—"

"I'll get my bag." Carly winced at the crude term her brother used even as she turned to dash for the cabin where she kept her medical supplies.

"No! Wait." Josh grabbed her arm. "He doesn't know whether he hit him or not. By the time they got across the canyon, they couldn't find a trace of him. Isaac's organizing the men to track him down. They'll get him this time. I just stopped to see if Wolf would like to go along."

"Luther shot at a stranger for no reason at all? Now they're tracking him down?" Her voice rose in incredulous horror. "Josh, this proves Isaac and the whole bunch of them are crazy. The poor man was probably lost or simply prospecting."

"Isaac isn't crazy. He's doing what he has to do to keep this mountain safe for people like us."

"You're talking about murder!" Carly was shouting now.

"Murder is what happened to Anna. Murder is what happens when people wait for policemen and judges to protect them. It's up to us to keep that kind of slime off this mountain. Now where's Wolf?"

"He isn't here. He's still fishing with the children." She was lying again. Merciful heavens, it was getting easier all the time to lie to her brother.

"I'll have to go without him. I really wanted him to come, but there isn't time to look for him."

"Josh, don't go."

"Don't be a fool." He brushed her hand off his sleeve. Long, angry strides carried him back to the river.

Tears burned the back of her eyes. She stumbled back into the cabin. Moving like an old woman, she lowered herself slowly onto a chair. She sat caught in the grip of horror, picturing the black man running, bleeding, trying to hide. And her own brother among the pursuers. *Dear God, save him,* she prayed. She wasn't certain whether she prayed for the black man or her brother. Maybe both.

Then another picture swam before her eyes. It was Wolf running and hiding. She nearly stopped breathing. What had she done? She'd sent him away, straight into the arms of a massive manhunt.

Four

Wolf paused to listen. No alien sound interrupted the peace of the mountain. Still, he took the time to carefully scan both the way he'd come and the terrain ahead of him. Light filtered through the thick canopy overhead, leaving a speckled pattern on the brown pine needles at his feet. He left the faint path he'd been following to step onto the boulders of an old rock slide. Crouching low to stay below the height of the thick scrub, he made his way to a rocky outcrop where he could rest. He still had a considerable distance to travel.

He welcomed the shady niche in the rock. From there he had a good view of the area, but no one could sneak up on him. He sat down, leaned back against a granite slab, and opened the package Carly had given him. He smiled at the sight of two thick ham sandwiches, a handful of cookies, and a small leather pouch filled with jerky, dried apples, and matches. He decided he'd better eat it all quickly. Carrying food around in bear country wasn't too wise.

At the bottom of the packet he found a handful of cartridges taken from his pocket before Carly got rid of his shirt.

From where he perched looking down the mountain, the compound was a good three miles to his right, at a place where the river backed up and was joined by several creeks to form a small lake. Isaac kept a light pontoon plane there. He and Bradley had scouted the area well before they had found the poachers. He frowned. How had they missed the Peterson cabin? They'd crossed the ridge several times, but had somehow missed the quiet inlet and the cabin nestled in the pines.

If it weren't for his shoulder, he'd push on, but five years with the Service had taught him not to exhaust his strength needlessly, to always keep a reserve. He'd give his rifle a cursory cleaning and rest an hour before moving on. Years of training had taught him to keep his eyes and ears alert even while his thoughts traveled elsewhere.

An image of Carly flashed before him. She had got to him in a way no other woman ever had. Wolf knew that she was strong and capable, but he didn't like leaving her. Gut instinct told him she could use a helping hand.

He deliberately shifted his thoughts to the task ahead. A couple of hours of hard climbing should place him at the observation camp. He didn't expect Bradley to be back yet. They'd been traveling light the afternoon they'd run across the poachers' camp, waiting for dark to push past the compound. After photographing the camp from all angles and gathering every piece of possible evidence, they'd wrapped the bodies in canvas ground cloths and placed them in one of the trappers' canoes. They'd worn cloths across their faces to cut the stench of both human and animal carcasses decaying in the sun.

Together they'd decided Bradley should be the one to take the bodies out, since Wolf was the more experienced mountain man and could be expected to fare better left on his own. Wolf had insisted Bradley take both their packs since he expected to be back at their own camp in a few hours where he could replenish his supplies. Bradley would need two, maybe three days going down, twice that coming back. It'd been five days. No, there wasn't much chance Bradley would be back yet. Wolf decided to rest awhile after he reached camp, then work his way around the mountain to where he could use the radio.

He bit into one of the sandwiches Carly had packed for him. He knew she assumed he was heading downriver to safety, but there was no way he'd leave the mountain until he was sure she and those kids were no longer at risk. Besides he still had a job to do. Even with her dislike and suspicion of Isaac, Wolf doubted she had any idea of just how serious the danger might be that they faced. He'd been tempted to tell her, but Josh clouded the issue. Wolf wasn't certain how involved Carly's brother might be with the separatists, and he knew without being told that Carly wouldn't leave without her brother, even if she did know of the cult's violent record.

Isaac should have been locked up a long time ago, but he had an uncanny knack for skirting the edge of the law and inspiring incredible loyalty among his followers. At least two men were in federal prisons on charges of munitions theft. Everyone knew they'd been following Isaac's orders, though they repeatedly denied he had any role in the thefts. Two young guards, both black, died in that heist.

For a moment Wolf considered moving closer to the compound for a visual check before continuing up the mountain, then decided against it. Getting to the observation camp and picking up the radio gear was more important. Between what he'd learned from Josh and the grisly cargo his partner would have delivered by now, this mountain would soon be swarming with agents from the U.S. Marshal Service, the Bureau of Alcohol, Tobacco, and Firearms, and the FBI. Most likely, the county sheriff, the reservation police, and the local game warden would want in on it, too! Wolf would insist they send someone to take Carly and the kids off the mountain first thing, whether she'd go willingly or not.

He finished his lunch, gave the slope one last examination, then slipped carefully back into the trees. He'd grown up in mountains a little to the east of these. He felt right at home.

High above the compound, the river emerged from a narrow canyon. Wolf paused in the trees at the mouth of the gorge before crossing the exposed area. His shoulder ached. Perspiration dampened his shirt and his head throbbed. A few miles more and he could rest. Traveling up the canyon would be easier than following the rim, but he'd be in the open for almost five minutes. His eyes swept slowly across the open terrain, then meticulously examined the trees and brush bordering the open area. It appeared safe. He searched the opposite rim, then he moved to another position along the fringe of trees and sectored the tree line once more. He listened for any variation in the call of birds or sudden movement of wildlife.

One last sweep of the area and he'd move out. He lifted his rifle to his shoulder. Through the scope he checked the opposite rim, and froze. Silhouetted against the sky were two tiny figures who hadn't been there moments before. Through the scope he watched two more men join them. He wished he had binoculars or the telephoto lens of his camera. He couldn't tell much from the scope, only enough to be certain the men were part of Isaac's army, not law officers.

Moving deeper into the trees, Wolf worked his way along the rim. At several points he stopped to examine the opposite side of the gorge. It became easier to pick out the moving figures. Isaac's army were neither woodsmen nor well-trained infantry. They swarmed en masse across the ridge heedless of the trail they left or the target they presented. Many were farmers and factory workers, displaced by government regulations and economic hardship. A few were army deserters, and a few were well-paid mercenaries. Almost all were religious or political fanatics who thought they'd found a cause.

By the time he'd counted twenty of Isaac's rifle-toting foot soldiers, sweat had beaded on Wolf's face and ran in rivulets down his chest. What was Isaac doing? They couldn't be hunting. A party that size would frighten away every animal on the mountain. Had Isaac sent his army after him? No, not unless Josh had suddenly realized that Wolf couldn't possibly be Dieter.

And why on the other side of the river? The terrain was much rougher, and several deep creeks fed the river from that side. Either Isaac was attempting some kind of training maneuver, or he was looking for someone.

There might be men on this side, too. They could be coming up behind him or lying in wait somewhere up ahead. Cautiously Wolf moved deeper into the forest, looking for a place to hole up until dark. He found a cave, but decided against it when he caught the rank sourness of bear. The cave might be abandoned by now, but he wouldn't risk tangling with another bear for a long time.

Finally he worked his way deep inside a tangle of deadfalls. Well protected by massive broken tree trunks and lush second growth, he couldn't be seen by anyone passing within mere feet of the thicket. If anyone approached his hideout, the snapping of dry wood would alert him.

He slept for an hour, awaking to the raucous quarreling of a couple of jays. Slowly he lifted his head to survey the area. As his eyes and ears searched for the tiniest movement or sound out of place, he worried about Isaac's militant followers making their way up the nearly impassable south rim of the canyon. He wished he knew the reason they were there. He wished, too, he had some water and a few more of Carly's cookies.

The sun was almost down and it was time to move. He did so cautiously. By the time full darkness fell, he wanted to be back near the canyon rim.

Once free of the deadfall he followed a game trail toward the gorge, always angling upward until he reached a rocky promontory he knew well. He and Bradley had camped there a few nights when they first arrived on the mountain. Flattening himself against the ground, he worked his way to where he could see both sides of the canyon for miles.

When the sun slipped behind the mountain, darkness was sudden. A chill wind swept down from the ice-capped peak, and Wolf huddled against the rocks where he lay prone. There were worse things than being cold. He'd been in some tight spots before, times that had taught him he could withstand Mother Nature's extremes much better than the extremes of some of his fellowmen. He scanned the closer rim, seeing nothing but darkness and darker shadows.

The other rim was another story. A blaze of fire leapt in the air a quarter mile further down that side. He could clearly make out a large number of men, at least fifty, maybe more, huddled around its warmth. It appeared they'd only made one camp and were unconcerned about being seen. Wolf didn't trust assumptions, but his hopes rose. He'd give them a little while to settle in for the night, then he'd go over the edge before the moon rose.

From the promontory he didn't need light to find the spot he sought. A massive force in the distant past had cracked a narrow fissure in the side of the mountain. A trickle of water from a small spring, aided by runoff from the ice fields above, followed the crack to the canyon rim. From there it plunged over the side, not to free-fall ninety feet to the canyon floor, but to skip from ledge to ledge, disappear in crevices, then appear again further down. Moss and brush had managed to find toeholds at places in the crevice and on the narrow ledges. For more than fifty years a fir tree had clung to one of those narrow ledges, sending roots deep into the fissure and pointing needled branches upward to the canyon rim. The winds and snows had bent and mangled the top, preventing it from growing higher than the canyon rim, but the trunk and branches, though gnarled and twisted, had continued to grow thicker and sturdier.

Now Wolf made his way to the great pine and slipped into its embrace. From that first camp on Steeple Mountain, Bradley and Wolf had searched for a quick way down the canyon wall to the river. They'd climbed down the tree and discovered it hid not only the tiny stream, but behind its branches was a small dry cave with a smooth stone floor. Wolf descended slowly, feeling uncomfortably aware of his injured shoulder. It wouldn't do to slip.

His foot found the narrow ledge he sought. Releasing his hold on the tree, he stooped to enter the mouth of the cave. Once inside, he straightened and felt something hard press into his back. His muscles tightened.

"Don't move unless you have a death wish."

Wolf froze. "Bradley?" he asked tentatively.

"Wolf? Wolf, it's really you? I thought sure that lunatic got you." Bradley caught Wolf in an exuberant hug.

"Take it easy." Wolf pulled back.

"What's this?" Bradley's fingers touched the thick pad on Wolf's shoulder. "Gunshot? They shoot at you, too?"

"Bear. What do you mean, *too?* Are you injured?"

"No. They missed. Couple of guys took a shot at me yesterday just as I came over the ridge on the south rim. I didn't wait around to give them a second chance. I took the first available route down the canyon, then made my way here. Scared me spitless when I saw you hadn't been here since we left together."

"That explains the posse on the south rim. How'd you get back so quick?"

"I hitched a chopper ride with a couple of rangers. They dropped me off at the Indians' fish camp, then I crossed the river and circled to the south."

"How'd the boss like the little present you brought him?"

"He said to tell you to keep your head down and that he hopes there's something in there that'll definitely link Isaac. ATF is putting together an arms warrant, but the Service wants to keep checking until we've got a murder charge we can take to court and make stick."

Wolf thought of the bloody trail stretching behind Isaac—his lieutenant in 'Nam who just happened to be black, the two guards in Kansas, the retired Hispanic colonel in Arizona who collected guns as a hobby, and Isaac's ex-wife as well as the well-insured daddy of Isaac's young, second wife, who had met with a mysterious accident in Texas. And now the poachers.

"How'd a bear get you?" Bradley wanted to know. "I thought it was only us city slickers who didn't know enough to stay out of the clutches of old Bruno."

Wolf told him about the bear and the Peterson family. He made himself speak of Carly in a matter-of-fact way, and the two men talked long into the night. Then they agreed they'd better get some sleep if they hoped to hike out to where they could safely call headquarters the next day.

Wolf slept restlessly. His mind insisted on dwelling upon Carly. He worried because someone from the compound had seen Bradley and therefore, Isaac now knew there was someone else on the mountain. How would that affect Carly and the kids?

Wolf didn't want Josh hurt either. Carly's brother might be bullheaded and bigoted, but Wolf figured Isaac had taken advantage of the big man's pain and loneliness and given him an outlet for his helpless rage over his wife's death. Wolf didn't excuse Josh's bigotry; he understood it.

Lying awake, Wolf stared into the blackness above him and found himself praying—something he hadn't done often since he was fourteen years old and been told his pa was dead. He didn't ask God to protect him. It was the woman and kids he worried about.

Carly paced the floor. It had been three days since Josh stormed off. During that time she'd kept the children close to the cabin. They didn't believe Wolf had left of his own free will. They were certain Isaac had taken him. Both children were troubled by bad dreams. She hadn't slept well either. Over and over she'd awakened with Wolf's image fresh in her mind. Perhaps his name wasn't really Wolf. There was so much she didn't know about the man she couldn't get out of her head. Would she ever know? All night she'd wondered where he slept and who would change his bandage when he got wherever he was going.

Absently she gathered an armful of firewood. It was barely light, but already she and the children were up. They'd sat on the dock huddled under a quilt and watched the sunrise. Then, unable to sit still any longer, she'd returned to the house to fix breakfast.

"Carly, somebody's coming. Maybe it's Daddy." Petra burst into the cabin.

"There are two canoes. Do you think he's bringing Wolf back?" Daniel was right behind his sister.

Carly, with the children at her heels, rushed to the dock. Her heart pounded with fear when she saw neither canoe held her brother.

"Where's Josh?" she demanded.

"He's fine." Luther caught a post and swung himself onto the dock. "He sent me to pick up you and his kids. He wants you at the compound."

"Is someone injured?"

"No."

"Then why should I go to the compound?" Something about Luther's jovial air alerted Carly she was missing something.

"It's time you went. That's all."

"For how long?" Her suspicions were fully alerted now.

"Doesn't matter how long," Luther snapped as a small bandy-legged man with a wreath of salt and pepper hair beneath a shining pate joined him on the dock. "Just get your things and let's go."

"No, thank you. When Josh returns, we'll discuss this."

Before she could walk away, Luther grabbed her wrist. "You're coming now, Carly. Isaac sent us to get you. We can go up to the house and you can pack a few clothes, or I can throw you over my shoulder and take you the way you are. It's up to you, but either way you're going."

Carly shuddered inwardly, but she was no match for the two men. There were also the children to consider. Her heart pounded and she wondered if there might be a way to deter Luther. He was a bully who enjoyed intimidating those weaker than himself. She'd have to be careful. Out of the corner of her eye she saw Petra's white face. If Josh wanted them at the compound, he should have come himself. How could he forget how hard Petra had struggled to overcome her fear of crowds and loud voices?

"Well, I certainly can't do anything about packing until you release my arm." She didn't struggle, but let her voice become snide.

"Don't get smart!" Luther jerked her closer.

"No!" Daniel flung himself at Luther. "Leave Aunt Carly alone! I hate you!"

Luther released Carly to deal with the small fury punching and kicking him. Lifting his boot, he sent the child sprawling on the dusty path.

Swiftly Carly swept Daniel into her arms. "Did that make you feel like a big man?" she sneered her contempt for Luther before turning toward the cabin with the little boy. Petra marched stiffly ahead of her aunt. The rigid set of the girl's back and the way her pigtails snapped with each movement of her head warned Carly she'd have to calm the children before they said or did something that might get them hurt. She'd have to conceal her own revulsion for Luther, too.

The children clung to her side, and Luther followed her from room to room as she packed. There was no opportunity to speak to them alone.

Carly took her time packing their clothes. When she began packing bed linens and towels, Luther objected.

"I'm not leaving them here," she responded flatly. "As soon as we leave, rodents will find their way into the house. They won't be eating *my* best sheets!"

"I'm in a hurry!"

"It won't take me long. I'll be all packed by the time you've caught the chickens."

"Chickens! Why should I catch chickens?"

"Well, you don't expect me to leave them here? If they didn't starve first, the foxes would get in the hen house and eat them."

"Who cares!"

"I do!"

"I'm not catchin' no chickens!"

"Fine! I'll catch them myself."

"No, you won't!" Luther turned to the other man. "Reuben, go catch the lady's stupid chickens!"

"Do you want I should wring their necks, too?"

"No!" shouted Carly. "I need them alive so they'll lay eggs. There's a wire hook for catching them hanging on a nail just inside the hen house door. There's twine too. You can use some of it to tie their legs together."

For just a moment her eyes met those of Luther's taciturn companion, and she saw a spark of humor lingering in their depths. For some reason, it brought her an instant's tiny measure of reassurance.

Before leaving, she cast one last despairing glance around the cabin she'd turned into a home. She had a sudden vision of Wolf lying on the floor, his massive chest moving rhythmically as he pretended to sleep, his big arms pulling her close for one long kiss that would have to last her a lifetime. Once again she saw his fingers tighten on his rifle before he disappeared into the trees. Her eyes jerked to the rifle Josh had given her and taught her to use. She reached for it.

"You won't need that!"

"It's mine and I'm taking it with me." She cradled the gun against her side.

"Women have no business playing with guns. You'll wind up hurting yourself."

"Josh warned me to never go anywhere without it."

"All right, just get moving." Luther ushered her toward the door. Carly started down the path, with Petra beside her carrying a small bag of her most treasured possessions. Daniel hovered so close to her side he nearly tripped her with each step she took.

Without warning, Daniel made a break for the trees.

"No, Daniel!" Carly screamed and started after him.

Luther swore as he flung the filled pillowcases he carried to the ground and leaped after the boy.

"Run!" Petra screamed. She moved to join her brother's flight, but Reuben's hands settled on her shoulders holding her firmly in place.

When Luther caught Daniel, he jerked him around by one arm and slapped him viciously across the face, then raised his fist to strike him again.

"Stop!"

Something in Carly's voice convinced Luther to look her way. She stood less than ten feet away, the rifle leveled at his chest. "Let him go."

Slowly he released the child. "Are you crazy? You can't shoot me."

"I will if you lay another hand on either of these children." At that moment she knew he recognized her words held no idle threat.

"This is ridiculous. You couldn't hit me if you tried." But he let Daniel go and made no move to take the gun from her. "Get in the canoe."

She was tempted to use the gun to insist the men leave, but she knew that would only delay the inevitable.

Reuben picked up Daniel and swung him into his canoe. Petra followed. Carly found herself sharing the second canoe with Luther and fourteen squawking Rhode Island Reds. The cords about their legs kept them from escaping, but they flopped and fluttered their protest.

Anger churned in Carly's breast though she schooled her face not to reveal her emotion. She wouldn't do anything to jeopardize the children now, but when she reached the compound she'd have it out with Josh. Surely he wouldn't condone the abuse and terror she and his children had been subjected to. It was time he woke up and got them away from these hateful fanatics. Tears burned at the back of her eyes, but she wouldn't humiliate herself nor alarm the children by letting them fall. This had to be some kind of mistake. Josh knew how she felt about the compound, about Isaac. Surely he wouldn't force her to live there.

The canoe hugged the bank and willow leaves fluttered against her face as Luther brought the canoe in close to shore to negotiate the curve. Carly caught a glimpse of a wide-eyed doe fleeing into the trees. The current tugged at the little craft, urging it to turn. Luther gave a powerful thrust to the oar and sent it flying against the natural flow of the river.

Carly turned for one last glimpse of the cabin as it disappeared behind the bend. A hard knot formed at the back of her throat as she bid it a silent farewell. It had lodged them well against snow and beasts, giving them time to heal from their terrible loss, but it hadn't been enough to keep them safe from violence and hate. Some premonition warned her she'd never return. And what about Wolf? Even if he came back, he wouldn't know where to find her. She hadn't realized until that moment she'd been dreaming he might return again someday. The lump, heavy as lead, caught in her throat and slowly settled to a deep ache in her chest.

Wolf tossed essentials into his pack. Socks, shirts, underwear, a couple extra pair of moccasins. He pulled the buckles tight and threw it angrily against the wall. "You finished yet?"

"Don't bite my head off. I'm not the one you're mad at." Bradley continued polishing the stock of Wolf's .30-30 Winchester. "Looks pretty good, don't you think?" He held up the rifle for Wolf's inspection.

"Yeah, great." Wolf barely glanced at the spot where his friend had removed the inscription plate and replaced it with a stag's head, carefully chiseled into the wood stock and stained with boot polish.

The two men had been friends a long time, meeting first as green rookies when the handsome and outgoing Bradley teased the quieter Wolf about being a "lone wolf" because he seldom dated any of the women who cast longing glances his way. When they'd been assigned to the same office three years ago, they'd become working partners.

"You're not scared, are you?" Bradley sat up as though examining a novel idea.

"Any fool with a lick of sense would be scared."

Bradley laughed. "But not the Wolf."

Wolf checked the safety on his 9 mm Blackhawk before slipping it inside his pack. He knew Bradley watched him as he stooped to tuck a knife in the special holster he wore about his right ankle.

"It's the woman," Bradley spoke triumphantly. Bradley's mind always worked like a computer, evaluating all of the data and coming up with only one answer—even when he had insufficient facts to input. "You should have told the Marshal. He'd have gotten her out if he knew you were personally involved."

"I'm not involved."

Bradley's look conveyed his skepticism. "She got to you. Your days as a lone wolf are numbered. I might not be a mountain man like you, but I can read wolf sign. One old timber wolf has met his mate—you might as well accept the fact. And you know the policy."

"Don't kid yourself. I'm the only one who can get in, and she's my ticket. Stewart wants Isaac real bad." He wouldn't admit even to himself how much thoughts of being with Carly again played in his mind.

Bradley's sigh was a kind of acknowledgment. Wolf knew he wasn't the only one who faced risks. Some higher-up should have had better sense than to send Bradley up here. What kind of fool would send a black man to scout out a white supremist nest?

"It'll be light in a couple of hours. You'd better get moving." Bradley held the silver gun plate in his hands. Wolf glanced at it, remembering the Christmas Day Bradley had given him the rifle. They'd just completed a difficult case where a crazed drug lord had held Bradley at knifepoint for what seemed like hours. Wolf had talked the man into putting the knife down and giving himself up. The dealer had whistled old western tunes between his teeth and referred to the deputy marshals as Matt Dillon types. When Bradley was finally free, he told Wolf he'd thought he was headed for the last roundup until the moment the knife clattered to the floor and the guy started whistling, "*There'll be peace in the valley . . .*"

Bradley had invited Wolf to spend Christmas with his family a few weeks later, and under the tree had been the rifle with its subtle reminder that all the battles they fought were in hopes that their efforts would eventually bring a better world. The rifle meant a lot to Wolf. Each time he looked at it, he saw Bradley sitting beneath a Christmas tree with his small daughter on his knee and his wife leaning over his shoulder, laughing with the joy of just being together. Something clenched tightly in his abdomen, and he felt a wave of envy for his friend. No, that wasn't right. He'd always been glad there was no one waiting for him. No wife and child to face life alone if he didn't return. Deep blue eyes and a crown of golden hair mocked his thoughts.

Wolf reached for Bradley's hand; their grip lingered. Wolf knew the handshake meant "Watch out, and whatever you do, be careful."

He answered silently in kind: "Don't set foot out of this cave in the daylight, watch for my signals, and don't take chances."

Hand over hand Wolf moved rapidly down the pine. Two days earlier, two-thirds of Isaac's army had stood below the tree and never once glanced up. They hadn't noticed the ledges and niches that formed a crooked, but natural staircase leading right to the tree. They hadn't crawled on their bellies to the edge of the rock shelf and peered over to examine the muddy cut left by a century of rampaging spring waters where a canoe was hidden beside a neat one-man kayak, a present to the black man from the salmon fishers. Swiftly and silently Wolf slid the small craft into the black water.

The ride downriver was uneventful, though nerve-wracking. A hidden snag, a surge of current, a too-observant guard, any of them could spell trouble. He clung to the shadows, floating in the blackness until early morning gray replaced the night. The first pink slivers of light could be seen between the eastern peaks as Wolf pointed the kayak into a shallow creek mouth a mile below Short Creek. A shiver of excitement shot through him. As soon as it was full light he'd head for the cabin. An hour, tops, and he'd see Carly again. He only wanted to be sure she was safe, he assured himself.

It wouldn't do to arrive at the cabin too early. He waited until the sun was fully up to begin his hike. His stride became longer the closer he got. He wondered if Carly would be glad to see him. He put aside his concern about using his friendship with the Petersons to visit the compound. The plan was for later. Right now he just wanted to get to Carly. He topped a rise. There. He could just make out the roof of the cabin. From this angle he couldn't see if Josh's canoe was at the dock.

He hurried forward. From the top of the last hill he got a good look at the buildings. His senses screamed an alert. Something wasn't right. The hen house door stood open and an eerie silence hung over the clearing. No smoke came from the cookstove chimney. Quickly he skirted the buildings. The house was empty and appeared to have been ransacked. A movement out on the water caught his eye and he peered upstream. Two canoes were rounding the bend, headed away.

Wolf closed his eyes as though that would shut out the sight. His fists clenched and unclenched. He was too late. His eyes flew open and his feet were moving almost before he ordered them to. He headed for the point where the canoes would have to hug the bank to avoid being caught up in the current. A startled deer leaped across his path and he swerved to avoid a collision. Seconds later he caught a last glimpse of the canoes as they disappeared around the bend in the river. They'd come after his Carly and he hadn't gotten there in time to save her. His Carly? Yes! He wasn't archaic enough to believe in literal ownership, but Ma had told him more than once that when the right woman came into his life he'd know his world couldn't be complete without her. He'd doubted and now she was gone.

The bags piled in the middle of the canoes and the chickens flapping in the bottom told him she wasn't going for some casual visit. He felt certain Carly wasn't leaving willingly. The boy, Daniel, wouldn't go willingly either. He frowned. What would Isaac do to the boy if he discovered Daniel had seen him shoot the two old poachers? And Carly? He had a hunch Isaac wouldn't appreciate her sass. He'd take the vinegar out of her one way or the other. A picture of Luther wielding the paddle as he carried Carly off buzzed an alarm in Wolf's head. He remembered the hungry, knowing look in Luther's eyes the morning he'd come to the cabin. Wolf hefted his pack on his shoulders and set off with quick, long strides up the river.

Five

Wolf moved silently through the trees. His moccasined feet left no trail. He could no longer see the canoes, but he never doubted that Carly and the kids were being taken to Isaac's compound. The canoes would be kept close to the north bank where the current was slow and two-way navigation possible. The river bank grew higher, becoming cliffs overlooking the river. Far below, water lapped at the stone walls where the river ran wide and deep with spring runoff.

Why were Carly and Josh's kids moving to the compound? Was this Josh's idea or Isaac's? Had Josh mentioned to Isaac that Daniel insisted that he'd seen the old trapper and his Indian friend shot and robbed? Josh wouldn't deliberately endanger his own child, but he trusted Isaac and thought Daniel's story was just a story. Josh didn't know Isaac the way Wolf did. Had Isaac become suspicious of Wolf? What would he do to Carly if he discovered her deception? Tentacles of cold fear clenched Wolf's stomach. The questions beat a relentless tattoo in his ear.

He broke into a jog, almost running, until a wide chasm opened at his feet. Far below he could see a narrow strip of white water foaming over boulders where a smaller stream joined the river. The men paddling the canoes would have to fight the current for a few yards here, then the river would become almost placid as it began to widen into a small lake.

In his headlong rush to follow Carly, Wolf had overlooked the change in elevation. Two miles up that creek it would be an easy matter to cross, but he didn't want to take the time needed for the detour. Ten feet was all that separated him from the other side, but it might as well be a mile. He considered scaling the sides of the crack, but without ropes he couldn't risk it. He chafed at the delay. Every minute he lost was a minute carrying Carly further away. He debated returning for the kayak, but he couldn't risk being seen in it. Turning, he began jogging along the edge of the chasm.

Trees grew thick along the way. They were old and many had branches extending across the distance he sought to cross, but the limbs were light and feathery by the time they reached far enough. They wouldn't hold him. Suddenly he spotted a dead tree pointing crazily in the direction he wanted to go. Its branches and bark had long ago been stripped away by the massive claws of the great bear who'd left his territorial claim on the tree.

Wolf leaned his weight against the trunk and felt the tree tremble, but it didn't yield. He wished the bear had finished the job by scratching his backside against it a few more times. Pulling his knife, Wolf hacked at the few stubborn roots that still held the tree anchored to the ground. His efforts were slow and ineffectual. Sheathing the knife, he studied the angle of the tree and estimated how far he would have to drop if he climbed to where its top hovered high above the opposite bank. He'd risk it.

The first part was easy; he could practically run up the side of the thick log with his rifle and his pack on his back. The further he went, the more narrow the trunk became until he had to slide to a sitting position and grip the trunk between his thighs. He was directly over the middle of the chasm when he heard the first crack. He eased forward. If the brittle old wood snapped he wanted to be over solid ground. Shifting his weight, he pulled himself another couple of feet, holding his breath at the sound of each ominous crack. He felt the tree sway. He moved again and heard a groan behind him. His shirt was damp and even the breeze, coming down the mountain fresh from banks of snow, wasn't enough to cool his straining muscles. With one last shove he reached the other side, but hung twenty feet above the ground.

He could jump and risk breaking his neck, or he could continue to climb the tree and hope his weight would carry the narrow top of the tree toward the ground. Of course the dry wood could break at any time and dump him on the rocky ledge below.

Going forward appeared the better choice.

He moved more rapidly now, and as he'd hoped, the tip began to bend toward the ground. When the tree shifted unexpectedly beneath him, he quickly glanced down. Only about ten feet separated him from the ground now. He slid to one side, tossed his gun and pack to the ground, then grasped the tree with both hands. He swung toward the ground, bending his knees and rolling as he hit. He heard a *whoosh* of air as the tree whipped upward without his weight. He turned in time to see the whole tree crash to the ground, snapping its trunk where it hit the rocky ledge.

Across the chasm a cloud of dust nearly obscured the great roots, pointing like fingers to the sky. He breathed a shuddering sigh, thankful his instincts had prompted him to jump. Ma would attribute that silent prompting to divinity. He looked wonderingly at the thick tree trunk that now lay neatly across the gulf.

"A little late to give me a bridge." He spoke irreverently to the sky. Instantly he felt apologetic. He'd thought a lot about Ma's religious beliefs lately. She'd become a Mormon after Pa died, and he knew she'd been disappointed that he and his brothers hadn't been converted, too. They'd agreed with Uncle Ulysses that Aunt Suzy's Bible reading on Sunday morning was all the religion they needed. Studying the religious philosophy of Jerome Isaac had him thinking back to the things Ma and the missionaries who visited her regularly taught. Their beliefs couldn't be more different.

His mind shifted into high gear as his legs cut across the distance between him and Carly. He cut across a ridge to where the cliffs disappeared and he could once more follow the river bank. Ahead he could see the stockade through the trees, and he stopped on a knoll to survey the scene. Isaac's plane floated near its mooring and he couldn't detect any unusual activity. If his estimate was right, the canoes should have reached the compound an hour ago. The peaceful scene gave him hope he wasn't too late.

He reached into his pack for his revolver, checked its load, and placed it in a holster beneath his jacket. He'd walk into the camp and openly ask for Josh. If anyone challenged him, he'd say he'd been away for a few days and returned to an empty cabin. Worried about his sister's family, he'd set out to find them. Pulling his rifle from his back, he clasped it easily in his right hand, took a deep breath, and broke cover. Silently he prayed Isaac's men wouldn't shoot first and ask questions later.

Aghast, Carly looked around the dark, dingy cabin. She could see only one dismal room with a rickety ladder leading to a loft. A sheet of yellowed plastic instead of glass covered the room's single window, letting in little light. The walls were untrimmed logs and the floor rough planks. A tiny potbellied stove stood in one corner beside an empty wood box. A double bed with a stained, lumpy mattress and a single blanket took up one wall. Next to the bed a row of nails pounded into the log wall at shoulder height served to hang clothes on. Josh's jacket hung from one of the nails. Two wooden benches completed the room's furnishings.

Luther dropped their things in the middle of the room. Carly didn't speak as she stared in dismay at the filthy, cramped cabin.

"Ain't what you're used to." Luther seemed suddenly aware of the stark contrast with her former surroundings. "God don't truck with all that rubbish vain women stash in their houses anyhow. Uhh, outhouse is that way." He jerked his head to the west and ducked out the door, brushing past Reuben.

Carly continued to stare. She didn't have any idea how long she stood there telling herself this couldn't be real. She'd wake up any minute. "Please, God, get us out of here," she prayed. The children huddled closer and she remembered an old adage of her father's she'd trusted all of her life. "Pray like everything depends on the Lord, then get up off your knees and go to work like everything depends on you." Slowly she straightened her shoulders, prepared to put on a brave front for the children.

"Ma'am?" Reuben hoisted the chickens. Carly turned toward the man she'd momentarily forgotten was even there. "If you like, I'll go build a pen for your chickens. I'll feed 'em every day too. I brought along that sack of grain I found in your woodshed. I'll take real good care of them poor ol' chicken birds for you."

Carly nodded absently. What was she going to do? This was no place to raise children. She should have told Reuben to leave the chickens here and go build a house for her family. There were no cupboards, no table, no chairs. Josh must have lost his mind!

"Carly?"

She turned to see her brother silhouetted in the doorway. With the light coming from behind him she couldn't see his face.

"Daddy!" Petra flung herself toward him. He hugged her to his side. "Luther was mean to us. He hit Daniel and made us come in his boat. He's mean! Mean! Mean!"

"He was!" Daniel added solemnly. "Daddy, how come you let Captain Isaac get us?"

"Josh, we have to talk. This place isn't fit for pigs, let alone children! You know how I feel about these bigots. You had no right to bring—"

"Are the children all right?"

"Yes, but—"

"And you?"

"Yes."

Josh was silent for several minutes and Carly sensed he was struggling in some way. "Okay, kids, take your things up to the loft. Right now. No arguing." Carly thought her heart would break watching their shoulders slump and the slow way they dragged their few things up the ladder.

"Josh, they're your children. How can you let them be mistreated and forced to live in a hovel like this?" She faced him fully, seeing for the first time fatigue and strain in his face.

"I didn't know Luther would be sent after them. I'm sorry about that, but it's really better for them to be here where they can play with other children and attend school. The place needs some fixing up, but it'll look a lot better after it's clean."

"Better?" Carly was practically screaming. She wanted to pull her hair out, better yet pull Josh's hair. "No amount of cleaning is going to make this dump fit to live in. Besides, this place is dangerous. The people here thrive on hate. Is that how you want Daniel and Petra to grow up, hating everyone who is different from themselves?"

"Carly, keep your voice down. You're tired and overreacting. Get some rest and think about all of the advantages. Here you can return to nursing, which I know you've missed. You won't have to be responsible for the children so much of the time. There will be other women to talk to, young men to get acquainted with, and no more worry about wild animals invading the cabin."

"Josh, there's a larger issue here—"

"Look, Carly, I've always taken care of you, haven't I?"

She nodded her head reluctantly.

"Believe me, I'm trying to do what's best for all of us. Trust me. Okay?"

She didn't answer. How could she? Josh wasn't being reasonable.

"Will you at least promise me you'll try to get along?"

"It's wrong and you know it. Why are you doing this to us?" Furiously she wiped away the tears running from her eyes. She turned toward the door.

"Don't try to leave, Carly." There was an unmistakable warning in his voice.

"Don't worry. You may turn a blind eye to what's happening here, but I can't. Petra and Daniel are going to need me more than ever now."

As Wolf approached the gates, a figure lolling in the shade of a nearby tree separated himself from his companions and started toward him. Someone called out, the man looked hesitantly toward Wolf, then back to the other men before retracing his steps. Wolf glanced toward the group, recognizing one of them as being among the men who had been sent to dispose of the grizzly. He saluted before passing, unchallenged.

Pausing inside the gates to release the breath he'd been holding and to get his bearings, Wolf scrutinized the shabby buildings and took measure of the few people in sight. He had to get to Carly as fast as possible, determine whether or not she'd been injured or threatened, and make certain they told the same story.

Two cabins away, a door opened and a young woman emerged, her bright hair glowing like a freshly scrubbed copper kettle. Wolf caught his breath. Rachel Isaac! What on earth was she doing here?

Marshal Stewart had shown him a videotape of the woman, made by a sheriff in Texas. She was Isaac's daughter from an earlier marriage, but she had chosen not to claim the kinship. Isaac had virtually abandoned her and her mother when the girl was an infant. Years later, after the woman's second husband left her a wealthy widow, Isaac had become embroiled in a vicious custody battle with his ex-wife over Rachel. Though Rachel's mother retained custody, Rachel was forced to spend a month with her father each summer. When her mother died in a fiery automobile crash two years ago, Rachel had gone to the sheriff seeking protection. She'd claimed that Isaac had killed her mother; since she stood to inherit her mother's estate when she reached twenty-five and Isaac was her only relative, she was in danger, too. The sheriff had dismissed her charge, but had been sufficiently concerned to send the videotape to the Marshal's office. Incensed by the dismissal, she'd dropped out of sight.

From everything Wolf knew of Rachel, she hated her father. While there was always the possibility she'd made up with her father, Wolf wondered if she, like Carly, was a prisoner here against her will. Perhaps she was playing some dark and dangerous game of vengeance. He'd need to find out all he could about Rachel Isaac.

Rachel looked up at him and gave a slight smile of greeting. Wolf stepped forward.

"I seem to have lost my family. Have you seen Josh Peterson?"

She didn't seem surprised by the question. Her smile widened as she held out her hand. "So, you're Josh's brother-in-law? I've been looking forward to meeting you, Dieter." Sparkling green eyes appeared genuinely pleased by the contact. She seemed much too cheerful for a prisoner, Wolf surmised.

With a smile of his own, he said, "Call me Wolf."

Carly walked out into the sunshine. The bright light blinded her until her eyes adjusted, then she stared morosely at the ragtag collection of buildings. Two rows of unpainted cabins staggered drunkenly on either side of a narrow, dusty road on one side of the compound. The cabin she'd just left was in the middle of the second row. At the west end of a heavily trampled open area that she'd heard referred to as the "common" stood a large structure that resembled a lodge with a wide front veranda. It was Isaac's headquarters. Two long barracks trailed down the north side of the enclosure.

She could see Reuben hammering boards together for a chicken coop behind the cabins. And at the far end of each row of cabins and barracks stood square structures she guessed were toilets and bath-houses. The log walls around the small community made her feel claustrophobic.

She glanced toward the fourth side of the compound. The wide gates stood open and she could see the trail leading down to the boat dock. Beyond the dock the river spread wide to form a small lake against a dramatic backdrop of pine-covered mountain. A small amphibious plane rocked gently near the dock and a sleek motor boat lifted with each rolling swell of water. As many as two dozen canoes were drawn up on the small beach. It looked deceptively calm and beautiful, but Carly knew it hid ugliness and evil. Steeple Mountain had become her prison, the log walls of Isaac's compound the bars of her cell. She could only pray her stay here would be short.

A movement caught her eye. She looked up to see a woman leaning against a post several feet ahead. Her bright coppery hair looked incongruous against the dusty, faded colors around her. A man's deep voice chuckled and the woman lifted her hand to point in Carly's direction. Deep blue eyes looked her way and Carly gasped. Wolf! Had he lost his way? Or did he belong here? Hurt and disap-pointment vied with fear. She'd taken a terrible risk by sheltering him and giving him an opportunity to leave the mountain. He was prob-ably behind her summons to the compound and her resultant loss of freedom.

Wolf said something to the woman, she smiled back and touched his arm. Carly turned away quickly, tripping in her haste, to seek refuge in her hateful new home. She had been a childish fool, entertaining fantasies about the mysterious stranger. She should have known better. Wolf's voice called her, "Carly! Carly, wait."

She increased her speed until she was almost running. She flung open the cabin door and hurried inside, but before she could close the door, Wolf followed her through it and grasped her arm.

"Are you all right?" The door slammed behind him, leaving the room in semidarkness.

Carly didn't try to pull free of his grasp, neither did she answer. He couldn't see her face clearly, but she appeared to be unharmed.

Thank God for that. Across the room he made out the shapes of two children. He breathed a sigh of relief. He didn't know how long he'd have with her before Josh or someone else arrived. It would be best to get right to the point. "Who knows I left your cabin?"

Carly hesitated before she answered. "No one but the children; Josh hasn't been back to the cabin since the morning you left." Her voice sounded flat.

"Why are you here?"

"Josh sent for us."

"Stupid fool!" He muttered under his breath, but he knew Carly heard him. Adjusting slowly to the half light, he took in the boxes and bundles in the center of the floor, the piles of dirt and debris, the soot-streaked logs behind the inadequate chimney, and the stark gloominess of the room. With one glance he absorbed Carly's sense of betrayal and the wide-eyed, scared faces of Daniel and Petra. What he'd give if he could snatch them up and march them right out of this stinking hole!

"Ah, Carly," he whispered as his arms came around her. He pulled her close and rocked her gently against his chest as her tears began. She was strong, and he never doubted she would rally to make the best of her situation. No matter what, she'd come through for the children. No mean-spirited fanatic like Isaac could keep her down. But for just this moment she needed a shoulder to lean on and he was glad his was there for her.

"Hug me too, Wolf. Please." Petra's little arms found Wolf's waist. He let one hand slide down Carly's back to cup the back of the little girl's head.

"Luther hit me." Daniel's arms firmly gripped Wolf's leg.

"Will you take us back home?" Petra lifted her face to Wolf.

"I wish I could, honey, but for now I'm afraid you'll have to stay here." Wolf hated denying the child. He'd like to kick Josh into the next county for involving his family in this nightmare. From the long talks he and Josh had shared while he recuperated, he suspected Josh was a good man at heart who cared about his family, but who was stupidly blind when it came to Isaac. Josh's whole being had revolved around his wife, and without her he felt himself teetering on the verge of a black hole. Isaac had fostered his hurt and confusion, filling the emptiness with hate. Fear was a factor in his actions, too. Wolf wished he knew just what Josh was afraid of.

"What are you doing here?" Carly whispered. "Were you looking for the compound when you stumbled onto that bear?" He could see the doubt in her eyes. She pulled away, leaving a space between them. He searched for a way to reassure her without revealing too much.

"I need to be here. Could you continue to trust me and let me go on being Dieter?" The kind of trust he asked for was more than he had a right to ask and he could see the uncertainty in her eyes.

"What if the real Dieter arrives? Josh got a letter two weeks ago saying he would come this summer."

"It's taken care of. Dieter won't be coming."

"How do you know?"

"I can't tell you that. Could you just take my word he's planning to lounge on a white sand beach and flirt with women in bikinis for a few weeks?" Carly looked skeptical, but she slowly nodded her head in acquiescence.

"Does Isaac own me, now?" Daniel interrupted, his small face scrunched with worry.

"No! Of course not." Carly's quick answer revealed the horror Daniel's question evoked.

Wolf dropped to one knee, grasped the child's shoulders, and drew him closer. He looked in the boy's eyes and spoke slowly. "Daniel, I want you to listen to me. Isaac may think he owns you and everyone else here, but he doesn't. He'll tell you to do things or he'll tell other grown-ups to tell you to do things. If you don't do what they tell you, you'll be punished. But he can't change what you think or know. What's in your head belongs to you alone." He wanted to reassure the boy, but at the same time discourage defiance.

"Sometimes we have to choose to do what someone else wants us to do to keep from getting hurt, but Captain Isaac can't change who you are on the inside. Only you and God can do that. Isaac will tell you he speaks for God, but that's a lie. If God has something to tell you, he'll whisper it quietly in your ear; he won't go talking to Isaac. There are always people like him who think they own everyone, but there are always other people like you, Daniel, who believe in being free." He brushed Daniel's hair back from his eyes, then gripped his shoulders. "You know how to keep secrets, don't you?"

Daniel bobbed his head solemnly.

"Keep what's in your head a secret. Don't tell anybody. Pretend you're like the other kids and do the things you're told to—unless it is something that would hurt you or your sister. If you think someone is going to get hurt, then tell your dad or Aunt Carly. Okay?"

"Or you. I can tell you, can't I?"

"Yes, you can tell me." Wolf's eyes met Carly's over the top of Daniel's head. He tried to send her a silent message of support. She wasn't alone in her concern for her small nephew and niece.

"Carly, there's—"

The door suddenly swung open filling the room with light, and Carly never heard what Wolf had started to say. She turned to see Isaac and Josh enter the cabin. With the light behind them, it was hard to read their faces, but she knew Josh well and his posture spoke of barely leashed anger. Isaac's movements were quick and jerky as though he too struggled to hide his irritation. Had the two men quarreled or were they both angry with her? She felt Daniel's small hand slide into hers and she squared her shoulders, ready to do battle.

She looked toward Wolf, really seeing him for the first time since his arrival. He wore a khaki green shirt under a tan leather jacket. It wasn't one of Josh's. Loose-fitting Dockers had replaced his 501's. On his feet were soft-soled moccasins that laced almost to his knees. Behind him, in plain sight, lay a backpack, and his rifle leaned against the wall.

Her pulse hammered against her temples. The name plate would give him away! No, this was a different rifle, she realized. The one she'd hid had a silver name plate; this one had a carved stock. Where did these things come from? Josh knew Wolf had arrived at their cabin without luggage or a weapon. How could she explain? What story would they believe?

Both men's eyes fell on Wolf. Some undefined emotion flickered quickly across Josh's face before he stepped forward to embrace him. "Wolf! They didn't tell me you'd come, too."

"He—" Carly began.

Wolf cut her off before she could invent an excuse. This time he had a story ready. "The pilot who brought me said he'd be picking up some salmon fishermen in a week, so I made sure I was there to meet him. When the sportsmen showed up I talked one of them into selling me his rifle." He pointed to the gun leaning against the wall.

"I lucked out since my pack was still on board the plane. But when I got back to the cabin the place was empty. Even the chickens were gone. I was worried sick wondering what had happened. I remembered you'd told me this place was a few miles up the river, so I headed this way to get help to look for you. I saw Carly right away, and she brought me here to wait for you." He grinned at Josh.

"Glad you're here." Josh patted his shoulder.

"Luther wouldn't let me wait for you, Wolf," Carly added a little too sweetly. "He didn't even give me time to leave a note."

Wolf shot her a warning look. He didn't want her to overdo it.

"We can always use another man," Isaac cut in. "Can you use that rifle?" He jerked his head toward the .30-30.

"You bet! Some of the places I've been required a bit of guerilla tactics. Even sitting on an oil platform or floating on an iceberg, there's not much entertainment other than target practice."

"I'll see how good you are tomorrow. Right now take your gear over to the barracks nearest the lodge. There's plenty of room there."

Carly and Josh both spoke at the same time.

"He can stay with us."

"We'll make room—"

Isaac said flatly, "Men without families stay in bachelor quarters."

"Wolf is family." Carly wondered if she imagined a desperate note in Josh's voice.

Isaac turned his back, making it clear there would be no discussion of the matter. At the open door he stopped to watch something he alone could see. Abruptly he turned back, obviously displeased. He spoke to Wolf. "When you get your things moved, get over there," he jerked his head toward the back of the cabins, "and help Reuben build that chicken coop. I shouldn't have let him stay when he wandered in here last fall offering to trade his carpentry skills for home-cooked grub and a warm bed for the winter. The stupid fool is getting senile. He doesn't even remember which end of the hammer to use anymore."

Carly shrugged her shoulders apologetically as Wolf gathered his pack and rifle before moving toward the door. There was nothing either of them could do.

Wolf was disappointed, but it might be for the best, feeling the way he did about Carly, a feeling he'd better get over, he reminded himself. Personal feelings had no place in this case. It would be much harder to sneak out or move around freely from the barracks, but he'd find a way.

He found an empty bunk and threw his pack on it to stake his claim, but kept his rifle with him as he went in search of Reuben. He couldn't help seeing a touch of humor in his situation. He'd entered the compound prepared to do battle, and here he was setting out to build a chicken coop. He could just imagine the scene when Carly insisted on bringing her chickens. He wished she'd had a cow. He could just see poor old Reuben trying to get a cow in his canoe, then attempting to build a barn.

Wolf approached the construction sight on silent feet. For several minutes he stood in the shade of a cabin watching Reuben struggle with tools and lumber. An awkward structure leaned against the fort's wall and Reuben worked in a swelter of boards, posts, and a confusing array of tools. His general plan obviously called for nesting boxes at the back, roosts on the side nearest the cabins, and a door on the side that would open from a small fenced run. Awkward, but Wolf guessed it would work. He shook his head. Poor old Reuben didn't have a clue how to measure before cutting.

Wolf watched the old man cut a post, run inside the ramshackle structure, only to return minutes later with the piece of wood and throw it on the ground. Immediately Reuben began cutting another.

Wait a minute. Wolf straightened his shoulders and squinted at the piece of lumber in Reuben's hands. He watched the wiry older man repeat the exercise a couple more times. Reuben wasn't a fool. He wasn't crazy either, except like a fox. The pieces Reuben carried out weren't the same pieces he carried in. Reuben was building a door behind the nesting boxes, one that led straight through the compound wall! Wolf relaxed his stance and began to whistle softly as he made his way toward the industrious carpenter to offer a helping hand.

Six

Carly stretched and opened her eyes. The lumps in the mattress were a painful reminder she wasn't in her own bed. The one window beside the door let in only enough light to tell her morning had come. She felt stiff and her muscles ached. Before climbing out of bed she eyed the cabin sadly. It didn't look much better, but at least it was clean. She and the children had scrubbed until midnight. They'd hung curtains and she'd spread the braided rug that she'd made for the other cabin on the floor. Still, the cabin looked like a shack.

In the loft she'd found two mattresses. Josh had helped her haul them outside for a good pounding. Once they were back in place, he'd disappeared. Grateful that she'd insisted on bringing clean bed linens, she made one mattress up with Daniel's quilt and one with the big double quilt for Josh. She swallowed a lump in her throat as she tucked in the quilt Anna had made with such hopes and dreams.

She turned to watch the sleeping child beside her. Dark shadows formed a hollow beneath each eye, and a tiny blue vein crossed the little girl's temple to disappear under a cluster of tangled hair. Today, Carly thought, she'd help the children finish unpacking, then take them for a walk. Perhaps familiarizing them with the compound would ease their fears. She'd have to find out about cooking arrangements, too. Last night Josh had brought them sandwiches, but they'd been too upset to eat them.

"Carly?" Josh descended the ladder. He was dressed and carrying his boots. "Can you get the children up and ready for school? I've been assigned to one of the hunting parties this morning, and the kids have to be there in thirty minutes."

"Today? Josh, they need some time to adjust."

"They have to start today." He settled on one of the benches to pull on his boots.

Carly jumped out of bed and ran to his side. "Josh, I can't. They're too scared. They haven't had breakfast, and I don't know where to go to prepare it. I don't even know where the school is."

"Children eat all of their meals at the school. Just take them to the cabin on the end, closest to Isaac's headquarters."

Stunned, Carly stared at Josh. "You mean children don't eat meals with their parents? What about weekends?"

"School's six days. On Sunday they have Bible classes."

"Josh!"

"Get a move on, Carly. You'll just make it harder for them if you keep delaying and make them late." He stood up and added one final warning before stepping outside. "Don't even consider keeping them here. They're to be in school today."

Carly blinked against the sting of tears. What had happened to Josh? He'd always been a wonderful brother and a kind and loving father. But since he'd met Isaac . . .

Reluctantly she awakened the children, and within the allotted time she had them washed, dressed, and Petra's long hair brushed and plaited. As she worked, she talked cheerfully to them about making friends and reading new books. They didn't resist leaving the cabin for school, but the way they gripped her hands as they walked along the dusty road revealed their nervousness.

Taking a deep breath, she released Petra's hand to tap on the schoolhouse door. After she had waited for several minutes, it opened a crack. A heavyset woman peered out suspiciously. "What do you want?"

Taken aback, Carly stammered. "I've brought my niece and nephew to school."

"Leave 'em."

"Of course." Carly smiled sweetly as her shoulder caught the door and pushed it wider. Holding Daniel's hand, she stepped inside. Petra followed. The startled teacher stepped back involuntarily, allowing them to pass. A wooden picnic table sat in the center of the square room. On either side of it were ranged nine children, boys on one side, girls on the other. The oldest appeared to be ten and the youngest barely three. At one end of the table was a chair for the teacher and on the table sat a single notebook, a primer, and a Bible. The remainder of the room was bare, save for a chunk of wood resembling a tree trunk in one corner. There were no pictures on the wall, no bookcases, no flag, not even a chalkboard. The children at the table didn't turn to look at the newcomers.

Carly's temper began to simmer. The school was worse than she'd expected. Swallowing an instinct to grab the children and run, she made an attempt to be civil. She turned to the teacher, "Petra is seven. She reads on a third-grade level. Daniel is six. He's ready for second grade. I see you have a shortage of textbooks and classroom materials. Tomorrow I'll send paper and books with them."

"That won't be necessary." The teacher's ample bosom heaved as she gathered herself for an attack. "The Bible is all we need. You will leave now, Miss Peterson. Parents are not allowed in this room. You've already caused considerable damage by appearing here dressed like a harlot."

Carly gasped. She glanced down at herself. Her buttons were all buttoned, her jeans zipped.

"And furthermore," the teacher shook her finger at Carly, "your niece is to be dressed appropriately in the future."

What was the matter with the way Petra was dressed? Her overalls were clean and her blue plaid shirt with the heart-shaped buttons and bit of lace on the collar was neatly tucked in place. Carly glanced toward the other children. The boys looked much like Daniel, except their hair was shorter and their pants didn't quite meet the tops of their shoes. The little girls all wore dresses! Dark ugly things without a scrap of trim. Heavy wool socks ensured that no bare leg peeked between hem and shoe.

"Come on, Daniel." Petra led her brother toward the table with a maturity that startled Carly. The little girl was attempting to make walking out the door easier for her! But there was no way leaving the children in that impossible classroom could be easy. It took all the will power she could muster to take the few steps to the door, lift the latch, and step outside.

Carly stood outside the door wondering which way to go, what to do. It felt so wrong to leave Petra and Daniel. Josh was gone; she couldn't talk to him. Behind her she heard hammering. Perhaps Wolf was still helping Reuben build the chicken house. If so, she'd talk to him.

She hurried across the dusty road. As she stepped around the corner of a cabin she saw them. Wolf was on one end of a crosscut saw, and Reuben the other. Wolf's jacket hung on a post and his shirt clung damply to his skin. Each motion of the saw revealed the smooth grace of his body; she was acutely aware of the attraction she felt for him whenever she was in his presence. She wondered if his wound had healed completely. It should be checked, but she wasn't certain he'd come to the infirmary to have it done.

A woman's laughter interrupted her thoughts. She glanced beyond the men to see the woman she'd seen with Wolf the day before. She said something and both men laughed. As Carly watched, the woman smiled warmly at Wolf and he sent her an answering grin. Quickly Carly stepped back. She had been foolish to imagine there was something special happening between herself and Wolf. No, she couldn't seek him out.

Her feet dragged all the way back to the hovel she'd have to call home until she could convince Josh to take them away. She pushed open the door and stood still. Someone sat on the bed. Scattered across its surface were her personal papers—birth certificate, nursing license, driver's license, bank book, letters.

"Captain Isaac! What are you doing? You have no right to invade my privacy!" She snatched at the papers. They contained nothing incriminating or embarrassing, but they were hers!

"You're late." He showed no qualms about being caught snooping through the papers. "You are to open the doors of the infirmary at 8 a.m. sharp and remain there until dark!"

"Infirmary? I don't plan to spend any more time in your stupid infirmary now than I did before I was forced to live here. I've told you before, you need a doctor. I'm not qualified to diagnose and prescribe treatment. Besides I have two small children to care for."

"The children are no longer your concern. They're spoiled and out of control. From now on they will be disciplined and trained as I see fit. If you interfere, I promise you won't like the consequences. It is Sister Hampton's job to see that they are educated and their natural heathenish instincts are curbed. Your job is to run the clinic."

"You have no authority over me and no right to search my belongings." She couldn't believe the audacity of the man. Temper sent her beyond caution. "You're either sick or a fool if you think Josh—"

Isaac's fist slammed into the side of her face, sending her reeling against the wall. Vicious fingers bit into her face as he grasped her chin to force her to look at him. "No one talks to me that way. Around here women do what they're told, and if you want to stay healthy you will, too. You will operate the clinic as I have instructed. You'll have nothing to do with Josh's children. You better understand this, too: I will not allow any daughter of Satan to tempt the unmarried men in my army to whoredoms. Unmarried women are an abomination before God. You have one week to accept one of the men in this compound as your husband, or I'll choose one for you. You will learn to submit to God's will in all things." He slammed her head painfully against the wall for emphasis before turning away.

Carly sank miserably to the floor. Leaning against the wall for support, she drew up her legs and folded her arms across her knees. Slowly she bent forward until her aching head rested against her arms. What was happening? She was caught in a nightmare. Captain Isaac claimed to be a man of God, and his compound was supposed to be a religious community. Her family had never been particularly religious, but she believed in God. Was this God's way of humbling her to accept his will?

Something small began to grow in her heart. She remembered the quiet peace of the small rustic chapel where her parents had taken her as a child, the hushed grandeur of the cathedral where Rita worshipped, and her heart ached for the calm assurance of Godly love she experienced each time she read from her mother's Bible. Certainty swelled inside her. Isaac was a charlatan. Surely Josh wouldn't insist on staying after this. But Josh was away somewhere, and she had the rest of the day to get through. She thought of Wolf briefly, but involuntarily shook her head. He had secrets of his own, and she didn't want to risk drawing attention to him. Besides she wasn't certain she could trust him. Right from the first, she'd sensed

Wolf was withholding information from her. He had his own agenda and she didn't know where—or even if—she fit into it. For today she'd have to go to the infirmary, but Isaac hadn't won yet. As soon as her head stopped pounding, she'd think of a way to get her family safely away.

The sound of the door opening brought up her head. Luther stood there. Didn't anybody knock around here?

"Get on your feet. Isaac said I should walk you over to the infirmary."

"Isaac can take a flying leap," she mumbled as she struggled to her feet. It hurt to move her mouth. Her ear ached and she suspected she'd soon have a goose egg on the back of her head. She wiped blood from the corner of her mouth with the back of her hand.

"Now, now." Luther shook his finger at her. "You'll learn it ain't smart to mouth off at Isaac." He reached for her arm, but she jerked it away. Luther's eyes narrowed. "The sooner you learn to accept authority, the better things will work out for you. Isaac don't allow women to flaunt God's laws around here. Until you learn what you're to do, keep your mouth shut and ask me. You do what I tell you, and you'll save yourself another clout on the head." He seemed perversely pleased with her discomfort. "Come on." He reached for her again.

"No thanks." She dodged his arm, dusted off her hands, and tried to think of a way out. She really didn't have much choice until Josh returned. Until then she'd have to swallow her pride and hope that treating people she wasn't qualified to treat wouldn't cost her her nursing credentials. She wouldn't turn her back on Petra and Daniel, however, no matter what Isaac threatened.

The "infirmary" was two dirty, disorderly rooms at one end of Isaac's headquarters. She surveyed the mess in disgust. It would take all day to scrub the place down. Each time she had been to the infirmary when she had visited the compound with Josh, she'd faced the same kind of mess. Isaac allowed his people to rummage through the supplies whenever they felt the need. She stared at the drug closet. Fortunately he had enough sense to keep it locked.

"Here." Luther offered her a small silver key. "Isaac said to give this to you each morning and you're to give it back to me before we leave each evening."

"Where will I find you?" Carly pocketed the drug closet key.

"Why, right here, honey. Didn't Isaac tell you? I'm your new assistant."

"You? That's ridiculous. You don't know anything about first aid, let alone anything more serious." Silently she added that any man as dirty as Luther would contaminate her patients faster than she could patch them up. Just being around him was enough to make her nauseated.

"Oh, I can be very serious." His arm snaked toward her waist.

Carefully sidestepping, Carly pointed to two buckets. "All right, Mr. Assistant, for your first assignment, pick up those buckets and bring them back full of hot water and I mean *hot* water, and see if you can find some soap."

He shot her a disgruntled look, but picked up the buckets. As soon as he closed the door behind him she dug out a couple of aspirin. She spent the rest of the morning scrubbing walls and arranging supplies while Luther leaned against walls or sprawled in a chair, boring her with his exploits and occasionally subjecting her to a poorly executed pass. She noticed several open boxes and pieces of equipment were stamped *U.S.S. Mercy* and she wondered how Isaac had acquired supplies meant for the Navy. Actually the small clinic was fairly well equipped. If she added her personal store of medicine and supplies she could cope with most emergencies, though she hoped she wouldn't see anything more serious than a few scraped knees or a case of sunburn.

A little after noon Luther strolled out the door and Carly breathed a sigh of relief. Her relief was short-lived, however. In a few minutes he was back with a plate of sandwiches and a couple of soft drink cans. The sandwiches didn't look any better than the ones Josh had found the night before, but she made up her mind to eat them. She'd worked hard and missed breakfast, and she felt weak and dizzy. She took a bite and washed it down with the cola. Someone didn't know how to cook venison. The meat in her sandwich tasted strong and gamey. Her stomach churned and she bolted for the door. Clapping her hand over her mouth, she raced for the outhouse. She barely made it before she lost the contents of her stomach. Headache. Fatigue. Nausea. What else could go wrong? As soon as she got back to the infirmary, she'd take something stronger than aspirin.

Luther smirked and lifted his feet to her clean examination table when she returned. She ignored the rest of her sandwich, but drained the soft drink can with a couple of pain pills. Before Luther could comment, the door opened and a young man walked in.

"You the doc?" he asked cheerfully.

"I'm not a doctor, I'm a nurse," she explained. "Are you sick?"

"Naw. I ain't sick, but I've got a sliver in my hand. D'ya think you could pull it out for me?"

"Sit up here." She knocked Luther's feet out of the way. It only took a minute to remove the small splinter of wood. She dabbed a touch of alcohol on it and told the boy he could go, but he took his time leaving. Slowly his eyes traveled over her, leaving her squirming uncomfortably. She'd barely ushered him out the door when another man appeared. This one had a blister on his heel. She stuck an adhesive bandage on it and advised her patient to wash his feet and wear socks. He grinned insolently and rubbed his bare foot down the side of her jeans.

"I'll see you later, Sister Carly." He winked before turning to walk out the door.

As the afternoon wore on, a seemingly endless supply of men with minor complaints sought medical treatment, and Luther's grin grew wider. Carly didn't think it was funny. The men weren't ill; they were inspecting her! And she knew who was to blame for the farce. If she were going to pick a husband it wouldn't be any of them. Briefly a picture of Wolf came to mind. No, she wouldn't marry him nor any other man just because Isaac said she had to get married.

Only one woman appeared that day. She looked pointedly at Carly's jeans and left.

By the time the sun set, Carly's headache had reached gigantic proportions. She wondered if her system could tolerate any more pain killers. She wrapped four tablets in a piece of paper and slipped them into her pocket. Her stomach rumbled, and she longed for a soothing hot bath and a place to lay her aching body. She worried about the children, too. They were pretty responsible, but she didn't like the idea of them being alone after school until she got there. She turned toward her family's quarters, hoping Josh was back.

Luther's meaty hand settled around her upper arm. "Supper time. Prayer meetin' first. If you're not there, Isaac'll send someone to fetch you."

"I've got to check on the children." She tried to pull free.

He laughed. "They're in bed and asleep by now. Isaac don't allow no brats in the dining hall, and he don't let 'em run around gettin' in people's way neither."

Isaac and his stupid rules! It was unreasonable to expect children to spend all day in a cramped school room, then go straight to bed. Daniel and Petra were accustomed to long hours of physical activity. They'd be stifled! But not for long. She'd caught a glimpse of her face in a small mirror included with the medical supplies. As soon as Josh saw her bruised and swollen face, he'd get them away from this nightmare.

Luther still held her arm as they entered the spacious dining hall, situated at the opposite end of Isaac's headquarters building from the infirmary. He pointed toward a long table at one side of the room where roughly twenty women sat. More than a hundred men occupied the other tables. With near desperation her eyes searched for Josh—and Wolf. She hadn't found either of them before Luther shoved her toward the table where the women sat.

Stumbling, she made her way to the only empty space on the split log that served as a bench. She sat down with her back to the tables where the men sat. No one spoke to her. She craned her neck to continue her search.

"Don't!" A shoe struck her shins softly.

"Why not?" She turned indignantly to the woman beside her, and was startled to see the young woman she'd seen with Wolf earlier.

"Sh-h-h." The girl whispered out of the corner of her mouth.

Reaching into her pocket, Carly withdrew two of the pain pills before reaching for the pitcher of water which sat on the table. She'd meant to wait until bedtime to take the pills, but the pain was unbearable. Her hands shook as she filled the glass in front of her.

"Stop!" The woman beside her hissed. Carly ignored her to down the pills and water.

"It is forbidden for women to serve themselves before the men."

Carly didn't know whether to thank her for the warning or not. More cautiously, she peeked along the double row of women. She recognized Mrs. Hampton's beady eyes peering nearsightedly like raisins from recently punched bread dough. Her shapeless dress couldn't conceal the mounds of flesh that hung over the back of the bench. Beside her sat the woman who had briefly visited the infirmary that afternoon. Most of the women looked tired and nondescript in their plain dresses, with no makeup, and their bedraggled hair hanging down their backs or coiled tightly against their necks. Those who looked her way revealed either contempt or pity when they saw her face.

At the head of the table sat a pretty young woman whose face shone as she gazed upward as though anticipating a glimpse of heaven. She was the same woman Carly had pitied the first time she visited the compound. Josh had said her name was Deborah, and Carly had seen her a couple of times since with a delicate-looking toddler.

Carly jumped when Isaac's voice suddenly boomed across the hall. She noticed everyone turned to watch him. He stood on a dais that extended across the front of the room, his arms raised. As he spoke he shook his fists in the air.

"Twin evils stalk the earth today," he intoned. "Women think to rise above their station. They defy their natural masters bringing evil among us." Most of the women at the table lowered their eyes and appeared to shrink into themselves. *I suppose he means me,* Carly thought. She was distinctly unrepentant, though she shivered at the wave of approval that swept through the crowd. As she tried to block out the insults and threats he heaped upon the women of the world, he shifted his tirade to vilify his second "evil": all dark-skinned peoples.

"When servants forget that God cursed their skin to set them apart to identify their place in the world, they must be rooted out and destroyed," Isaac ranted. Shouts of amen greeted his words. "My army will destroy these evils. I have been chosen to raise up a pure nation. Each of you must subject yourself to God's mouthpiece."

God's mouthpiece! Carly caught herself before an unladylike snort could escape. *Surely Josh has better sense than to accept this nonsense!*

By the time Isaac's speech ended and he began praying, Carly had difficulty concentrating. She bowed her head when the others did, but while Isaac droned on, her head slipped nearer her plate. She was exhausted and the pain pills on an empty stomach pulled her toward sleep. A sharp jab to her shins brought her head up, leaving her uncertain whether she sat beside a friend or foe. She probably shouldn't have taken those last two pills.

The men were served first and a number of them, including Captain Isaac, were leaving the hall by the time the women were served. Two young girls, barely in their teens, lugged heavy trays to the tables and placed bowls and platters on the plank tables. Carly stared suspiciously at a piece of meat she couldn't identify. Reaching for her fork she decided the rice and canned beans couldn't hurt her. Surprisingly light dinner rolls accompanied the meal. The men conversed and moved around the room freely, but the women continued to sit quietly as they ate their nearly cold meal.

Out of the corner of her eye she saw Josh walking toward the door. Hastily she sat down her fork and rose to her feet. If she hurried she could catch him before he went far. She skirted the edge of the room, keeping her goal in sight until a hand touched her shoulder. Fighting an instinctive urge to slap away the hand, she turned her head.

"Sister Peterson." A gaunt, nervous woman spoke to her. "I'm the cook here. It's a difficult job when I don't always have the supplies I need. Isaac promised the Lord would provide and that he did. Reuben and that new man, Wolf, said you brought your chickens so's I'd have eggs for making raised biscuits, cakes, and things. I sure do thank you. And I thank Isaac for walking hand-in-hand with the Lord and seeing to our needs."

"Uh-h, the rolls were delicious." She didn't know what to say. Josh was out the door and she needed to hurry.

"Brother Reuben brought me six nice brown eggs today. I knelt right down and thanked the Lord. Reuben said there'll be more when the chickens settle down and get used to their new home."

"I'm glad you can use the eggs. I didn't want the foxes or a bobcat to get the chickens. Please excuse me." She tried to sidle past.

"That would have been a real shame. For foxes to eat your chickens, I mean. Brother Reuben built a real fine chicken coop for them, so you needn't worry about beasts getting them now."

"I know he did and I appreciate—"

"It looks kind of funny, but it'll do. Some folks say Brother Reuben isn't quite right in his head, but I think he's a fine man. Always polite, always—"

"I've got to go. I really do. Perhaps we can talk again soon." Carly backed rapidly away, but when she reached the porch there was no sign of Josh. She concluded he must have gone to the cabin. She glanced nervously over her shoulder to the open door behind her where she could see Luther starting toward her. Hastily she moved toward the steps. A line of men lounged there, several of whom offered to walk her to her cabin. She shook her head and quickly took to her heels. The cool night air brushed back the drowsy cobwebs still lingering in her head.

With his elbows resting on the table, Wolf leaned his chin against his clasped hands. He'd spotted Carly the moment she'd come to the door. He didn't like the way Luther held her arm then shoved her toward the women's table. There was something proprietary in his actions that disturbed Wolf. Carly looked exhausted, and the way several old biddies at her table turned up their noses when she sat down wasn't helping. When the meal ended, he'd make certain she got back to her cabin safely.

He'd noticed during the afternoon that something was going on concerning her. He'd made a point to discover where she'd been assigned, and he'd noticed the number of men that made their way to the infirmary. He'd also noticed how closely Luther stuck to her. Something wasn't right.

When Carly stood up and began her dash to follow Josh out the door, Wolf choked on his drink. Rich, dark anger roiled to the surface. He wasn't a man who lost his temper easily and he never picked a fight, but someone was going to pay. The right side of Carly's face had been turned away when she entered the room, she'd eaten her dinner with her back to him, but now he could see the purple-black bruise covering her cheek, the split lip, and the yellow discoloration of her eye. Was Luther responsible? He'd soon find out.

He saw the cook intercept her and waited. He gave her a few minutes then rose to his feet. He reached the porch at the same time as Luther, and by then Carly was out of sight. He hesitated, waiting to see which way Luther went.

Luther leaned back against the porch rail. He slowly lit a cigarette and sucked in a heavy drag before speaking. "Want one?" He extended the pack toward Wolf.

"No thanks. I spent too many years working oil rigs to take up the habit."

Luther chuckled and returned the pack to his pocket. "That was some mighty fine shooting out on the hill this morning." Wolf shrugged at the compliment. At Isaac's orders, he had gone though quite a test to demonstrate his skill level.

"Carly seems to be settling in okay," he said neutrally, inviting the other man to reveal his thoughts. The mention of her name triggered a complacent smile on Luther's face that put Wolf on his guard.

"Got uppity with Isaac this morning." Wolf narrowed his attention to Luther's words. "He belted her a good one. She had it coming. Dumb woman, she won't listen to me, but that's going to change. One week, that's all, and she'll learn real quick."

Isaac! There was one more strike against him. Wolf recognized the need for revenge churning in his gut and knew he'd passed some invisible line. This case was personal now. Through narrowed eyes he watched Luther. Though Luther hadn't hit Carly, he was a threat to her in some way too, and Wolf had no intention of letting anyone threaten her.

Ahead of her Carly saw a flash of red hair. As she watched, the woman ducked behind a cabin. Her action appeared furtive and roused Carly's curiosity. Without stopping to consider, she followed. Seconds later she caught a glimpse of the other woman disappearing behind a cabin on the second row. A quick glance in all directions assured Carly no one was watching, so she rounded the side of the building. Now she could hear muted voices, a soft feminine whisper followed by the deeper rumble of a man striving to keep his voice down.

Carly's heart sank. The woman must be meeting Wolf. She should turn around, go back, allow them a moment's privacy. Knowing she was being childish, she inched forward. She had to see, to know. Her eyes watered. She blinked to clear them before peeking around the corner of the log house.

No! It couldn't be. But it was. Josh stood in the shadow of the fort wall with the woman in his arms. He leaned forward, kissing her mouth, while she wrapped her arms around him tightly.

Carly pulled her head back. Her legs began to shake, and she leaned against the rough log wall until they felt steady again. Is that what this was all about? Could Josh be placing his family's needs second to that woman? Who was she anyway? Just a woman easy with her favors, or someone really important to him?

A spasm of guilt flushed her cheeks as she realized she was glad it wasn't Wolf with the woman. Being careful not to make a sound, she retraced her steps. She'd go back to the cabin, check on the children, and wait for Josh.

As soon as Wolf could leave without drawing attention to himself, he made his way to the kitchen where he sweettalked the cook into giving him a chunk of ice wrapped in a thick rag. When he reached the Peterson cabin, he could see a faint light flickering behind the nearly opaque window. He tapped twice on the door without getting a response. He tried the latch and found the door unlocked.

Stepping cautiously inside, he paused a moment then hurried to the side of the bed. Fully clothed, Carly lay in an exhausted slumber. No doubt she'd planned to wait up for Josh. Wolf wondered what the big man would do when he saw his sister's face, then remembered something he'd heard earlier. Josh wouldn't see Carly's face for several days. Isaac had ordered Josh to guard duty that night, and before morning he would leave for some mission Isaac had sprung on him just before dinner. Josh had expressed his reluctance to leave his family when they'd only just arrived, but Isaac had over-ridden his objections. By the time Josh returned, the damage would have faded.

"Carly." He shook her shoulder gently. She mumbled some-thing unintelligible. "Carly, Josh isn't coming back tonight. Get into bed and hold this ice pack against your cheek."

"Wolf?"

"Look, get out of those clothes and lie down." She agreed, then promptly fell back asleep. Wolf smiled tenderly and reached for her buttons. He undid two, then froze. After a moment he decided to leave the shirt on.

He unsnapped her jeans, but didn't try to remove them. He jerked her shoes off her feet and pulled back the quilt. He gathered her in his arms and slid her into bed. It wouldn't hurt her to sleep in her clothes one night.

He placed the ice pack against her cheek and pulled up the quilt, noticing for the first time that Petra lay curled in a ball in her aunt's bed. It seemed curious to him that the child hadn't wakened. Carly might have taken pain medication; there was no way she couldn't be hurting. Even aspirin, as tired as she was, would put her out for the night. But Petra? He reached for the girl's pulse; the count was slow. Thoughtfully he picked up the lantern and climbed the ladder.

"Daniel?" He knew from the nights he'd spent in the other cabin the boy was a light sleeper, but he didn't respond when Wolf called his name. Wolf shook the child's shoulder. He didn't stir.

He clenched his fists in helpless frustration. It didn't take a medical expert to know the children had been drugged. And Carly? She may have taken pain killers herself, but he'd bet his boots she wasn't the one who drugged the kids. She'd sedated him once, but she'd thought she had good cause. He couldn't see any possible reason for sedating Petra and Daniel.

Seven

The soft thud of the door latch came from below. Wolf blew out the lantern and edged closer to the ladder. A shadow appeared in the doorway for an instant before the door closed, plunging the cabin into blackness. Wolf's hand strayed toward the holster beneath his jacket. A flashlight clicked on, aimed at the floor. Quick steps made their way across the room. Wolf couldn't see the person behind the light, but he knew it wasn't Josh.

"Carly?" The whisper was low. He couldn't make out the voice, but he shifted his weight, prepared to spring if the visitor became a threat to Carly. The light played across the sleeping woman's face, causing her to stir uneasily, but she didn't open her eyes. Wolf watched as the unknown person below placed the light on the bed, then reached to replace the ice pack, which had slipped to one side. The light caught a hand, a face. Rachel Isaac stood revealed in the faint glow.

Wolf saw her shake Carly again and whisper her name, then stand back silently. For several minutes she watched Carly without making any further attempt to awaken her. She looked toward the other occupant of the bed.

"Petra? Petra, wake up." The little girl didn't respond to Rachel's whisper. Rachel reached across Carly to pull Petra free of the covers and onto her lap. "Wake up, honey. Petra!"

She shook her gently. "Petra!" Wolf could hear the growing alarm in Rachel's voice. Suddenly her arm reached out to snatch the ice from Carly's cheek. She unwrapped it and ran it down Petra's arms and brushed it against the child's face. Petra mumbled and tried to pull away. Rachel repeated the action until Petra's eyes opened.

"Aunt Carly," the child whimpered. "I want my daddy."

"Aunt Carly is sleeping. Her head hurts and she needs to rest. Your daddy sent me here to give her a message. Will you give her the message in the morning?"

Petra nodded her head.

"Your daddy had to go away for a few days. Tell Carly not to worry, I'll watch you and Daniel after school." Rachel's face lifted. She turned her head toward the door as though she heard some sound that hadn't reached Wolf's ears. Quickly, she thrust Petra back in bed before reaching for her flashlight. The room was instantly black again.

Now Wolf could hear the scuffle of heavy boots on the planks in front of the door, followed by the rattle of the latch. Silently he moved down the ladder. He fingered the grip of his Blackhawk as a rectangle of lighter blackness separated from the deep black of the cabin wall and a man stood silhouetted in the doorway. He was shorter than Josh, but heavier than Isaac. Wolf gripped the gun with both hands. He wouldn't shoot unless the intruder made a threat he couldn't defuse any other way. He didn't want to arouse the camp, and besides, he had no idea where Rachel might be.

A solid thump answered his question. The flashlight clicked back on, revealing Luther lying slumped on the floor. He shook his head several times as though clearing some obstruction. Wolf edged closer but stayed clear of the beam from Rachel's flashlight.

Rachel didn't hide from the man sprawled on the floor. She continued to stand on the bench with the heavy flashlight in one hand. It wouldn't be much protection if Luther went after her. Wolf opened his mouth, prepared to warn Luther off when Rachel's words stopped him.

"Oh, it's you, Luther. You frightened me. I came to check on Carly. She didn't look well at dinner."

"You had no call to hit me."

"How was I supposed to know it was you? You didn't knock, and Carly didn't seem to be expecting a suitor to come calling. Does Daddy know you're here?"

"Mind your own business." Luther lumbered to his feet to

tower over the petite redheaded woman. He raised a heavy fist. Wolf rocked on the balls of his feet, ready to leap.

"Don't try it, Luther. Or Daddy might learn about the offer you made me before I disabused him of the idea you and I were headed for wedded bliss."

Luther snarled and called Rachel an ugly name before lowering his hand and moving toward the door.

"Don't come back. Leave Carly alone or I'll tell Daddy all about your little plan to appropriate my money for yourself instead of dedicating it to Daddy's Steeple Mountain Movement."

"He won't believe you."

"He will when I show him the paper you gave me, that had I been stupid enough to sign, would have transferred all the income from my holdings to your Swiss bank account." She stood in the doorway for several minutes after Luther left, then followed him into the night.

Wolf didn't move until they'd both gone. Interesting. He didn't know what to make of the scene he'd just witnessed. Rachel had seemed genuinely concerned about Carly. Rachel also seemed to have a strong hold over Luther. There was obviously no love lost between the two. He'd like to question her, but he couldn't risk his cover yet.

With a sigh, Wolf returned the Blackhawk to its holster, retrieved the lantern, and returned to the attic to assure himself that Daniel was in no danger. The boy was restless and muttering in his sleep. Whatever he'd been given, it was wearing off.

"Don't like green punch. Don't tell her I spilled some on purpose."

"I won't tell," Wolf whispered with a smile.

"Not going to drink it. Don't like green punch."

"Sh-h-h, it's okay." Wolf held Daniel a moment, assuring him he didn't have to drink green punch if he didn't want to, and the boy soon drifted back to sleep.

Petra too seemed to be sleeping naturally. Wolf took a moment to restore the ice pack to Carly's face and allowed his fingers to gently stroke her battered cheek. Then he shook himself and slipped out the door. He had some thinking to do. Somehow he had to find out who had drugged the children. He'd have to keep his eyes open and make certain Carly didn't face a repeat of this day when she awoke.

"Sister Hampton isn't going to like either one." Petra examined the two dresses Carly held up. With a sigh Carly acknowledged that she was right. Neither short red pleats nor just-above-the-knee white organdy would suit Mrs. Hampton, but they were the only dresses in Petra's wardrobe. Both were a size too small. There hadn't been any occasions calling for dresses since they'd come to Steeple Mountain. Overalls made more sense for an active seven-year-old.

"She could wear one of Daddy's shirts," Daniel giggled. "If she tied a belt around the middle, it would look like a dress."

"That just might work." Carly had run out of both ideas and time. She'd had difficulty rousing the children and her own head still ached. She'd awakened to find herself hugging a wet towel to her face. Some of the swelling had gone down, but she still felt tender. Josh hadn't returned during the night and Carly seethed with anger. How could he have changed so much? A few months ago she would have staked her life that her brother's first concern was his family. All she needed now was Mrs. Hampton's dictum that Petra show up for school wearing a dress!

Carly rummaged through Josh's shirts until she found a soft black wool he used to save for special nights out on the town. On Petra the shoulder seams drooped to her elbows and the square cut hem reached her ankles. Grabbing a pair of scissors, Carly slashed small holes around the bottom of the sleeves. Through the holes, she laced strips she cut from the bottom of the shirt. Once the strips were tied, the sleeves would stay put above the little girl's elbows. She used tape to baste a new hem, fastened a belt around Petra's waist, and stepped back to take a look.

"You better put on tights, too." Petra looked pathetic. The makeshift dress was a mess, but the child didn't seem to care. She seemed listless and Carly worried she might be catching a summer cold. She couldn't be tired. Both children had been soundly asleep when she reached the cabin the night before. Neither one had said much about their first day of school and in the rush to get them ready this morning, Carly hadn't asked questions. She made certain they each had a tablet and pencil, but decided against sending books with them.

"She said Daddy wouldn't be back for a few days, but she'd look after Daniel and me." Petra fiddled with the ties on her sleeve. She appeared reluctant to leave for school.

"Who, Petra?" Carly suspected Petra was stalling.

"The lady I dreamed about."

"Dream people aren't real, honey. Go to school and maybe your daddy will be here when you get back."

"I dreamed about Wolf," Daniel announced importantly. "He said I don't have to drink green punch."

"No, of course not. We never make you drink green punch."

"Sister Hampton doesn't know. She said I had to drink it cause God said so."

"Silly." Carly smoothed his cowlick in place. "God doesn't care what color punch you drink." With a hand on his shoulder she urged him toward the door, then stood in the doorway and watched them walk away, hand-in-hand.

A movement caught her eye. She looked across the street in time to see Wolf cross the common and enter a barracks. A sudden memory of his voice and the soothing touch of ice on her face reminded her she'd awakened that morning in bed with her clothes loosened. Had he put her to bed and ministered to her injury or had she dreamed it? And where was Josh? She didn't dare search for him. If she didn't show up at the infirmary on time, Isaac would beat her or send Luther to drag her there bodily. She seethed with frustration, but didn't dare openly defy Isaac.

Her first patient when she reached the infirmary was Luther. He sported a sizable lump on his head. He claimed he bumped his head on a low door frame, but he wouldn't look her in the eye. She suspected whatever caused his injury was something he didn't want her to know about. That was fine with her. There wasn't anything about Luther she wanted to know.

She dressed the wound, gave him a tetanus shot, and offered him a couple of pain pills. To her relief he accepted them and drifted to sleep in a chair with his feet propped on the supply cabinet she used for a desk.

An endless train of men with minor or nonexistent ailments

once more paraded through the door. One young man with a faint trace of pale fuzz on his upper lip came twice. The second time he stammered a proposal.

"What?"

"Will you marry me?"

"I heard that, but I don't believe it! I can't marry you. I don't even know you."

"But I know you. Ever since you first came here a couple of months ago with Josh, I've dreamed about marrying you. I think that's a sign from God."

"Get out of here, kid!" Luther growled from the chair where he sprawled. "You've got work to do."

Carly frowned, but didn't say anything as the boy hurried out the door. Luther closed his eyes and snorted a couple of times as he settled more comfortably in the chair. A short time later Carly pressed a wooden depressor against the tongue of a man seated on the examination table and peered at a perfectly healthy throat. As she bent forward to look more closely, she felt a hand slide up the back of her thigh. She quickly pushed the hand away.

"Keep your hands off her or I'll break your arm, Swenson. I don't share." Luther managed to rouse himself again.

"I don't need your help." Carly turned on Luther. "I don't belong to you or any other man!" Not only could she take care of herself, but Luther's implication that there was some kind of understanding between the two of them sent shivers up her spine.

He laughed. "Isaac's giving you just one week."

"Nonsense! This isn't the dark ages."

Nevertheless she heard something sinister in Luther's laugh that sent an uneasy tremor through her. Isaac couldn't really force her to marry, could he? She recalled the parade of men who had passed through the clinic the past two days and shivered. They hadn't been looking for medical care. Her stomach tightened as she glanced toward Luther. She was glad he had fallen asleep again.

She took great care to make certain no one else got a chance to touch or propose. As she worked, her anger and frustration mounted. The men ogling and maneuvering to touch her made her feel cheap and fueled her anger. There was no way she would marry anyone associated with this place. *Liar.* She'd marry Wolf. Carly started at the thought. Where did it come from? She knew nothing about his background; for all she knew, he might already be married. Then, too, he seemed to be showing a lot of attention to a certain redhead, the same redhead she'd seen kissing Josh.

Wolf stood in the kitchen where preparations were underway for dinner. A tall, gaunt woman looked up and he smiled.

"Reuben is busy, so I brought the eggs." He held out a basket to the cook. Without seeming to, he studied the room carefully. None of the cabins had kitchens. All meals were prepared in this one room. The dining hall and kitchen occupied half of the building Isaac called his headquarters. The other half housed Isaac's office and personal quarters except for two rooms on the far end that had been turned into a small medical clinic. His thoughts turned to Carly, and he determined to get her alone and have a real talk with her.

Wolf knew Reuben hadn't wanted to forfeit the task of carrying the eggs to the kitchen, but he also knew the other man wanted some time alone for a little fine-tuning of the chicken coop. He'd been careful to keep his awareness of Reuben's secret door from the little man. His offer to deliver the eggs had put Reuben in a terrible quandary, but eventually he'd made the choice Wolf knew he would.

Wolf had been looking for an excuse to enter the headquarters building ever since Isaac left in his plane early that morning. With Luther nursing a sore head and Isaac gone, Wolf planned to do a little snooping.

Instead of arriving through the kitchen door, he'd walked right through the front door and into the main hall. In a glance he'd taken in the three doors leading from the hall. One led to the kitchen, one to Isaac's living quarters, and the third directly to Isaac's office. He'd leave by the front door too, but with a little luck he'd make a short detour on the way.

His eyes lit on a row of trays resting on a counter. There were eleven of them. Two women placed scoops of potatoes and beans on them. A third woman filled cups.

"Thank you for bringing the eggs," the tall cook effused. "I've been after Captain Isaac for months now to get me eggs. I told him the young ones are starting to look right peaked. He said God would watch over them, and if they'd take their vitamins every morning they'd be fine. Vitamins just aren't the same as fresh eggs, now are they?"

"No, ma'am." Wolf started backing toward the door. His mind was racing. Vitamins? What kind of vitamins? But if they took them in the morning . . . ?

"If you ask me, the good Lord—"

"Uh, I've got to go." Wolf ducked through the door. He took a deep breath and glanced around. The door to Isaac's quarters stood open, and indistinct sounds were coming from somewhere beyond the room Wolf could see. Furtively he stepped across the hall to the office door. He tapped twice, and when there was no response he twisted the knob. The door opened easily beneath his hand.

Once inside, Wolf faced a luxury found nowhere else in the camp. A thick carpet muffled his footsteps, a leather couch sat before a stone fireplace, and a gleaming mahogany desk looked out over the common. A laptop computer sat on the desk and beside it a sophisticated radio system.

Taking care not to disturb anything, he began leafing through Isaac's calendar. Three late summer dates had been circled. Why? His hand reached for the top drawer, and an icy prickle ran down his back. A sudden vision of a woman pouring green punch into eleven tin cups swam before his eyes.

He tipped over a fancy leather swivel chair in his haste to get out of the room. He righted it quickly, cracked the door, and seeing no one about, raced across the hall.

Back in the kitchen he could see the trays were gone. He tore across the room and wrenched open the back door.

"Whatever is the matter?" The cook's voice followed him as he dashed past her. The women were almost to the building that housed the school. Two of them carried the children's dinner trays on a stretcher between them. The third woman walked alone carrying the drink tray, eleven tin cups of green punch and one tall glass of iced tea. Wolf raced after them. His shoulder crashed into a woman's back.

"Oops! Excuse me. Oh my gosh, I'm sorry." Wolf fought to

conceal his triumph at the sight of tin cups rolling at his feet, their contents sinking into the dirt. "You aren't hurt, are you?" He helped the woman to her feet.

She began to whimper. "I'm fine. But Captain Isaac will be angry, and the children will be fussy without their drink. He said they must have it every night right at six."

"Don't worry." He patted her comfortingly on the back. "It was my fault. I'll explain to the cook and get something else for them."

"Oh, no. It's my responsibility—"

"No, it was my fault, I'll do it." Wolf was already gathering up the cups.

"No, I'm the only one who knows how to mix it right. Isaac said it was my job." Wolf insisted on carrying the tray. Now what? She'd just mix more of the stuff, and he couldn't get away with running her down a second time.

As he carried the tray to the sink he watched the woman's actions. From a cabinet a few feet away, she pulled out a large can of powdered drink mix. From it she dumped two plastic measuring cups of powder into a clean pitcher. Replacing the plastic lid on the can, she shoved it to the back of the shelf then reached for a smaller can. From it she measured two carefully leveled scoops of another powder. He watched as she filled the pitcher with water and slowly stirred the mixture.

"Are the cups ready?"

"Just a minute." Wolf took his time scrubbing them.

"Need some help?" Startled he turned to see Carly leaning against the counter on the other side of him.

"No. I can manage." Manage? There was no way he could manage. If his suspicions were correct, he had two choices. Let the kids be doped again or blow his cover.

"Sister Hazel, you're shaking too much to fill the cups." He made his voice sound solicitous. "You go help Sister Marian set the tables. This little accident has upset you and put everyone behind. I'll finish up here. By the time you get back the cups will be washed, filled, and ready to go."

"Well, all right, Brother Wolf, but I hope it doesn't take long. Sister Hampton gets upset when the children don't get taken care of on time." She scuttled from the room to join the cook as though she expected a reprimand for shirking her duty.

"All right, what was that all about?" Carly's hands joined Wolf's in the soapy dishwater. "And don't tell me you sent that lady flying by accident."

She must have been watching from the infirmary and saw everything. He weighed his choices. He could insist it was an accident or gamble on the truth. Carly had access to drugs, but he'd bet his life she had nothing to do with the green concoction. Carly, of all people, could be trusted where the children were concerned.

"Um-m, it's Daniel. He doesn't like green punch."

"Daniel doesn't like green punch?" Carly's eyebrows shot upward and she stared at Wolf incredulously. "You did that because Daniel doesn't like green punch?"

"It makes him sleepy."

"Sleepy?" Carly's eyes grew narrow. "How do you know—?" She glanced at the pitcher then back at Wolf. Wolf knew the moment she made the connection. Less than a second later the green punch was washing down the sink.

"How dare he—?"

"Sh-h, there's no time to talk."

They worked together quickly, each anticipating the other's need without speaking. Carly found frozen lemonade in the freezer and quickly mixed it with water. Her hands shook and he could see she was on the edge of an explosion.

"How did you escape your watch dog?" Wolf spoke out of the corner of his mouth.

"He's asleep. I gave him something for his headache."

Wolf grinned at the irony. "You'd better get back to the infirmary before he wakes up," he whispered as Carly filled the last cup with lemonade.

"What are you going to do?" Carly whispered back. "Hazel won't take this to the children when she sees it's the wrong color."

"Don't worry. Just get out of here before Luther comes after you."

"Better do as he says."

Wolf glanced toward the door where Rachel stood framed in

the doorway. Out of the corner of his eye he saw Carly blanch. He had no idea how much Rachel may have overheard. He didn't even know whether she was friend or foe, but from what he'd seen last night, he didn't think she'd hurt Carly or the children. The important thing was to send Carly back to the infirmary.

"What about tomorrow?" Carly spoke quietly to Wolf, but her eyes remained on Rachel.

"Go on. I'll take care of it." He ushered her past the other woman and watched until she closed the front door behind her. He turned in time to see Rachel pick up the tray and saunter toward the back door. A faintly mocking smile curved her lips.

Hazel dithered when she found the tray gone and Wolf scrubbing the pitcher, but finally agreed that in the interest of time perhaps it was all right this one time for Rachel to carry the tray.

That night Rachel paused beside Wolf in the dining hall to give him a quiet message. He smiled and nodded.

Across the room Carly swallowed her hurt. What kind of woman was the redhead? Would she give away what she and Wolf had done? And why did she have to monopolize both Josh and Wolf?

She was glad Isaac was still away. Not only did his absence spare her having to listen to his preaching, but it gave her time to consider what she and Wolf had done that afternoon. Did the children's punch really contain a sedative? If so, she'd have to make certain it didn't happen again, but how? She looked toward Wolf and wondered what had made him suspect something was wrong with the drink.

Carly glanced down the long table and saw Mrs. Hampton. Did she know the children were being drugged? The thought made her uncomfortable and she turned her attention back to her plate. She ate quickly so she could return to her cabin and wait for Josh. He had to be told as soon as possible. He hadn't returned last night, but surely he'd be back tonight.

Before she got out of the dining room two men asked to walk her to her cabin. She refused them both politely, but firmly. She pitied the young men in the camp. There were so many of them, and no women they could spend their spare time with. They were all so starved for feminine attention they were driving her crazy, appearing in droves at the infirmary and declaring their love every time one managed to catch her alone. She had a horrible suspicion Isaac had added to the problem by telling them she'd choose one of them to marry. Isaac was wrong; she wasn't marrying anyone.

When Carly arrived at the cabin Petra was reading to Daniel. She played with them for almost an hour before getting them ready for bed. Josh hadn't appeared yet and her irritation grew as she helped the children with their prayers and tucked them in bed. Why was he staying away when his family needed him? She sat on the edge of the bed and waited until her eyes grew heavy, then gave up on him and crawled into bed with a sinking feeling in her heart.

She was almost asleep when she heard a light tap on the door. Josh had returned! She ran across the room to lift the latch, then stood back in surprise as Wolf stepped into the room and quickly closed the door behind him.

"What are you doing here?" His actions were so furtive she found herself whispering. Disappointment at Josh's continued absence warred with the pleasure of seeing Wolf.

"I came to check on you," Wolf spoke matter-of-factly. He stepped closer and took her chin between his strong fingers, turning her face toward the light. His touch was firm, but gentle as a caress. The muscles in his jaw flickered and his mouth became a grim line. A tiny tremor rippled down her throat from the spot where his hand cradled her face. She brought her hand up to touch the back of his. Their eyes met, and for several long seconds she felt caught up in an emotion too powerful to permit movement.

He swallowed hard and released her face, allowing her hand to flutter back to her side.

"He'll pay for this, I promise you that."

"I'm not concerned with vengeance, only with getting my family away from here." She took a couple of agitated steps away from him, then turned back as she spoke. "I thought you were Josh when you came to the door. Once he sees my face, I know he won't want anything more to do with Isaac."

"Josh won't be back for a few days. Isaac plans to keep him away until your bruises fade."

She stared at him as though his words were gibberish, yet at some deeper level she knew he spoke the truth. She looked at him as if he made no sense. Nothing about Wolf made sense, a voice in the back of her head reminded her. He knew things no stranger to Isaac's community could know.

"Who are you? Why are you here?" Fear and uncertainty crowded her throat, making her words harsh.

"I'm a friend. There are things I can't tell you, but I swear I'll do everything possible to keep you and your family from getting hurt."

"You really aren't one of them?" A look of pain crossed his face. Two fingers brushed her cheek in a feather-light caress.

"No, I'm not one of them, but for now I must convince them I am. Will you keep my secret?"

She looked deep into his eyes and whispered, "Yes."

"One more thing." There was regret in his voice. "Will you pretend to settle in here, act as though you accept your situation?"

Could she do that? What about Isaac's order to marry? What about the children? How could she bear Luther's presence day after day? She didn't voice her doubts. Instead she bowed her head, and while fighting a sudden surge of tears threatening to break free, she nodded her agreement.

She suspected she was a fool to trust Wolf without knowing more. Perhaps loneliness and her sense of estrangement from Josh were clouding her thinking, but at the moment Wolf appeared to be the only friend she had.

The next day was much like the day before. She occasionally caught a glimpse of Wolf, but not Josh. She grew worried about his continued absence and more concerned over her forced association with Luther. Luther was evidently feeling better. He'd trapped her against the examining table once and had her cornered in the back room when a worried mother brought in her nine-year-old son.

"Doc?"

Carly acknowledged the woman. She'd given up trying to make her patients understand she wasn't a doctor. "There's something wrong with Luke." She pushed forward a shy, frightened boy.

"Jump up on the table." Carly smiled, attempting to set him at ease. When she finished examining him, she turned to the mother. "His pulse is a little fast. Is he a nervous child?"

"Not usually." The woman chewed her lip. "When he was littler he cried and fussed a lot, always wanted to do things he shouldn't, but he's been much better since we came here. He comes straight home from school and goes right to bed, but last night he had an awful stomachache and his head hurt. He whined while I was getting him ready for school this morning and he threw up his lunch . . ."

"Did Mrs. Hampton send him home?"

"Oh no, she's not allowed to do that, but as soon as he got home he said he was cold. He just sits on his bed and shakes instead of going to sleep."

Carly was stumped. Something about the child's symptoms sounded vaguely familiar, though not serious at this point. His temperature was normal in spite of the glazed, feverish look in his eyes. The mother, however, seemed to be overreacting.

"He probably has the flu. But if he continues to vomit and shiver, you should get him to a doctor. Watch him closely for a day, then bring him back to me. If he's in pain, come to me right away." She couldn't rule out appendicitis, but it didn't seem likely. She chewed the inside of her lip in frustration. She simply wasn't qualified to diagnose the child's illness.

After the woman left, Carly handed the drug closet key to Luther and turned away to pick up her jacket. Her mind was still on her last patient, and she didn't dodge quickly enough when Luther grabbed her from behind. An elbow to his midsection brought an angry growl, but he released her.

"You won't get away with that next week." He slammed the door behind him, leaving Carly staring after him with dawning horror. He thought she would marry him! He'd hinted broadly enough before, but the idea was so absurd she'd never taken it seriously. Not even Isaac would expect her to marry Luther, would he?

Josh didn't appear at the table that night. Isaac was back and after his sermon he and Luther conversed in whispers through the meal. Several times Carly felt them watching her and felt icy tremors snake down her back. She was glad to escape back to the cabin.

She took the children for a short walk to visit the chickens before putting them to bed. They both seemed withdrawn and reluctant to talk about their day. Daniel insisted on undressing himself, and by the time Carly climbed back down the ladder Petra was already in bed. Keeping the light low, she picked up her sewing basket to work on a dress for her niece while she waited for Josh.

He returned late that night. Long after the children were asleep, Carly heard his step at the door. She lay down her sewing and flew to his arms.

"Josh, oh Josh. Where have you been? I've been so worried."

"Worried? I sent you a message, telling you I'd be away a few days. Didn't you get it?"

"No, no one told me anything. Josh, we've got to leave here. The school is terrible. There are no books and the children are held there like prisoners. The children are drugged to keep them quiet. They never play or do things with their families. Luther works at the infirmary with me, and I spend all my time avoiding his hands. Isaac hit me and said I have to get married in one week. I think he expects me to marry Luther. It's already been three days and I'm scared." It all came out in one frantic outburst.

"Oh, Carly. I know you didn't want to come and it's not easy for you here, but it can't be that bad. Please be patient a little while longer. Now what's this about Isaac hitting you?"

"The first morning, right after I took the children to school, he was here waiting for me when I got back. He was snooping through my things. He ordered me to run the infirmary and when I objected, he hit me in the face."

"What?" Josh reached out to touch her. Slowly he turned her face from side to side. Carly knew the bruises had faded and in the dim light Josh would have no idea of the severity of the blow. "I'm sorry, Carly. It won't happen again."

"You can't be sure. The only way to be sure is to leave here."

"Carly, I can't leave. If you wouldn't resist Isaac so fiercely, everything might go better." Was she imagining or did Josh's voice carry an element of fear?

"Nothing is going to get better here. You know that. Next time it might be Daniel or Petra who displeases him. And what are they being taught in that school? What if he does force me to marry one of the men here?"

"Now, Carly . . ." His big arms came around her. "I don't believe the man exists who could force you to marry him if you don't want to. Isaac's bluffing. You're pretty direct, and he's not used to that from women. You must have made him mad, and he latched onto the first threat he could think of."

"He was angry, but I think there's more to it than that."

"No, Carly. Trust your big brother. You're not marrying anybody you don't say yes to of your own free will. I'll have a talk with Luther tomorrow and make it clear I won't stand for him harassing you. Now get to bed. You look as bushed as I feel."

She lay awake after the lamp was extinguished mulling over all that had happened the past few days and Josh's words. She was sure that if he'd seen her face three days ago, he would have been furious. Was it possible Isaac had kept Josh away for that very reason? So he wouldn't see her face until the bruises faded? Wolf had said as much.

Carly felt more optimistic the next morning when she walked the children to school, then hurried to the infirmary. With Petra and Daniel's pleas added to her own, surely Josh would take them away from the compound. The two of them had been happy to see their father, and they'd lost no time letting him know how much they disliked the present arrangement. She didn't feel so alone anymore. Wolf was on her side and so were the children; if she were patient, everything would work out. She'd taken Isaac's threat too seriously; he really couldn't force her to get married. This wasn't the dark ages. She'd try harder to get along until Josh could make arrangements for their departure.

Dodging Luther was beginning to feel like part of the routine, and she stepped around him easily as she tidied up the examining room. He disappeared as usual to collect sandwiches for their lunch, and when he returned he was in a foul mood. He planted himself in a chair and glared at her, but he didn't try to grab her. She surmised Josh had kept his word to have a little talk with him.

The door opened so abruptly it crashed against the wall. Rachel burst into the room with a limp, unconscious child in her arms.

"Over here. Lay him right here." Carly indicated the padded table. Immediately she bent to check the child's respiration. He was breathing—barely. Blood ran profusely from a deep scalp laceration, and his little face and arms were covered with bright red welts. She barely recognized the blond toddler she had seen in company with his mother, the woman called Deborah.

As Carly recognized the signs of a severe beating, her lips tightened to an angry white slash. She'd seen plenty of similarly abused children in the trauma center in Los Angeles. Scarcely aware of the conversation behind her, Carly concentrated on stopping the bleeding.

"Does Deborah know you brought her brat here, Rachel?" Luther's voice revealed his lack of concern for the child.

"I don't care whether Deborah knows or not. Benjamin is going to die if he doesn't get help."

"Maybe I ought to tell Isaac about this."

"Maybe you should, and while you're at it you can tell him for me that if Benjy dies, our deal is off."

Carly was aware with some part of her mind that the door opened and closed, but her attention was focused on her small patient. Frantically she fought to stop the bleeding.

"He needs oxygen and I'll connect an IV. Luther, hold this gauze right here while I—"

"I've got it." Rachel's hand reached out to hold the bandage.

Carly worked quickly. Four years of trauma-room nursing in Los Angeles' inner city guided her actions. As soon as the IV was taped in place and the boy's breathing stabilized, she cut away the child's shirt and removed his pants. Rachel helped her.

Rachel gasped. The little body was covered with bruises and welts, and one leg turned at a grotesque angle. While Carly set the leg and wished for an orthopedic surgeon and an x-ray machine, she had Rachel rub a soothing ointment over the many abrasions.

"That witch! I'd like to take a rod to her!" Rachel exploded.

"Deborah? Deborah did this?" Deborah was a little strange, but Carly hadn't once thought of her as the violent type. Still, after all her years as a trauma nurse, she should have remembered there was no such thing as a "violent type."

"No, not Deborah. Although she's one of those wives who agrees with her husband on everything, and he says sparing the rod spoils the child."

"Who is her husband?" Carly only half listened for the answer as she began the delicate task of closing the deep wound on the child's head. She glanced up to see a strange expression on Rachel's face.

"Deborah is married to Captain Isaac."

"This poor baby is Isaac's son?"

"Yes. Does that make a difference?"

"No, but did he do—"

"No. Rebecca Hampton did this."

"Mrs. Hampton? The school teacher?"

"Yes, Isaac gave her carte blanche to beat any of the children who don't behave. Benjamin didn't sleep well last night, and when he started crying at school this morning and wouldn't stop, she beat him until he did. Daniel escaped from the classroom and came after Josh. He found me instead."

"But this boy's too little to go to school." Reaching to check the boy's pulse again, she found that it was steadier. His breathing was more regular, too. If he didn't wake up soon she'd have cause to worry, but right now she felt optimistic the child was going to make it. When he woke up, he'd be in a lot of pain; but Carly didn't dare sedate him because of his head injury.

"What about the other children?" She felt a sudden dread of the consequences to Daniel for his heroic action.

"Wolf is with them. Reuben and Wolf were hanging around the chicken coop, and I called for them to help me. Wolf stayed at the school while I came here."

Carly breathed easier until the door suddenly burst open. She glanced up to see Isaac coming toward her, his face like a thundercloud. He never even glanced toward his small son. She sucked in her breath and prepared for battle, but the attack didn't come immediately. It was Rachel he turned toward.

"I've warned you, Rachel. Since you refuse to take charge of the school, I won't tolerate your interference with Sister Hampton's discipline. Being my daughter doesn't exempt you from following my rules."

"Your rules, Daddy, almost got Benjamin killed. He still isn't out of danger. If Benjy dies, you'll no longer have any hold on me." Rachel spoke softly, but her words sounded an alarm in Carly's head.

Rachel is Isaac's daughter? No! How could Rachel and Benjamin both be Isaac's children? Rachel was older than Deborah. A picture of the woman in Josh's arms swam before her eyes. With shaky hands she reached for a blanket to cover her patient. How involved were Rachel and Josh? Josh and Isaac's daughter! She shuddered.

Carly glanced down at the unconscious child, her heart filled with pity and fear.

"Leave now, Rachel. Go to your room. I'll deal with you later." Carly heard the unspoken threat behind the words.

"Benjy needs me." Rachel's voice dropped to a whisper.

"Carly will take care of Benjy. That's her job."

Green eyes sent a beseeching plea to Carly before Rachel left the room, with noticeable reluctance. Not speaking, Carly concentrated instead on adjusting the drip that ran into the pathetically thin arm of the little boy.

"Sunday, Carly. On Sunday you pick a husband."

"No, Isaac." Caught off guard, Carly responded instinctively. She took a deep breath and reminded herself to stay calm, retain her poise. "I'm not getting married. I won't marry until I'm ready."

Isaac was silent for a moment before he said, "Daniel disobeyed. He didn't have permission to leave the school. He'll have to be punished unless—" Isaac turned his head to stare pointedly at Benjamin. "When someone disobeys my commands, my wrath is fierce to behold."

Carly reeled with shock. As her knees began to buckle, she grabbed the bedrail to support herself. Isaac's fanatical religion obviously meant more to him than even the life of his young son. She stared at Benjy and saw Daniel. A man who felt nothing at seeing his own child in this condition wouldn't hesitate to carry out his threat against another child.

She bowed her head submissively. *Oh, Josh,* she cried silently. *You were so wrong. With Daniel as a lever, Isaac can make me do anything he wants. Even marry a man I detest.*

Eight

"Don't take it too hard, Joe."

"But Isaac said she could choose." The young man stood before a narrow mirror, combing his hair. Laughter greeted his words.

"Sure she can choose, so long as she chooses Luther." The other man lounged on his bunk.

"She wouldn't choose you anyway." Another man joined the conversation.

"She might!" The younger man bristled.

"You and fifty other guys can dream, but face it kid, you're not man enough for a woman like that. Isaac'll make sure she has a husband who can keep her in line. Luther's big enough and mean enough." Several men snickered.

"The only choice that matters is God's choice, and Isaac speaks for God." Another voice joined in.

"Rachel wouldn't have him, maybe the doc won't either." The young man's voice sounded almost desperate.

Wolf stiffened. They were talking about Carly! He pretended to be asleep, but watched through slitted eyes and listened more closely. Most of the men in the barracks were getting ready for bed, but a few were leaving shortly for guard duty. A dozen men had already left with Luther for some secret night maneuver. The way Joe had been primping all evening he obviously planned a detour past the infirmary on his way to his assigned position. A surge of annoyance passed through Wolf.

At the other end of the long barn-like building, half a dozen of Isaac's soldiers were gathered around a table with an open Bible before them. One guy stood in the aisle methodically pelting darts into a magazine photo of a black rock star. The would-be suitor picked up a khaki jacket. He was trying valiantly to ignore the heckler.

"Doc won't have any choice. Isaac gave her a week. After that, something just might happen to those brats she brought with her if she decides she don't want old Luther."

"Don't say things like that." There was an edge of desperation to the young man's voice. "Isaac wouldn't hurt those kids; he's a prophet. Anyway they're not her kids. They belong to Josh, and Isaac likes Josh."

"Aw, come off it, kid. You know why he likes Josh. If Snakes Johnson wasn't in prison, Isaac wouldn't need Josh to build his bomb."

"You're a cynic, Schmidt."

"You talk too much." An older man with narrow eyes and tightly cropped hair cut in with a warning. "I doubt either Isaac or Luther would be happy if they heard you discussing Josh's special talents."

Wolf watched beneath his eyelashes as the men in the barracks looked around nervously. He felt sick. Carly couldn't marry Luther. Luther would break her spirit—or kill her. Wolf decided he'd get her up the mountain to Bradley. It would be risky, but for her to stay would be riskier.

"That child was beaten!"

"There might be another explanation."

"No, Josh. Benjamin, Isaac's own son, was attacked by his teacher, and Isaac doesn't care. Daniel or Petra could be next. How can you still refuse to take them some place where they will be safe?"

"Is there any place where they can be really safe? They're as safe here as anywhere." Josh's voice sounded desolate. Carly looked at him sharply and her eyes narrowed. Josh didn't look well. Why hadn't she noticed he'd lost weight and his eyes looked dull? It was probably fatigue, combined with the poor light in the cabin, but it provided extra impetus to her determination to convince him they must leave.

"There's something strange about the children here. I told you I thought they were being drugged. The first two nights we were here, I never saw or heard a child anywhere in the compound, then Wolf dumped the powder that was being added to the punch the children were given. Last night I heard children cry several times, and tonight while I sat with Benjy I noticed that in every cabin where there are children, the children are fussy and restless. I've examined a few of them. They don't seem ill, yet they complain of stomach pain or headaches and they're restless and unable to sleep. I think they're going through some kind of barbiturate withdrawal."

"Carly, you're carrying your concern for the children too far. Isaac has a lot on his mind, and he carries a great load of responsibility. You said yourself it was the teacher, not Isaac, who struck the boy. You've misunderstood the situation. I'm sure Isaac cares about his son. He cares about everyone here, even you. He told me how badly he felt that you'd been injured. He said he didn't mean to hit you, but when you rushed in here shouting wild accusations, he jumped up too quickly and jostled you so you tripped and fell against the wall. Sometimes he lacks patience, but he'd never harm little children." Carly sensed Josh was trying to convince himself more than her.

"He's a liar."

"Don't stir up trouble."

"Trouble? I'm trying to keep Daniel and Petra safe from trouble!"

"Nothing is going to happen to the kids. You've carried the responsibility for them too long and have become overly protective."

"I love them."

"I know you love them, and I appreciate more than you'll ever know all you've done for them and for me. But, Carly, it's time you got on with your own life. You should be married with little ones of your own, but you gave all that up to come here with us." He reached out to take her hands. "You don't have to stay here if you're unhappy. Go on back to Los Angeles or anywhere else you'd like to go. The children and I can't go right now, but I think Wolf would take you as far as one of the lodges, then you could get a plane out."

"Josh, you know Isaac isn't going to let me or anyone else just walk out of here. Besides I can't leave Petra and Daniel—or you.

You're all the family I have. But it's not me I'm worried about, it's the children."

Pulling her head against his chest, he patted her shoulder. "You don't have to worry about them any more. I've decided to get married again. You can get on with your life and know they'll be taken care of."

"Married?" Carly jerked her head back and craned her neck to look up at her brother. His eyes didn't quite meet hers.

"Yes. Rachel and I will be getting married in a few weeks."

"Rachel? Rachel Isaac?"

"Yes, of course. We've been seeing each other for several months, but she only agreed a week ago to become my wife."

"You're out of your mind. She's Isaac's daughter." Carly's voice dropped to a whisper revealing the full horror of her reaction to Josh's words. "That's why you brought us here. You placed your desire for that woman before the safety of your children! Have you forgotten Anna? Sweet, gentle Anna would never agree to her children being raised here, with these people!"

A spark of anger flared in Josh's eyes before he spoke. "No, I haven't forgotten Anna. I'll always love her, but there's room in my heart for Rachel, too. She loves children and she will be a good mother to Daniel and Petra."

"Josh, don't do this. Isaac—"

"Rachel isn't Isaac."

"Like my friend Rita isn't responsible for Anna's death?" She took no pains to hide the bitterness she felt at his betrayal. "Josh, I want to get away from here and take the children with me. Even if you choose to live here and marry into this hate-filled cult, please let me take the children where they can grow up in a normal setting and attend a school where they don't have to watch a classmate be sense-lessly beaten."

Josh turned his back, and Carly watched his shoulders heave with great emotion before he turned back to her. "They are my chil-dren. I will not let someone else be responsible for them. They will stay here where I can watch over them." He tried to smile. "Perhaps Isaac is right. It is time you find a husband and have your own babies to worry and fuss about. Since none of the men here suit you, go on back to Los Angeles. Perhaps you can find someone there."

Every time she thought the nightmare couldn't get worse, it somehow did. Was Josh ill? Had his grief finally caused his sanity to snap? Not only was he prepared to become Isaac's son-in-law, but he could actually suggest she leave him and the children in this place! She couldn't even reason with him.

"I have to get back to Benjy. I only left because his mother wanted some time alone to pray over him. I only hope she hasn't finished the job started by his sadistic teacher and sick father!" She pulled open the door and slammed it shut behind her.

A dim light flickered in one window of the infirmary. Carly was still there. A wave of guilt washed over Wolf. He suspected he was partially to blame for what had happened to the little Isaac boy. He hadn't given a thought to the possibility the children might be addicted to that foul green punch. Their withdrawal symptoms were driving their parents crazy. It had driven the old dragon school teacher to nearly kill Benjy. He'd glimpsed bruises on several other children, too. They probably hadn't been drinking the stuff long, and the dosage was still relatively low or their symptoms would be a lot worse. Obviously it had affected the littlest guy the most. He wondered if Carly might know some way to help the other children. But then he remembered that Carly wasn't going to be around to help them; he was going to get her out of the compound somehow.

Following the shadows, Wolf made a point to be as silent as his namesake. The door made no sound when he eased it open. Luther was nowhere in sight; Carly was alone with her small patient. She sat on a wooden chair, her head bent forward, and her shoulders slumped, but she wasn't asleep. Her breath sounded as ragged as the child's.

"Carly." He hadn't meant to startle her, but she lunged protectively toward the child. Wolf's eyes narrowed. Did she expect another attack on the kid? "It's all right. I wanted to talk to you alone."

"Wolf!" She turned so swiftly the chair fell backward. Wolf made a grab for it and without quite knowing how it happened, he found Carly in his arms, crushed against his chest, her mouth inches from his. He breathed deeply, which didn't help. He should open his arms, let her go. But he didn't. He knew by the sharp intake of her breath that she felt something, too. His hand slid down her back, pressing her closer. She didn't resist. Instead she snuggled more comfortably against him. The first soft brush of their lips was like silk. Silk turned to fire. He'd never felt nearer to heaven.

"That's my love." What was he saying? He realized he cared about her, but love was for men who punched time clocks or raised cows, not for someone who followed his dangerous line of work. Slowly he drew back, allowing a hint of space between them. His breath was coming hard, and he could hear Carly's soft gasps.

"I'm sorry," he tried to apologize, but he knew he was lying. He wasn't at all sorry he'd held her or kissed her. He was only sorry he'd started something he couldn't ever finish. He glanced around quickly, assuring himself they were still alone. "You've got every right to haul off and hit me, but please wait until I've said what I came to say. I found out yesterday a little more about the drug that was being given to the children at school. It was supposed to put them to sleep so they wouldn't cause any trouble or make noise until it was time to go to school again the next day."

"What?!"

Knowing that Isaac's office was just on the other side of the wall, Wolf quickly placed his hand over her mouth. "It's okay . . . they're not being drugged anymore. But what I didn't consider was that the kids would go through cold turkey withdrawal when the drug was eliminated so abruptly."

"*Mffph.*"

"Oh. I'll move my hand, but please don't yell or make any noise. Isaac's apartment is real close."

"Barbiturates! I suspected as much."

"Sh-h. Is there anything we can do to help them?"

"No, they're probably through the worst of it, unless another one gets beaten." He wished she hadn't said that. He felt guilty enough. "Isaac must know the children are no longer being drugged. Won't he find another way to give it to them?"

"He might not have any more on hand, but I intend to watch for that possibility."

"If he finds out you're responsible, it will mean trouble."

"I'll deal with that if I have to. Right now I'm more concerned with helping the kids through withdrawal."

"Exercise might help. If they are physically tired, it will be easier for them to sleep without the drug. They need exercise anyway; it's not good for anyone to be confined all day."

"Okay, they need exercise. Anything else?"

"No. Yes! Fluids will help. They'll need to be handled with a lot of patience and care for a week or so. Except Benjy." She looked down at the little boy lying on a padded gurney. Wolf didn't miss the troubled look in her eyes. "He's going to be in a lot of pain when he wakes up, and I won't be able to give him anything strong enough to keep it at bay."

"Carly, there's something else."

She looked at him expectantly.

"Isaac has plans to force you to marry Luther."

"I know."

"You know?" Wolf almost forgot to keep his voice down. "Do you want to marry him?"

"No. Of course not, but I don't have a choice."

"Yes, you do. I can help you get away."

"Could I take Petra and Daniel?" Hope flared in her eyes, but died a sudden death when he shook his head sadly.

"No, not without their father's permission, or unless they're in imminent danger. The way you're going would be too difficult for them anyway."

"Then I won't be going."

"Carly, listen to reason. You can't marry Luther. The first time you stand up to him, he'll beat you until you look like that poor kid." He jerked his head toward Benjy.

"And if I don't marry Luther, that will be Daniel." She stood with her arms folded, her back rigid. He could almost feel the pain behind her eyes from the tears she refused to let fall. She'd marry Luther if that's what it took to keep Daniel from meeting the same fate as Benjy. Wolf felt a tremendous blaze of anger and behind the anger, fierce admiration for Carly's courage.

He gritted his teeth and struggled to hold back his rage. Overlying his frustration and the black emotion he fought was a desire to go to Carly, hold her, tell her it would be all right, that he admired her strength and courage, that he would somehow save her. But he didn't know if he could save her if she refused to leave, and he wouldn't lie to her or give her false hope.

Tight, hard fingers clenched deep in his chest, and he swore Luther wouldn't have her. A moment's brilliant clarity mocked him. Who did he think he was kidding? It wasn't just Luther; he wouldn't let any other man have her. She was his! He slammed his hat on his head. "I'll be back." The words came out in a half snarl. He opened the door more forcefully than necessary, then stepped into the night.

The night was dark and thick clouds obscured the stars, but Wolf didn't need light. He knew the way. His only concern was that he might be missed in the barracks. He'd been able to slip away a couple of times to leave a message for Bradley, but this time he had to meet with his partner face to face and time was short. Bradley would be hard-pressed to get the information to Stewart and get papers back in time.

Carly watched Wolf leave. One minute he was there, then he was gone. She wished she understood him better. Why was he here? Several times he'd shown her a side of himself that was gentle and caring. There had been compassion mixed with anger when he looked at her small patient. He'd discovered the children were being sedated and he'd done something about it, then blamed himself for the attack on Benjy. He was patient with Daniel and Petra. He'd offered to get her away from the compound, but in the same breath he'd indicated he wouldn't be leaving the cult himself.

Wolf didn't have the characteristics she'd learned to associate with either the political or religious fanatics in the camp, but he might be a mercenary. He certainly knew his way around guns. The first day after she arrived in camp Wolf had helped Reuben build that sorry-looking chicken house, so she knew he wasn't a carpenter. But since then Isaac seemed to be using him as some kind of war games instructor. From the window of the infirmary she'd seen him with small groups of soldiers, showing them how to tear their guns apart, clean and oil them, then put them back together. The young men who came to the clinic "courting her" spoke almost reverently of the drills he led.

He'd held her like he cared, but only after she'd tripped and practically thrown herself at him. Possibly any normal man would have reacted the same. It was wishful thinking to imagine he might be staying because of her. She couldn't allow herself to be distracted by personal emotions anyway. She must concentrate her entire attention on keeping Daniel and Petra safe.

A small movement drew her attention back to Benjy. His little face twisted in a grimace. No, even if she were selfish enough to accept Wolf's offer, she not only couldn't leave her own nephew and niece, but she wouldn't be able to leave Benjy to struggle on his own for quite a long time.

By the time Wolf returned to the ledge overlooking the compound, it was too light to sneak back in the way he'd left. He couldn't risk being seen coming in that way. Bradley had been glad to see him and agreed to do as Wolf asked, but seemed to think it was all a marvelous joke. He'd stopped laughing long enough to let Wolf know that the Bureau of Alcohol, Tobacco, and Firearms was now investigating Isaac as well. A couple of their agents were late checking in. Also that Stewart was getting antsy about the evidence Wolf was supposed to find.

Wolf would have to wait until more people were wandering about, then join them unobtrusively. There seemed to be a buzz of activity around the gate. He counted sixteen men. At this hour there should be just the four guards. Luther and Isaac were both there, increasing Wolf's concern. Luther had taken a group of men out on patrol earlier, but unless something unusual had happened they should have returned hours ago and gone to bed. He wondered if he could get close enough to discover what the excitement was about without alerting them. He'd have to try; otherwise he could walk into a trap.

Patiently he worked his way closer, using trees and brush for cover. The sun coming over the mountain revealed streaks of wetness on the sand where four canoes had recently been pulled from the river. Whatever Isaac was angry about had to do with the returning night patrol. He couldn't get close enough to hear, but Isaac's gestures made it clear he was upset. He pointed to the canoes, then Wolf watched as two men pushed one of the canoes into the water. It appeared to carry a heavy, tarp-covered load. The men returned for a second canoe, which they boarded and used to tow the first.

Wolf wished he could be in two places at once. His gut told him there was something he should know about in the canoe disappearing from sight, while some instinct warned he'd better get back inside the compound in a hurry.

Luther and one other man were both carrying heavy packs and rifles. Some of the others were carrying guns, too, and several rifles leaned against the log gate. Wolf couldn't get an accurate count from where he crouched, but there appeared to be more guns than men. He glanced back toward the river, and a sick suspicion began to grow as he remembered two agents were missing on this mountain.

Abruptly Isaac headed for his headquarters. The other men followed him. Halfway there, Luther turned to bark orders for the guards to return to their posts, but by that time Wolf had already taken advantage of the moment to slip inside and duck behind the first barracks. A sharp whistle sounded and men began pouring from the buildings. Wolf stepped from the shelter of the log wall to be swallowed up in their ranks.

"Evidence has been found," Isaac shouted to the crowd from his position on the porch, "clearly indicating the puppet of evil has sent devils among us to spy and destroy. They shall not succeed! My army shall prevail!"

Wolf eased back into the shadows. Did Isaac refer to the ATF agents or had he been alerted somehow to Wolf's identity? If he had to run, he'd stay behind the buildings until he reached the chicken coop. Fortunately Isaac's spartan ethics when it came to his followers' comfort precluded windows at the back of buildings. Casually Wolf moved his head, checking who carried a gun and where certain men were positioned. By this time he had a pretty good idea who could shoot and how well. A white face far to Isaac's right caught his eye. A look of terror showed on Rachel's face.

"Federal spies were found last night by our night patrol. They were watching us and preparing a trap. Luther led his men into their midst, and they ran from the sword of justice."

Wolf thought of the tarp-covered canoe. *Ran nothing,* he thought bitterly.

"We must not relax our guard. This is just the beginning. Other sons of Satan will come to take their places. From this day forward our camp will be encircled about by warriors of God to protect our mission. No one will enter or leave this compound without my permission."

Oh great! Wolf didn't relish dealing with tighter security.

"Luther!"

"Yes, sir." Luther strolled casually from the infirmary. Wolf frowned. He hadn't seen the man enter the clinic. The last he'd seen, Luther was passing through the door into Isaac's headquarters.

"Double the guards tonight, and I want two men on that ledge." He pointed in the direction of the ledge where Wolf had paused an hour ago.

Isaac called out several other names and ordered the men who answered to start constructing towers at both the front and back of the compound.

"Wolf!"

"Yes, sir." He stepped forward easily. Not by a glimmer of emotion or tremor of muscle did he betray his surprise. Why was Isaac singling him out?

"I've got a couple of big guns that need to be assembled and mounted in those guard towers. Can you do it?"

"Bigger than M-60s?"

"Yes."

"I'll take a look." Wolf leaned against a log wall with feigned nonchalance. What did he have? A missile launcher? Once more he caught sight of Rachel. Her color had returned to normal, though she still looked unhappy. She wasn't looking his way. Wolf turned his head to follow her glance in time to see Josh send her some kind of signal. Wolf's eyes narrowed. It was time he found out what secrets Rachel was hiding. Josh would bear a little scrutiny, too.

A few minutes later Isaac dismissed the assembly, and Wolf made his way to where he'd last seen Rachel. She'd just turned away and when he placed his hand on her shoulder, she jumped.

"Guilty conscience?"

"What do you mean?" She was instantly wary.

"Sorry." Now wasn't the time to confront her with his suspicions. "Just thought you ought to know anyone coming down from barbiturate dependency tends to be nervous and emotional and in need of a lot of exercise, mega fluids, and in extreme cases a milder sedative for a short while to help them sleep."

"What?" She looked at him blankly.

"The green punch, lady." Her eyes widened in horror, then turned to hard jade. She understood. Like him, she hadn't associated drug withdrawal with Benjy's fussy night and beating. She might not be aware of the difficulty other parents and Mrs. Hampton were facing, but Isaac soon would.

Wolf continued. "You're as guilty as I am of getting rid of the miserable stuff, so what do we do now?" He had two aims—to protect the children and to find out how far Rachel would go as a co-conspirator.

"I'll take care of it." Rachel's voice was hard as flint and Wolf had no doubt she would. "Daddy wants me to be the children's teacher. We disagreed over the curriculum and he ordered that old dragon, Rebecca Hampton, to teach. He warned me the children would suffer if I didn't do as he wished. Once again Daddy wins."

Wolf was sure of one more thing. Rachel wasn't here because of any tender feelings toward her father. Something else held her and unless he was mistaken in the way he read her reactions, she was planning a move against Isaac, a move that had been hampered by this morning's events. Revenge might be a factor in her plan, but he hoped not. Revenge tactics had a way of backfiring and injuring more than the intended target.

Giving her a mock salute, he walked away and headed straight for the men's washroom. The facilities were primitive, but he needed a shower if he was going to make it through the day without sleep. He stepped behind a wooden barrier and stripped. Minutes later cold water sluiced down his face and poured over tired muscles. He shivered, but appreciated its revitalizing sting. He jerked a cord and the water dwindled to a trickle, then stopped altogether. He stood still deep in thought for long minutes until the cold spurred him to action.

Wolf reached for a towel, then froze as Luther's voice reached his ears. "I took care of it. Even if they burn this place down, there's nothing the feds can link to us. It's all hidden. Can you believe one of those pigs was carrying 600 bucks, cash?"

Wolf caught the sound of low laughter. The other man said something, but he spoke too softly for Wolf to hear the words.

"Right! He won't be needing it any more."

Another low rumble followed, then Luther spoke again. His voice sounded testy.

"No way, Schmidt. Not half. A hundred, and count yourself lucky. If you even threaten to squeal to Isaac, I'll cut your tongue out." Wolf pursed his lips as though about to whistle. Luther was playing a dangerous game, but then he'd suspected the man was more con-artist than religious zealot. He'd served time once for swindling, and Wolf never doubted he'd run another scam if he got the chance. Recalling Rachel's words the night Luther visited Carly's cabin, he suspected Luther was using every opportunity to line his own pockets.

The door slammed and Wolf waited. He didn't know if they'd both gone, or just Luther. He didn't have long to wait until the door opened again and closed more quietly this time. He reached for his pants while he mulled over what he'd just heard and what he'd pieced together from papers in Isaac's office and some research Marshal Stewart had forwarded to him through Bradley. If Luther hadn't hesitated to double cross Isaac for $600, Rachel's $6 million must be enough temptation to keep him awake nights.

Luther wasn't the only one with underhanded plans. Isaac was planning something big, something for which he needed both Rachel's fortune and Josh's familiarity with explosives. Isaac hadn't been able to force Rachel to marry his lieutenant, but indications were he'd found a new plan, and Wolf had a strong hunch that plan involved Carly.

Wolf's expression was grim as he finished dressing. He'd have to let Bradley know the ATF men were dead. With extra guards and Isaac alerted to the presence of federal agents, getting messages to Bradley would become harder. He'd have to wait a couple of nights. Sneaking out of the men's barracks wasn't easy. By the time he dared risk it again, he might even know where Luther had hidden whatever he'd hidden.

Wolf went in search of Isaac. He might as well find out what kind of guns he was supposed to put together.

Wolf spent the next two days with pieces of two guns scattered across the wide porch of the headquarters building. He had no idea what kind of guns he was building. They were something new, probably experimental, and required some kind of programming. Bradley could have them operating in nothing flat, but Wolf wasn't a computer man. He'd need time and several consultations with his partner before he'd have them operating. Hopefully he could stall long enough to keep them from ever being used.

While Wolf worked, he had a first-rate view of the compound. He grinned when he saw Rachel with the children instead of Mrs. Hampton. The older lady was rumored to be too ill to teach, but he suspected Rachel had brought about the change. Rumor also indicated that Isaac was pleased his daughter had finally accepted the assignment he'd given her. Apparently she'd refused when she first arrived at the compound. A cynical part of his brain wondered if Isaac had used his fists to persuade Rachel as he had Carly.

Rachel took the children out for an hour each morning to play rough-and-tumble games in the open common area. Wolf would give a lot to know how she had convinced Isaac to allow physical exercise to be interspersed with the dogma he expected her to teach. Unless drugging the children had been a ploy to get Rachel to change her mind, and now that Isaac's plan had worked, he recognized the need to restore the children's health.

Wolf felt grimly satisfied. He still didn't know what game Rachel was playing, but he was convinced she shared his determination to do all that was possible for the kids.

He caught glimpses of Carly as she ran between her cabin and the infirmary or quickly gulped down her dinner. Sometimes he heard Benjy cry out, followed by the soft rhythm of Carly singing to the child. Sometimes he wanted to punch all the men who pestered her with their attention; other times he was grateful their persistent wooing kept Carly from being alone with Luther. Though he stayed outside the infirmary, he positioned himself each day where he could keep an eye on her.

Being stuck with guard duty until five o'clock Sunday morning had Wolf seething with impatience. Time was running out. He needed just an hour to reach the message point he and Bradley had agreed upon, but could he disappear that long in broad daylight and get away with it? If his plan worked, he'd soon be out of the bunkhouse and in a cabin where his comings and goings would be less noticeable. And Carly would be a whole lot safer.

Instead of returning to the barracks when his shift ended, he knocked on Josh's door. Silence greeted his knock. Wolf fidgeted and knocked again. Finally he heard the scraping of a bar. That pleased him. Maybe Josh was finally getting a little sense if he'd installed a bar to protect Carly from unannounced visitors.

Josh blinked startled eyes when he saw his early morning caller. "Is something wrong?" He looked quickly toward the infirmary.

"No, nothing has happened." He felt a quick urge to tell Josh of the danger Carly faced, then decided the risk was too great. Josh might not believe him and go straight to Isaac. He knew Josh wouldn't deliberately hurt his sister, but his actions so far indicated he was deeply involved in Isaac's schemes. Wolf was uncertain to what extent Isaac controlled Josh, but if rumors were true, Josh was building a bomb, a bomb Isaac intended to use to destroy a major gathering of ethnic minorities some time in the fall.

"Sorry to wake you, but it's Sunday and I've got a couple of free hours before Isaac starts preaching. I wondered if I might borrow your son and a couple of fishing poles?"

Josh scratched his head. He opened his mouth to speak, then closed it. "You'll take care of him?" he finally asked. The question asked more than the simple words conveyed and gave Wolf hope that the other man might be more aware of the danger to his family than he'd previously indicated.

"He'll be safe with me." Wolf's answer was the right answer. While Josh went after Daniel, Wolf looked toward Carly's bed where she was curled up, her back to him. She didn't stir. Wolf knew she was tired. She'd only returned to her cabin from Benjy's side an hour ago when Rachel had tiptoed in to relieve her.

"Hi, Uncle Wolf." Daniel whispered as Josh urged him down the ladder. Ten minutes later he and the boy approached the gates, fishing poles in hand. After a few minutes' discussion with the guards and a promise not to go far, they followed a faint trail leading up the river. They stopped to dangle their lines in the waters of several promising holes. Wolf was pleasantly surprised when they each pulled in a nice-sized trout. About a mile from camp, Wolf dropped to his knees beside the little boy.

"Daniel, I'm going to leave you alone for a little while. I don't want to, but someone is going to hurt Carly if I don't go get something that will help her. I'm going to put my coat and hat on you and set you on a rock, so if anyone sees you from up on the hill they'll think you're me. Okay?"

"Okay." Daniel grinned for just a moment, then his face grew serious. "Is Isaac going to hit Aunt Carly again?"

"No, Daniel. I'll make sure no one hits Carly ever again."

Carly couldn't think of anything she wanted to do less than listen to Isaac preach. What she needed was sleep. Benjy was past the worst now and would be perfectly safe with Rachel. But he wasn't with Rachel; he was with Deborah. She wished she felt as confident of the boy's mother. Deborah had insisted on taking the boy home this morning, and though Carly didn't believe Deborah would actually hurt him, the woman spoke so strangely she made Carly uncomfortable.

Carly pulled on a dress. She knew Isaac wouldn't approve of it, but it was the only one she owned. Its pleated skirt of pastel blue fell to mid-calf. It was sleeveless with a white lace collar. A cluster of embroidered daisies drew attention to her waist. For just a moment she wondered if, when Wolf and Daniel returned from fishing, Wolf would notice how small the dress made her waist appear. She dismissed the thought and brushed out the length of her hair before quickly braiding it to form her usual coronet. Petra had dressed herself, but needed Carly's help with her braids.

When the three of them were ready, they joined hands to walk the short distance. Carly was glad Wolf had taken Daniel fishing. Neither she nor the children had been beyond the walls of the compound since they'd arrived, and Daniel missed the freedom he'd previously enjoyed. She just hoped they'd return before Isaac began preaching or he and Wolf would both be in trouble. She shifted from one foot to the other and wondered crossly why Isaac couldn't allow his followers to sit in the dining hall during his Sunday sermon. She felt much too tired to stand on the common while Isaac spouted his hate-filled, racist diatribe this morning.

Isaac's threat to force her to marry crossed her mind, but she had one more day before she had to choose. For a moment she prayed Isaac's ultimatum was the idle bluff Josh had said it was, but with the threat to Daniel she knew it wasn't. She knew, too, that she couldn't talk to Josh about it again either. Isaac intended her to appear willing; if she failed Daniel would suffer. She gazed around at the compound. It was squat and ugly, a terrible blight on this beautiful mountainside. Everything about Isaac's tightly controlled community was ugly, and she didn't intend to be a part of it any longer than she could help. Tomorrow she'd have to accept Luther as her fiance, but before a wedding could be arranged she'd find a way off this mountain.

She heard her name spoken and swung around. Isaac had taken his place at the front of the crowd of people standing in the sun on the dusty trammeled common.

"Carly Peterson and Zedekiah Luther will exchange vows immediately following this morning's sermon."

"No!" Carly gasped aloud, stunned by the pronouncement. She took an involuntary step backward. He couldn't do this to her!

"This is too fast!" Josh exploded. "You said you'd give her time to choose." He looked angry enough to hit someone, and out of the corner of her eye Carly saw half a dozen skinhead guards start toward them.

"She *has* chosen." Isaac's voice was cold and hard. Carly felt his eyes compelling her to look where he looked. She turned her head slowly and saw Daniel walking toward her, carrying his fishing pole. A string of trout dangled from one hand. An icy fist clutched her midsection and she gasped for breath. This was no bluff. If she didn't obey, Daniel would suffer. She bowed her head.

"That's right. She has chosen." Carly's head jerked up at the sound of Wolf's voice. He walked beside Daniel with a broad smile on his face. "She chose me. We've been engaged for more than two weeks."

Carly's head swam. Wolf was trying to save her! He was lying to protect her, just as she once lied to protect him. Isaac wouldn't allow it, but . . . oh how she wished it were true. He was beside her, his arm about her waist, and Josh pumped his hand, saying how happy he was.

"Now just a minute," Luther roared.

"Isaac said she could choose," a young man shouted above the murmuring of the crowd. He had visited the infirmary every day all week with some minor ailment. "There's still one more day," he added, as though one more day still gave him a chance.

"Seems the fox got the chicken." Reuben's sly voice came from behind her followed by a rusty chuckle.

Isaac and Luther whispered together for several minutes, then Luther triumphantly waved a piece of paper in the air. Isaac spoke.

"The Peterson woman was given until today to accept a husband. God has decreed that she marry on this day. In spite of the corrupt government of this land, property and family claims must be protected by those pieces of paper the government recognizes, and Luther has a marriage license issued by this state. Had Carly Peterson really chosen to marry someone else she would have—"

"She knew it was unnecessary, since I already have a license for us." Wolf, too, waved a document in the air. "As soon as Carly accepted my proposal, I hiked back to meet the plane that brought me in. I didn't just pick up my belongings, I gave the pilot $200 to fly me to the county seat and back. Carly had given me all the necessary documents, and we planned to tell Josh as soon as I returned. We haven't had two minutes together since then to tell him or anyone else of our plans."

Afraid to speak up, Carly huddled against Wolf's side. Luther stomped back to stand beside Isaac. "Well, who's she going to marry? Him or me?" he bellowed.

Nine

Carly closed her eyes against the horror for just a second. When she opened them again it was to look down at her nephew's wide grin. His six-year-old round face and near-white hair faded to be replaced by the memory of a smaller boy with hair the color of honey, a little boy battered and bruised almost beyond recognition. No, she didn't have a choice. Daniel must be kept safe. Agony tore at her soul; for precious seconds she leaned against Wolf's supporting arm, then drawing on more courage than she knew she had, she lifted her head.

"I have to marry Luther." She meant to speak firmly, to not let them think she was beaten, but the words came out in a nearly inaudible croak that carried no further than Wolf's ears.

"She said she's marrying me," Wolf shouted triumphantly.

"No, I can't. Daniel . . . He'll hurt Daniel." The words tumbled out in a whispered sob.

"He won't. Trust me, Carly."

Trust him? She knew almost nothing about him, except that she loved him. Yes, she loved him, but why did she have to discover that now? Loving Wolf would make marrying Luther that much harder. Luther was glaring at her. Instinct told her to snuggle into Wolf's arms for safety, but good sense told her to put distance between herself and Wolf. There was no sense in antagonizing Isaac or Luther further. She tried to step away, but Wolf's arm tightened about her until it nearly cut off her breath, leaving her incapable of speech.

Gradually she became aware of the hush settling over the crowd that had turned expectantly to Isaac. They were waiting for *him* to decide whom she would marry! A surge of bitterness swept through her. These people were so completely brainwashed by Isaac, they accepted without question his right to control the most intimate details of their lives. She had no allies against him, with the possible exception of Wolf and Josh, and she wasn't sure of them. Like everyone else, she thought bitterly, they were likely to cave in to Isaac the moment he said it was God's command she marry Luther. In her heart, she knew God had no part in this travesty. Her experience on the mountain had made one thing clear to her: *obedience to God and mindless submission to a self-proclaimed despot are not the same thing.*

"It makes no difference who she marries so long as she is decently wed this day." Isaac dismissed the subject as of little importance before opening his Bible and beginning to read.

In stunned silence, Carly shut out Isaac's attempts to validate his bigoted conspiracy theories with scripture. Did he mean it? Would she really be allowed to marry Wolf? Her heart skipped a beat. But, no. A sick certainty settled over her. Isaac hadn't changed his mind. He'd made it clear what he expected of her and the consequences if she refused. There was no question but that she'd choose to save Daniel, and in the process everyone would believe she had chosen Luther. She didn't want to see Luther's reaction to Isaac's words, but his furious face was impossible to avoid. There was no mistaking the hate and anger Luther directed toward her—and Wolf.

Wolf had gambled and won. Or maybe lost, depending how he looked at it. By marrying Carly, he would be setting himself up as a target. Luther would hate him for spoiling his plans. What those plans were he didn't know, but he suspected that Luther thought he had some financial advantage to gain by marrying Carly. Oh, he didn't doubt Luther wanted Carly in a much more elemental way, but something more was involved, something to do with money. Rachel and Carly would soon be related by marriage.

Was that the key? Luther had failed to get Rachel's money by becoming her husband; how could being her brother-in-law benefit him? Wolf didn't know and he didn't like the suspicions niggling at the back of his mind. Nevertheless he felt certain the man had some scheme in mind.

Wolf wasn't surprised by Isaac's willingness to switch grooms. Though the cult leader depended on Luther, he was too smart to entirely trust a man with Luther's record; Wolf had a strong hunch Rachel's money was a major factor in Isaac's plans, too.

He felt certain that by now Isaac must have a nice fat dossier on Dieter Karlis, the man Wolf was supposed to be. He'd know Dieter had no living relatives other than Josh's children, and that no one would come looking for Dieter if he suddenly disappeared. What's more, if he disappeared there would be no one outside the cult to ask questions about Josh and his family. Isaac was very good at surrounding himself with people without outside ties, people who were expendable.

Wolf didn't doubt that Isaac assumed he could control him, and through him, Carly. If he couldn't, no doubt Isaac had an accident or quiet disappearance in mind.

Wolf had made a dangerous enemy of Luther and drawn more attention to himself than was perhaps wise. On the other hand, marriage would give him access to a cabin and diminish the number of people aware of his movements. Most important, it would place him in a position where he could protect Carly. He wasn't sure how much he could tell her, though, and that was a problem. Nor had she said yes to this marriage he proposed. Her fear for Daniel overrode everything else. There had been a subtle shift in Josh and Isaac's relationship the past few days, and Wolf's instincts told him Isaac wouldn't hazard his hold on Josh by punishing the children at this point. But how could he convince Carly?

He cast a surreptitious glance at Josh's face. He seemed caught up in some stark emotion, part gratitude and part fury. Perhaps Isaac's grip on Josh wasn't as strong as the militant preacher believed it to be.

With an arm around Carly, he could feel her tremors as Isaac stood on the porch and preached to the crowd assembled on the dirt-packed common. Isaac expected silence from his followers when he preached, and Wolf didn't dare risk whispering encouragement to Carly. Several times Josh reached over to squeeze her hand. Each time his features revealed barely controlled rage, a rage Wolf didn't doubt was directed at Isaac.

Isaac's ranting stretched on, adding the torment of aching legs and a blazing sun to already stretched nerves. The man was a devil, no two ways about it, and Marshal Stewart was right. Agents shouldn't work on cases where they were personally involved. When this case finally came down, Wolf might have to be restrained to keep him from strangling Isaac with his bare hands. His work revolved around protecting people; he'd become a peace officer because he believed that a strong, peaceful society could only exist where the weaker elements of that society were safe from predators. But he'd never experienced such a compelling need to protect anyone before as he now felt for Carly.

The preaching finally stopped and Wolf felt Carly draw in a deep breath.

"It'll be all right," he tried to reassure her. Anger toward the man preempting Carly's right to choose her own future made his voice gruffer than he'd intended.

"Joshua," Isaac raised his voice. "Bring Carly and Dieter forward."

"Josh, please get the children away from here." Carly made a last whispered appeal to her brother, who refused to meet her eyes.

"Wolf, don't do this." Tear-filled, pleading eyes turned to him. He smiled encouragement and ached to give her the reassurance she really needed.

He removed his arm from her waist, laced his fingers through hers, and swallowed a sudden lump in his throat. Whether she wished to or not, Carly was about to become his wife. A stab of regret pierced his heart. He'd never planned to marry and here he was forcing a woman to marry him. And no matter how honorable his intentions, the fact remained she hadn't consented.

Wolf and Carly, followed by Josh and the children, moved toward the porch steps. Luther turned his back and stormed inside the building. As Carly stared after him in confusion, Isaac began to speak. Not until Wolf made his response in a firm, clear voice, did she realize the ceremony had begun. She spoke her vows in a daze, not understanding why Isaac was allowing her to marry Wolf instead of Luther. She'd seen Isaac and Luther whispering together as she and

Wolf approached the porch and had steeled herself to say she would marry Luther.

Brief dreams of being Wolf's wife had crept into her thoughts during the past few weeks, but she didn't want to be the object for his sacrifice. He was only marrying her to protect her. And what about Daniel? She groped for her nephew's hand. Would he suffer because she'd lacked the strength to call Luther back? She could feel tears running down her face, but could do nothing about them without freeing her hands, and she couldn't let either Daniel or Wolf go.

The ceremony was brief, and at its conclusion Wolf slipped a plain gold band on her finger, then rushed her to sign her name to the paper he held. Isaac signed, too, as did Rachel and Josh.

"The fourth cabin on the back row is empty. Move your things there." Isaac spoke abruptly before he, too, disappeared inside the building. He was already out of sight when Wolf added his own name to the marriage license and quietly slipped the document into an inside pocket of his jacket.

Carly stood still, as if she might shatter if she moved. Around her she saw with a terrible clarity the bare ugliness of weather-warped wood, the dirt and weeds. Beneath the squalor, a greater ugliness thrived—the ugliness of hate and domination, and the loss of personal will. A picture of Anna floating down the aisle of St. Paul's on a cloud of satin and lace to meet Josh intruded into her thoughts. Anna had glowed with happiness while smiles and warmth had filled the church. Here there were no smiles, no well-wishers. When the brief ceremony ended, everyone turned away to go about their business.

Carly shook her head, forcing herself to face reality. Josh pried Daniel's hand loose from hers and gave her a fierce hug. Tears glistened in his eyes, and his voice was husky as he whispered. "I never believed Isaac would go so far. But it'll be all right. Wolf will make a good husband."

Carly spoke softly but urgently. "Until you can get the children away, don't let them out of your sight!" She stooped to kiss them both, then stood biting her knuckles as Josh led them away. Numbness settled like a thick cloud in her mind, stealing the strength from her legs, freezing her tongue, and robbing her of the will to fight for survival. She felt herself sinking into nothingness until Wolf touched her hand, igniting a tiny fire in her heart. No, she wouldn't quit. She wasn't beaten yet.

Wolf carefully wrapped his arm around Carly's shoulders, but she seemed scarcely aware of his presence. He glanced uneasily at her. She seemed to be in some kind of trance. He'd seen soldiers look like that; young men who had seen too much trauma, too much loss. Tenderly he drew her to his side and began looking for the cabin they would share beginning today.

Not knowing what they'd find when they reached the cabin they'd been assigned, he detoured toward the chicken coop. He sat her down on a log Reuben used for a chopping block and dropped to a crouch in front of her. Her face was wet. That was a good sign. She needed the emotional release of tears.

Lifting both hands to her face, he used his thumbs to brush away her tears. "Carly, I wanted to speak to you sooner, but I wasn't certain I could get the license in time. I couldn't let you marry Luther. I considered kidnapping you and hauling you bodily off this mountain, but you would have hated me for separating you from your family. The last thing I want is for you to hate me."

"I don't hate you." She spoke softly as from a great distance, each word weighted with pain. "What you did was brave and noble, but what about Daniel? I told you what Isaac said would happen to Daniel if I didn't marry Luther." She raised tear-drenched eyes to his face.

"Daniel will be all right. Isaac has some kind of grand plan, and he needs Josh's help to carry it out. His treatment of you has driven a rift between them, and Isaac won't risk antagonizing Josh any further for a while." He didn't add that he planned to have her and her family miles away before Isaac could put his plan in action.

"Why does he need Josh?"

Wolf didn't share his suspicions concerning Josh's expertise with blasting components. He didn't want to add to her worries by telling her of the bomb Josh was rumored to be making.

"I don't know for sure. Whatever he's doing is important enough that Isaac realized he'd made a mistake when he hit you and that he couldn't risk Josh seeing your injured face. That's why he had to send him away until the bruises on your face faded. He doesn't have as much control over Josh as he would like, and whatever he's doing, he doesn't have anyone else who can do it. He won't hurt Daniel as long as he needs Josh."

She shivered. "He's doing something with explosives, isn't he?" Wolf didn't answer. There really wasn't anything he could say. She stood up and walked with halting steps to the mesh wire enclosing the chicken run. She stood with her fingers laced through the wire staring at the red hens scratching in the dirt, but he doubted it was the chickens she saw.

"Do you believe in God?" she asked without turning to face him.

"Yes. Yes, I do."

"Isaac talks about God. He says everything he does is God's will, but I don't believe it. Ever since I was a small child, I've had this feeling deep inside me that God is real, and I've been comforted by a sense that he loves me. I can't reconcile that feeling with Isaac's religion."

Wolf came to stand beside her. His big hand covered hers where her fingers gripped the wire. He didn't know what to say. He wanted to comfort her, but didn't know how. A picture of his mother kneeling in the soil between the rows of her garden came to his mind. She looked up at him and with the back of one hand pushed a floppy brimmed hat further back on her head. Moisture gleamed on her skin as she pointed a trowel in his direction and spoke from her heart. He repeated her words aloud to Carly.

"Everything good comes from God. People tend to blame everything on him, but it so happens, Satan goes around planting seeds, too. You have to look at the harvest to tell who planted it. If you get good corn and beans, it's because good corn and bean seeds were planted and nurtured. If you get weeds and thistles it's because you didn't trouble to root out the devil's planting. People are like good rich soil. The ones who accept the Lord's seeds in their hearts produce goodness. You can tell by a person's actions and accomplishments if he serves God. People who abuse and take advantage of others serve another master."

He paused, then added his own conclusion. "There's no goodness or honor in Isaac. Your instincts aren't wrong, and that faith you have is something precious. Hold to it."

They stood motionless for a long time, then Carly spoke in a halting whisper, "Who are you, Wolf? And why are you here?"

Wolf barely heard the softly voiced questions. He couldn't answer. Not just because his orders forbid his telling, but because saying he was a deputy U.S. Marshal would no longer suffice. There was something between them that went far beyond the law he'd sworn to uphold.

"Carly, let's go find that cabin. You need to rest." He put his arm around her, and she cringed as though he had threatened her in some way.

"Carly, don't be afraid. I won't hurt you." He hated to think she was afraid of him, but little during the past weeks had given her reason to trust anyone, even him. He suspected she hadn't had much experience with men either and might be worrying how he would act when they got inside the door. That was something else he'd have to explain. He didn't intend to consummate their marriage. Though Bradley had assured him the marriage was legal, he couldn't consider a union valid that was based on fear and coercion. He didn't know what rules the Service may have bent or twisted to get him that license, but as long as the marriage was unconsummated, Carly could get an annulment when this was over. He wouldn't be a party to eliminating her right to choose whether or not she wished to be married. Wolf released her hand to open the door.

The door swung wide and Wolf glared in speechless fury. He heard a soft gasp beside him and turned in time to see a kangaroo rat scurry across Carly's foot. Hesitantly she stepped inside and Wolf followed. If this was the cabin Luther had planned to share with his bride, he was a sadist. In the middle of the room lay a thin pallet. Heaped on it were a pile of dirty army blankets and a case of beer. A length of narrow rope lay beside these. No furniture graced the room. The cabin was unfinished with a raw, unplaned plank floor. There was no glass in the square cut for a single window, and he could see the sky through the hole left for a stovepipe. The loft was a narrow ledge without a rail, reached by a birch pole with nails protruding along its length. Kangaroo rats had eaten away one side of the cardboard beer case and left a liberal sprinkling of droppings about the room.

"I didn't think any place could be worse than the cabin Josh was assigned, but I was wrong." Carly looked so tired, Wolf's heart ached.

"You go back to Josh's cabin and get some rest," he urged. "You'll have to stay there until this place is habitable."

"That wouldn't be a good idea." They both turned to see Rachel standing in the doorway. "Daddy wouldn't like it. He told you to come to this cabin, so you'd better stay here." She walked inside and slowly navigated the room. Her lip curled in contempt. "Luther's idea of a honeymoon suite, no doubt."

"I gather there's no love lost between you and Luther," Wolf probed cautiously.

"You guessed that one right. You might as well know, since everyone else does. I was supposed to marry Luther." She looked pointedly at Carly. "I'm an heiress. Someday I'll have piles of money, and Daddy's cause requires a lot of money. He promised Luther that if he'd find me and bring me here, he could marry me."

"You didn't?" Carly gasped.

"No. Poor Luther's been jilted at the altar twice now. He brought me here, but he couldn't marry me after Daddy discovered I don't inherit until I'm twenty-five, and only then if the executors of my mother's estate approve of the husband I choose. Their guidelines call for a squeaky-clean background and specifically exclude felons. Luther didn't qualify. Dear Luther has a record," she added sarcastically. "He was terribly upset since he had plans for my money that didn't include Daddy's little kingdom." She attempted a cocky grin, but a vicious kick aimed at the pallet on the floor revealed her anger.

Wolf had a few answers now about Isaac's daughter, but she was still a wild card. Why weren't the executors she'd mentioned hunting for her? She answered that question with her next breath.

"Daddy flew Josh to Seattle last week to meet with Mom's lawyer and the other two executers. They approved of Josh, so we'll be getting married as soon as I turn twenty-five in a few weeks and they mail me their formal endorsement. We'll be sisters then; I hope we can be friends." She directed a hesitant smile toward Carly.

"You're using Josh." Carly made no attempt to hide her indignation.

"No, I love him. I really do. I'd marry him today if I could. I don't care about the money."

"I don't know whether you love him or not, but I wonder what kind of love drags two innocent children into this nightmare."

Carly's words brought tears to Rachel's eyes. "Carly, please believe me. I never intended to cause you or the children any harm. It wasn't my idea to bring them here. Daddy did that on his own, and Josh agreed because he didn't want to be separated from them, or me. I care about Josh's children, and I'll do whatever it takes to be a good mother to them. I promise." She glanced hesitantly toward Wolf then back to Carly. "As soon as I realized what was happening to the children, I took steps to stop it. I didn't know there would be that kind of danger to them."

"How could you not know? You're his daughter; you knew what he was capable of before you dragged them into this. If anything happens to them, you'll be as much to blame as your tyrant father!"

Rachel reached out to Carly, but Carly shook off her hand.

"You don't understand . . ." Rachel's words ended in a sigh.

"Perhaps you'd better leave." Wolf spoke to Rachel while his arms turned Carly to where she could bury her face against his shoulder. He'd like to keep Rachel talking; he sensed she was on the verge of trusting him, but he doubted Carly could take any more right now. She was tired and distraught, incapable of understanding the risk Rachel was taking in coming to her.

"I'm sorry." Rachel's voice caught as she stumbled toward the door. "I'm trying to tell you, I'm doing all I can for the children," she choked. "You need to worry about yourself."

Wolf listened as her steps receded. He'd gotten Rachel's message; the children were safe for the moment, but Carly still faced some kind of threat. He wouldn't upset her further by making certain she understood. Now didn't seem like a good time for that frank talk he'd planned earlier either.

While Wolf debated whether to leave Carly alone or take her with him to collect their things and hunt up some cleaning supplies,

Josh arrived at the door with a bundle for Carly. He left and returned again with two buckets of hot water and Reuben. The men stepped outside while she changed into jeans, then the four of them scrubbed all afternoon in near silence.

Carly objected when Josh tossed her braided rug on the floor and stacked linens and quilts on the narrow pallet. "You need those for the children, Josh."

"Rachel brought over a rug and some things she's been making for after we're married. We'll be fine. These things are yours and you should keep them." He seemed ill at ease when he mentioned Rachel, yet defiant, too.

Carly compressed her lips together and turned away. She tacked a thin muslin square to the window, then added curtains and reswept the floor after Reuben patched the hole in the roof. Reuben's carpentry job was another disaster. The hole became much larger before he managed to place a shaky patch over it.

Wolf tried to talk her into sitting in one of the chairs Reuben unearthed from somewhere, but she insisted there was too much to do.

The cabin was clean, the rat holes plugged, the pallet turned into a bed, and a few simple pieces of furniture scattered about the room by the time Carly finally sat down. Reuben had built two wooden chests with leather hinges to hold their clothes and a wobbly bookcase for Carly's books. A lantern sat atop the bookcase casting a faint glow over her weary features. Tendrils of pale hair escaped the tight coil to form a golden frame about her face. Wolf stood in a dark corner and watched his bride drift into sleep. Tenderness welled in his heart, mingled with admiration and something more. Could it be love he felt for Carly? He shook off the question, not wanting to delve too deeply into the possibility.

Josh nudged his arm, returning him to more practical thoughts and he followed his brother-in-law outside.

"Wolf, take care of her." Josh rested a heavy hand on his shoulder. "I haven't done a good job of that, and I'm afraid I've lost her trust. I want you to know, I wouldn't have let her marry Luther. I'd have stopped it somehow if you hadn't stepped forward. I don't know whether she really wanted to marry you either, but she does consider you a friend, and I don't believe you'll hurt her. If I ever find out different, I'll pound you into pieces so small your mother won't recognize you." Josh removed his hand from Wolf's shoulder and without waiting for a response started toward his own cabin.

Wolf watched until Josh was out of sight. Dieter's mother had been dead for many years. Had Josh's statement been rhetorical or had Carly's brother let him know he knew Wolf wasn't Anna's brother?

Wolf stood absorbing the night sounds and watching lights appear in the barracks. Dim patches of light on the dirt further down the row of cabins told him lanterns were lit there, too. No light was coming from the dining hall, which reminded him he and Carly had missed dinner, lunch too. He hadn't even had any breakfast and he doubted Carly had either. With all the stress she'd gone through, the lack of sleep and skipped meals, she'd likely be sick soon if he didn't do something about it. Tomorrow he'd make sure she ate.

Josh's words echoed in his mind. He hadn't been wrong about the big man. He did care about Carly, and he was fighting some tough demons of his own. He hoped some day soon they would be able to sit down and really talk.

"Wolf." His name came out of the darkness beside the cabin.

"Is that you, Reuben?"

"Yeah. Your missus didn't get no supper, so I fried up them fish you and the little tad caught this morning." He placed a tin plate in Wolf's hand.

"Thanks, Reuben. I appreciate your help this afternoon."

"Weren't nothing. Just you remember, only a fool lives in a house with no back door."

"And you're no fool." Wolf smiled as heat seeped through the plate in his hand, telling him that Reuben had a secret cooking spot somewhere on the other side of the chicken coop door. He wondered briefly why Reuben had joined the cult. He didn't appear to be militant or religious. He could shoot and was one of the best hunters of the group. He had a hunch Isaac was being bamboozled by one of the best, and Wolf humorously figured that when Reuben left it would be with a new rifle and enough supplies to keep the old mountain man comfortable for a long time to come.

When Wolf stepped inside the cabin and discovered scrambled eggs and fresh greens alongside the trout piled high enough for two, he smiled in appreciation of the secretive little man and his back door. In a small way, the gloom that pervaded the compound lifted just a little by knowing Reuben was there.

"Carly. Carly, wake up." He hated to awaken her, but he wanted her to eat, then get into bed where she could rest comfortably all night. Softly he brushed her arm and she stirred restlessly. "Carly, you need to eat." She blinked her eyes and stared owlishly at him. Impulsively he bent forward to place a quick kiss on her lips. A tiny smile began at the corner of her mouth and a little light flickered in her eyes, then went out.

A twinge of regret moved inside Wolf, and he wondered what it would take to bring that light back.

"Here eat this." He forked a sliver of trout toward her mouth. Automatically she accepted it.

"You don't have to feed me." She reached for the fork when he would have followed the fish with egg. Wolf produced a second fork and together they polished off the food. When the plate was empty, a heavy silence gathered around them. Each time he looked her way, she quickly glanced away. The next logical step was to go to bed. He needed to reassure her, but it wasn't an easy topic to bring up.

"Wolf, are we really married?" He jumped, then felt foolish. There was no reason to feel so awkward. He stood abruptly to reach into his pocket, and she scooted back a fraction on her chair. His temper flared briefly and he reminded himself she didn't have much cause to trust him. He'd asked for a lot of trust, but he'd given her little to go on.

"Here!" He slapped a piece of paper on her knees. Then softening his voice he said, "I'm not the kind of man to ask for a lady's trust, then only pretend to marry her."

"You signed it last, didn't you?" Her fingers stroked the raised seal at the bottom of the document.

"Yes."

"Because your name is really Dwight Eisenhower Wolverton?"

"Yes." She'd married him without even knowing his name. In all his concern over keeping his identity safe from Isaac, he hadn't once considered how it would be for her to marry a man whose name she didn't know. He hadn't thought beyond scheming to get the marriage certificate back to Bradley without Isaac getting another look at it.

"I never think of Eisenhower as a military man, just as a president. You told me once that you have three brothers and you were all named after military men. Is that true?"

"Ike was a general first. My brothers really are Jeb Stuart, William Westmoreland, and George Patton; Jeb, Will and Pat. Jeb died a few years ago, but I'm looking forward to introducing you to Will and Pat."

"Oh." She sounded like a little lost kitten.

"You're tired. I'll step outside and give you a chance to get ready for bed." He had to clear his throat. Sitting across from her in the shared circle of light cast by the lantern and acknowledging he was her husband did something strange to his voice. Her eyes were round and solemn; they seemed to be searching for an answer to a troubling question.

"I'd like a shower. I'm so dirty." She spoke hesitantly.

"It's late and the lights are all out."

"I have a flashlight." She pointed toward her trunk.

"Okay. I'll walk you there, but leave the flashlight here. I don't think it would be a good idea to announce we've left our cabin tonight."

Ten minutes later she disappeared inside the bathhouse and he stood outside shivering in the cold night air. He hunched his shoulders and paced to the corner of the building and back. He stopped and stared toward the closed door. Why was he standing outside? It was warmer inside and so dark Carly wouldn't even know he was there if he ducked inside out of the wind.

Once inside the building he cocked an ear for sounds of Carly. He could hear the faint rustling of clothing being removed, but she hadn't turned the water on yet. A manual check confirmed that the outer room was identical to the men's facility. He should have gone there. He needed a shower, too, and possibly Carly's insistence on taking a shower was really a hint that he needed one. Besides, a cold shower might be a good idea about now, and indeed it would be cold since the generator that powered Isaac's headquarters and the bath-houses had been shut off a couple of hours ago.

The women's shower room was likely the same as the men's with four small, separate cubicles. He could shower right here. After all, they were married. Still, he'd have to warn Carly or he would startle her. He eased his way to the opening of the showers.

"Carly," he whispered. A startled squeak sounded in the darkness.

"What are you doing in here?"

"I just thought I'd take a shower, too."

"Here?"

"It's dark and there's more than one stall isn't there? Just tell me which one you're using and I'll choose a different one."

"There are only two, and I'm in the first one." Her voice definitely held a suspicious note. She hadn't turned on the water on her side of the partition by the time he reached for the handle, which released a jet of water onto his head. It wasn't completely cold, but it didn't encourage lingering either.

"I can't find any soap." Carly's whisper barely carried above the sound of the water.

"I'll hand you mine. Do you want it over or under the partition."

"Over."

Wolf trailed his arm along the top of the barrier until he encountered Carly's. He could feel water splashing from her side. Their hands grappled until the soap had safely exchanged hands. Carly was tall and the divider wasn't as high as he'd expected. If it were light, he'd be able to see the top of her shoulders.

"Would you like to borrow my shampoo?"

Good sense told him to say no, but when he opened his mouth he heard himself say, "If I bend over a little bit, you can reach across the partition and pour some on my head. That way we won't be struggling to exchange the bottle in the dark."

In seconds he felt her hand touch his face, then slide up to his hair. The water didn't feel cold anymore.

"Oops! I think I spilled too much. You'd better rub it in before it runs down your face."

His hands encountered hers as he reached to follow instructions. For a brief moment he forgot where his hands were headed. They slid easily up her arms until they reached her shoulders. Her wet skin was like slippery satin. Their heads were inches apart and the darkness was no hindrance to finding her mouth with his own. He forgot the cold shower and shampoo dripping from his hair as her lips answered his. Showering with Carly invoked warm possibilities in his head, but he released her and backed away. One more time he ducked his head under the spray, which was decidedly cold now, then reached for his towel.

He dressed swiftly. He knew Carly must be freezing, but she wouldn't leave that shower stall until she was sure he was in the other room. What a wedding night! Of course, he hadn't planned to ever have a wedding night, but if he had, he wouldn't have planned to spend it shivering in the cold, trying to think of anything except making love with his bride.

They almost ran back to their cabin. Wolf held Carly's hand to make certain she didn't stumble in the dark. Inside the cabin he lit the lamp, but kept it turned to a low glow. He saw Carly had changed to a sweat shirt and pants and carried her jeans in a bundle in her arms. She'd wrapped a towel, turban style, around her wet hair. He watched her remove the towel and give her head a little shake. Her hair tumbled down her back, stopping just short of her waist. His hand seemed to have a will of its own as it reached out to lift a damp strand away from her face and stroke it gently behind her ear.

"Here, let me help you dry your hair." He reached for a dry towel.

"I can do it."

"No, I want to. Just sit in that chair."

Carly sank hesitantly to the seat he indicated. "Where's your brush?" he asked from somewhere behind her.

"On top of the chest Reuben made for me."

She steeled herself not to flinch when Wolf pulled the brush through her wet tangles. But it wasn't the brush Wolf first touched to her head. It was a towel. Slowly and methodically he separated her hair into thin strands, which he then blotted with the towel. Next, he finger-combed each strand, then air-fluffed with another towel. Each movement calmed and relaxed, bringing a measure of peace. By the time he finally ran the brush through her tresses, her head was nodding.

"Come on, sweetheart. Let's sit on the bed. You can lean against me and be a lot more comfortable while I finish drying your hair."

"I could braid it. I've slept on damp braids before."

"No, you might catch cold." He maneuvered her to the bed, where he sat on the edge and settled her in front of him between his legs. He could smell the clean scent of her hair as he slowly moved the brush through it.

The motion was soothing and Carly found herself relaxing against Wolf's bare chest. Turning her head she felt hair tickle her cheek. His skin was warm and smelled like soap with just a hint of something strong and masculine. An urge to turn her face toward his warmth startled her. A flutter of panic prevented her fitting thought to deed, but as the brush strokes continued, she relaxed once more into a dreamy world where being Wolf's wife held increasing appeal.

Wolf set down the brush and leaned over to turn off the lamp, then his hands returned to her hair. They followed the same motion the brush had. Starting at her crown, they skimmed the back of her head and stroked down her back. He trailed a hand along the side of her face and over her shoulder to smooth her hair. A shiver rippled through her body.

"Cold? Let's get you under the quilts." Smoothly he shifted her weight. Her head touched a pillow and Wolf pulled the quilt to her shoulders. He paused a moment, a moment in which Carly suspected he shed his pants before he slid in beside her. He wrapped his arms around her and pulled her close. "Better?" he whispered.

He felt her nod her head and he smiled into the darkness. At least she was no longer afraid.

"Carly, I'm only going to hold you, nothing more. Go to sleep." She made no response and he knew the long hours tending Benjy and the emotional trauma of her wedding day had caught up to her. She was asleep.

He lay beside her and wished sleep would be equally merciful to him. Lying beside her, feeling her relaxed and warm in his arms with her hair spread across his chest, made sleep impossible.

When it became obvious he wouldn't be getting any sleep and if he stayed in bed with Carly curled against him, he'd forget his good intentions, he decided to get up. A little midnight prowling might bring him closer to the answers he needed, and the sooner he uncovered that secret stash Luther had mentioned, the sooner he could get Carly away from here.

Ten

Carly's eyes drifted open. She felt a chill where before she'd been warm and content. Her hand slid across the sheet seeking—Wolf! He was gone. A shadow stood beside the bed. The shadow moved and she knew it was Wolf dressing, preparing to leave. She wanted to cry out, to protest, to beg him to stay beside her, but before she could speak a brilliant light swept through the room followed almost at once by heavy, rolling thunder. The flash of light revealed Wolf standing as he placed a black handgun in a leather holster he wore across one shoulder.

Carly squeezed her eyes shut against the image of Wolf with a gun in his hand. She'd become accustomed to rifles, but the pistol brought back all the painful memories of that awful night of violence when Anna lost her life. She didn't want to see Wolf holding a pistol or wonder where he was going and why he needed the gun. She thought of the loose leather jacket he nearly always wore and knew she'd never be able to look at it again without associating it with the gun it hid. She didn't want him to leave their bed. Most of all she didn't want to face the fear that he might not come back.

An infinitesimal movement near her face had her reaching for his hand to hold him by her side. But he only tucked the quilt securely around her shoulders, then slipped quietly from the cabin. His touch lingered, filling her with warmth. Slowly the warmth faded and a tear slid across her cheek. What kind of man had she married and why did he marry her? He'd convinced her their marriage was valid, then spent their wedding night soothing and comforting her, a gentle prelude, she had thought. Now he was gone into the night without taking what she would have willingly given. Was the real Wolf the gentle man who had made her his wife or the secretive shadow carrying a concealed weapon? She asked the futile question over and over until eventually she drifted into restless sleep.

Carly knew before she opened her eyes again that she was still alone and the day would be rainy and cold. Wolf hadn't returned. Grimly she faced the dull certainty that if he cared about her he would have been beside her when morning came. But then, caring wasn't the reason he'd married her, was it? At least not the romantic kind of caring. Slowly she pulled herself to a sitting position. Behind the gray predawn gloom, she could see the mud-chinked walls, shabbiness, and squalor of the rough, unfinished cabin. For a little while last night in the dark it had been beautiful. She had felt peace and been unafraid, but with the first hint of morning her fears had returned.

She wanted to burrow back beneath the quilt and relive those feelings. She wanted to dream of building a home with Wolf and having his babies. What she must do is think carefully about her changed position. She was more convinced than ever that Wolf did not share Isaac's religious or political philosophies, yet the compound had to be the destination he'd been seeking when he was attacked by the bear. His ready acceptance by Isaac and his men as a weapons expert suggested the militant cult leader may have hired him to train his army. But if Isaac had hired him, why hadn't Wolf denied he was Dieter when she first identified him as Josh's brother-in-law?

As she stepped out of bed onto the braided rug, she appreciated its protection from the cold of the unheated cabin floor. Mornings at this altitude were always cold, but the stormy night had added to the chill. Dawn was an hour or more away and even the man who started the generator wouldn't be up this early, but her thoughts were making her restless. The more she thought, the more certain she became that she didn't want to still be in bed when Wolf returned. If he returned. She reached for her jeans. She couldn't bear to stay in the cabin any longer.

She'd go to the infirmary. She could count on being alone there for several hours. Luther wouldn't show up until after breakfast. No one would miss her at that meal since she'd skipped it all week. A couple of times Rachel had brought her juice and a roll after everyone else had eaten. Thinking of Rachel made Carly uncomfortable and reminded her of the things she'd said to the other woman the day before. Rachel had never been unkind to her and her genuine concern for her little brother set her apart from her father. Her brother's relationship with Rachel was something else Carly needed to think about.

The thought of Josh binding himself permanently to the cult by marriage appalled her. If Rachel were anyone other than Isaac's daughter, her devotion to her little half brother and the real effort she was making to help all of the children would weigh heavily in her favor. But how could she forgive the younger woman for being the magnet that had drawn first Josh, then herself and the children into Isaac's nightmare world?

Carly glanced toward the large building at the end of the row of cabins and wondered how Benjy had fared his first day back in his parents' care. He was another reason why she should go to the infirmary. She might be needed. If not, there were things that should be done anyway and she always did her best thinking while her hands were busy. Besides it would be hard to accomplish anything once Luther arrived. She shuddered. She'd have to face him sometime. If she went now, she'd have at least two hours before he arrived. He, no doubt, would be difficult.

Making her way toward the infirmary, she pulled the collar of her jacket tighter against the cold air. She stumbled once in the darkness and looked up toward the thick cloud cover obscuring the sky. Only grim grayness hinted that the sun would soon rise where the clouds thinned toward the east.

Once inside the infirmary Carly pulled the blind over the one small window, then went to the second room and closed the door behind her. In the larger, windowless room she lit a lamp and began the task of straightening and organizing. Between caring for Benjy and warding off would-be suitors, she'd been so busy all week that she'd failed to put away supplies properly; and as an assistant, Luther was worse than useless. She picked up several boxes of gauze and stacked them neatly by graduated sizes on a shelf. Scissors and tweezers needed to be sterilized. She placed them in a small basin and poured alcohol over them. She found a clean pillowcase for the little pillow on the gurney and slipped it in place.

Paperwork was a waste of time since there would never be a doctor to read her notes, but training prevailed. Besides she needed to keep busy. As though even hard work would keep her thoughts from Wolf!

She sat in the chair where Luther usually lounged and reached in a drawer for the notebook she used to chart her patients' symptoms, treatment, and progress. Her hand encountered a small brown bottle she recognized as the pain pills she'd given Luther. Beside the bottle was the key to the drug closet. She would put away the pills, but when Luther came she'd remind him of how dangerous it could be to leave the key where anyone coming through the unlocked outer door might find it.

Fitting the key in the lock, Carly swung open the door to the small walk-in closet and stepped inside. She pushed the button to a battery-operated lantern, then frowned at the haphazard condition of the small space. It badly needed to be organized.

She worked rapidly, shifting bottles and boxes to their proper places, making notes in the log. She looked at the small refrigerator in the closet. That should be organized and the medications logged, too. Placing one hand against the wall, she gave the handle which sometimes stuck a sharp tug. She almost lost her balance as the wall where she'd braced her hand moved several inches.

She staggered to regain her footing, then looked carefully at the gap exposed by the shifting wall. A deliberate shove against the wall moved it easily, revealing steps leading to a dark cavern below. A thrill of danger crawled up her spine. This was why Luther kept the key to the drug closet. Whatever waited at the bottom of those stairs was something Isaac didn't want her to know about. Still, she lifted the lantern from its hook and shined it down the stairs. She couldn't see much without moving down a couple of steps.

From the second step the lantern revealed a room the size of the two infirmary rooms combined. She let the beam from her light shine across the open space. A long table surrounded by chairs filled the center of the room. On the wall at the far end of the table, huge sheets of paper, which might be maps or posters, were taped to the wall. A shelf heaped with miscellaneous clutter ran the length of the room. Under the shelf were several wooden crates. At the opposite side of the underground room, another stairway led upward in the direction of Isaac's office.

She'd stumbled on to something she shouldn't have. If Isaac or any of his followers caught her, she'd be in serious trouble. Lifting the lantern for one last sweep before retreating, the light caught a small object, one that looked vaguely familiar. She had to get closer. She took several hurried steps, then paused. Uneasily she glanced behind her, hesitated just a moment, then retraced her steps to the closet. Once she went down those steps one hurried peek might not be enough, but she couldn't risk getting caught.

It took only a few seconds to turn off the small lamp she'd left burning in the examining room. On tiptoes she hurried to the window and peeked behind the blind. It wasn't light yet. She listened for the hum of the generator, but all was silent. There was time.

Carly made her way back to the closet. This time she pulled the door shut behind her and left only a crack in the secret doorway. A terrible premonition told her she didn't really want to see what was in the cellar room, but some stronger sense insisted she must know. She shook as she made her way down the stairs. She gripped her flashlight and wished it was Wolf's hand locked in hers.

Before her was the long shelf. Her hand reached out, hesitated, then she let one finger trace the large turquoise stone. Her fingernail ran across the intricate silver design. Two-Toe Johnny's necklace!

"Isaac shot Frank. They was mean to Two-Toe Johnny too. They put a rope on his sore foot and pulled him right through the weeds and dirt to the boat." Her eyes dropped to a little leather bag. It didn't look as full as when old Frank had pulled it out of his pocket to show gold nuggets to two wide-eyed children. Closing her eyes against the pain, she acknowledged what she had known deep inside all along: Daniel had witnessed cold-blooded murder.

Panic gripped her. Isaac must never know what Daniel saw! She had to get the children out of here. She had to make Josh believe her. Perhaps Wolf . . . In her haste, her lantern caught the strap of a backpack. Frantically she clutched at it to prevent it from falling and making a noise. She caught it, but not before several items slipped to the floor.

She bent to retrieve them and found two wallets in her hand. Without weighing whether or not she should, she opened one, then the other. Anger, nausea, and terror raced down her spine to form a tight knot in her stomach. The wallets contained I.D. for two men—two Bureau of Alcohol, Tobacco, and Firearms agents—the two men Isaac said had run away from a squad of his soldiers.

As she returned the wallets to the pack, her fingers encountered cold steel. Knowing what she'd find when she looked inside, she looked anyway. The small black gun and leather shoulder holster looked familiar. Carefully she leaned the pack back against the two rifles. She had to think, but she wasn't sure she could even breathe. Why were there two I.D.'s, two rifles, but only one handgun? Over and over like flashing strobe lights in a disco, she saw Wolf silhouetted in the glare of a flash of lightening, saw the gun in his hand.

No! She clapped her hand over her mouth to keep the scream from erupting. There was no connection. The man who had saved her from Luther had no connection with the grisly mementos in this room. He couldn't.

Slowly she moved down the length of the room, walking without plan or purpose, past crates of guns and boxes of ammunition until she stood before one of the papers taped to the wall. Several minutes passed before the faces on the poster registered on her conscious mind. The Dreadnaughts! Why did Isaac have a poster of black rock singers hanging on his cellar wall? She glanced at the next paper, a city map. Moving closer she began to recognize street names and bridges. It was a map of San Francisco. A route from the airport to Candlestick Park was clearly marked in red.

Rachel and Wolf had both mentioned Isaac had a plan, a plan that involved Josh. Were the Dreadnaughts and the sports arena part of Isaac's plan, too? Shivers shook Carly's body. Josh wouldn't . . . But he had joined in the manhunt for a black man . . . no, her brother wouldn't . . .

A faint shuffling sound reached her ears, sending tremors of fear coursing down her spine. She extinguished her light and stood motionless in the dark listening for the sound to repeat itself. She had no doubt that if Isaac found her in this secret room, he would kill her. The sound came again, a tiny scraping. She listened intently, willing herself to not even breathe. The sound came from Isaac's office. Like a many-fanged beast, fear tore at her throat. He was there, right at the top of the other flight of stairs! Only one door separated her from him.

The hairs at the back of his neck warned him someone was near. Though Deborah and Rachel's bedrooms were at the back of the family quarters, well away from Isaac's office, had he disturbed them somehow? Had he stayed too long? No, there was close to an hour before the generator would signal the beginning of another day for the compound. When it started up, the lights would go on in the barracks and the men would awaken. Some would relieve the guards at the gate, the others would grumble and go back to sleep for another hour. The cook and her assistants would head for the kitchen.

Wolf wasn't worried about Isaac catching him. He'd seen Isaac board the plane early last evening; he would have heard had it returned. The guards never patrolled inside the compound, and the only other person awake at this hour was Carly.

He'd seen the thin trace of light as she left their cabin and made her way to the infirmary. His first instinct had been to go to her. A moment later he'd conceded that wouldn't be fair. She had a right to a brief hour of privacy, and he would be the first to acknowledge she needed time to think through all that had happened. He could argue his motivation was superior to Isaac's, but he hadn't given Carly any more choices than the cult leader had. She should have been able to freely choose whether or not she wanted to marry. Isaac had forced marriage on her, and she'd been given no voice in choosing her husband. Wolf had chosen for her.

He didn't doubt she liked him, even trusted him on some level. He thought that if he had sought greater intimacy last night, she would not have turned him away. But he didn't want gratitude or comfort to be the reasons she gave herself to him. He loved her and wanted nothing less in return. And loving her was no justification for initiating a physical relationship while she remained in a state of shock. Leaving her side last night had been one of the toughest choices of his life. Bittersweet memories of the time they had shared together distracted him for long minutes.

Wolf gave himself a sharp reminder to pay attention. Agents got killed when they let their minds drift from their jobs. He listened with nerves stretched taught. Nothing. He must have imagined it. Nevertheless, he took particular care to make no sound as he pulled thick folders from the file cabinet he'd jimmied open.

The file was incredible. Isaac kept a dossier on every person at the compound plus dozens on cult followers living elsewhere. He'd been right about Isaac doing some checking on Dieter Karlis. There was a file with his name on it containing the pertinent details of his life. He smiled in grim satisfaction when he read a note attached to the file indicating Isaac believed Dieter to be the German weapons expert recommended by Snakes Johnson shortly before Snakes was sent to Leavenworth where he'd died in a knife fight with another inmate.

Wolf opened the folder bearing Carly's name. Nothing new there. He already knew her birth date and that she was a nurse. Josh and the children were her only family. Only one item stood out; the name of a former roommate was underlined, undoubtedly because the name was Hispanic.

Josh's file held no surprises either. It outlined his work experience and training in demolition and contained a copy of his life insurance policy and a simple form notarized in Los Angeles eighteen months ago transferring guardianship of his children to Carly in the event he should die while they were still minors.

Wolf glanced at the next folder spread on the desk before him, the thickest file he'd pulled. He adjusted the tiny pen light he held and read the name. Rachel Isaac. He thumbed through the papers finding a birth certificate, high school diploma, passport, her mother's will and her own, a university diploma. Rachel really was a teacher. Behind a copy of her mother's will were two more papers, a marriage license and an adoption agreement signed by Josh that would make Rachel Petra and Daniel's mother the moment she married their father.

Hurriedly, Wolf thumbed back through the papers until he

found Rachel's will and placed it beside her mother's. He examined them closely. Rachel would inherit a vast fortune on her twenty-fifth birthday, a date a little over two weeks away and the first date circled on Isaac's calendar. A stipulation placed in both wills prohibited Isaac from inheriting from Rachel. If Rachel died without issue, the money would go to specified charities.

The marriage license would expire ten days after Rachel's birthday, which most likely made the second date circled Rachel's wedding day. That left the third date, Labor Day, as the day for Isaac's great plan. Wolf held the light closer to Rachel's will and read rapidly. He knew what he would find, but finding it made him ill anyway.

Rachel's children, natural or adopted, were her heirs. If Josh and Rachel were to both die, Carly, as the children's guardian, would control Rachel's money. Wolf doubled up his fist, barely resisting the urge to pound it against the desk. No doubt Rachel had already figured it all out. That's what she'd been trying to tell Carly. It wasn't the children who were in the greatest danger, it was Josh and herself—and eventually Carly. No wonder Isaac wanted Carly in the compound where he could control her through force and intimidation. He'd meant for Luther to break her spirit and force her to turn the children's money over to the cult.

Wolf's eyes narrowed. Isaac would only get to Carly across his dead body—and that was most likely just what Isaac planned. It was also the reason Isaac had approved Wolf's marriage to Carly. Not just because he had doubts about Luther's willingness to turn the fortune over to him, but because if Carly couldn't be cowed into obedience, he could eliminate her. And if he got rid of Carly, he would also have to get rid of Dieter, the children's maternal uncle, in order to gain control of them and their inheritance. An accident that claimed a married couple would be much easier to believe than two separate accidents.

A slight sound caught Wolf's ear reminding him he'd been pouring over the documents longer than he should have. It was probably Carly moving around in the infirmary, but he'd stayed in Isaac's office as long as he dared. There was much more in the file he wanted to see, but he'd have to wait until the next time Isaac left the compound overnight. Picking up the papers, he returned them to their folders, then replaced the folders in the metal file case in a closet at the back of Isaac's office. Metal scraped against metal as Wolf closed the drawer. He held his breath and swore next time he'd bring a little WD-40 with him to make the drawers slide smoothly and silently.

Carly struggled not to panic. Isaac hadn't found her yet. Even if he were in his office, she still had a little time before Luther arrived at the infirmary. No way would she wait around for either man to open one of those doors and find her. Cautiously she edged her feet across the stone floor until her shin banged against the first step. Seconds later she stood in the drug closet. Her heart hammered and she gulped in a lung full of air. She pushed against the secret door and watched it swing silently into place, once more merely a wall.

On trembling legs, she made her way out of the closet and to the desk. Her hand shook as she placed the key back in the drawer. She no longer planned to mention the key to Luther. Wearily she sank into the chair. The room in the cellar changed everything. Not only would she not mention the key to Luther, she wouldn't tell Josh of her discovery either. Josh was her brother and she loved him, but he planned to marry Rachel, and Carly had no way of guessing what he might tell his fiance. Nor what Rachel might tell her father. No, she couldn't tell Josh.

She buried her face in her hands. There was another reason she couldn't tell Josh. Josh was involved, how deeply she didn't know, but she had no doubt Isaac was using her brother's expertise with explosives to build a bomb that could destroy Candlestick Park and anyone who might be in it. She couldn't bear thinking of Josh involved in such an evil act of destruction.

She longed for Wolf's arms and ached to confide the awful secret to him. But no, she couldn't tell him, and not just because she didn't know if she could trust him. A more compelling reason was the danger his knowing would place him in. Sharing her discovery might renew his offer to take her away, but she doubted he would agree to take the children with them. And he might confront Isaac. She no longer had any doubts about how far Isaac would go if someone got in his way. Her awful discovery would have to remain her secret alone.

Tears trickled down her cheek. Poor Frank and Two-Toe Johnnie. She'd liked them and had been amused by their wild tales of trapping and panning for gold. They'd called themselves trappers, but she knew the law would have called them poachers. They were really harmless old men living a life that had disappeared for most people nearly a century before. What about the agents? Did they leave behind wives and children who would never see them again?

The outside door opened and Carly jumped guiltily. She quickly wiped her face to remove any sign of tears. It was time for Luther to arrive, and he was the last person she wanted to see any vulnerability in her. By the time the inner door opened, the tears were gone and Carly was bent over her record book.

"Well, if it isn't the little bride." Luther's voice was a sneer. He adopted an exaggerated swagger as he crossed the room to stand in front of her. "What's the matter? Doesn't old Wolfie know how to keep a woman?" His arms shot out and he dragged Carly against him. "Maybe you just figured out you made a big mistake and came looking for a real man."

She pulled against his grip. "Let go of me. You'll never be half the man Wolf is." The moment she said the words she knew she'd made a mistake. The comparison only goaded his temper.

He crooked an arm around her neck and began to squeeze.

"You're hurting me," she croaked.

That seemed to please him. He moved his arm and grasped her chin with his fingers. "You think Wolf is so great," he snarled. "He doesn't know the first thing about women. When I get through with you, you'll know what a real man is." He wound a fist into her hair, dislodging her braids and bringing tears to her eyes.

Carly's head swam. Struggling only increased the pressure Luther exerted on her face and scalp.

"I see you get the picture." His eyes glittered as he shook her face. "I'll show you who's the better man."

She tried to scream, but Luther moved too fast. His mouth cut off her breath, and she tasted blood as his teeth bore into her tender mouth trying to force her lips apart.

Carly brought her knee up with all the force of her agony to connect with his groin. It wasn't the disabling blow she'd hoped for, but his gasp freed her hands and she doubled up her fist. A right to his eye brought a grunt of pain. Like a maddened bull he grabbed for her. She dodged out of his reach just as the door opened once more, and Deborah walked into the room. Carly breathed a sigh of gratitude for the interruption and edged further away from Luther.

"Good morning, Sister Carly. Hello, Brother Luther," Deborah chirped as she placed her white Bible on the desk and pushed Carly's ledger out of her way. She seemed oblivious to the tension between the two. "I see you've already explained to Carly," she spoke sweetly to Luther. "You're such a thoughtful man and the Lord loves you."

"I'm not through with you." Luther's voice was too low for Deborah to hear. The menacing message in his eyes made Carly's skin crawl. Deborah continued to smile until Luther slammed the door behind himself on his way out.

Tapping one foot, she turned to Carly speaking severely. "Now, it was too bad of you to encourage Luther all this time, but your flirting has to stop. You're a married woman now and God will punish you if you continue to cast wanton eyes toward dear Brother Luther. You may not have chosen wisely, but you have chosen."

"Flirting! That maniac attacked me!"

"Loose women are not tolerated here," Deborah went on as though Carly hadn't spoken. "God delights in the chastity of women, and wives should submit themselves to their husbands only."

"Fine by me." Carly answered tartly as she dug through a jar of paper clips in search of a couple of safety pins to fasten her blouse. While Deborah looked on disapprovingly, she rewound her braid about her head.

"It's not too late to repent. Even Rachel is beginning to see the light and will soon be on her knees begging for forgiveness. God must sometimes use evil to accomplish his purposes, and Rachel has been an unnatural, evil daughter. But God has let it be known she is a chosen vessel and through her will come a miracle. God stayed Isaac's righteous wrath when he would have whipped her for defying his commandments. Marriage will redeem her, then blessings will flow down on all our heads."

Vague embarrassment overrode Carly's anger. Deborah was making a fool of herself. By what right did she or Isaac judge her? Or for that matter, Rachel?

"How is Benjamin this morning?" Carly decided changing the subject might be best. She wasn't certain why Deborah had come, nor how much of her company she could take, even if the other woman had saved her from Luther.

"Benjamin is fine. I'm sure he's learned his lesson and won't need to be disciplined again."

"Disciplined? Your son was nearly killed. That isn't discipline; it's child abuse. Mrs. Hampton should be prosecuted."

"Oh, no. She merely did what had to be done. Benjamin allowed an evil spirit to enter his body, and Sister Hampton had to chase it away. That's why dear Isaac explained to her that God has forbidden us to spare the rod or we will spoil the children. Jesus said, 'Suffer the children to come unto me,' so you see, if they don't suffer, they won't go to him."

The woman was crazy. Insane, the world would call her, but that description was too tame. Anyone who could twist Jesus's words into something so evil was dangerous beyond belief. In a just world, that precious little boy would be taken from parents like Isaac and Deborah, and given to parents who would allow him to have a normal childhood. Carly trembled with rage and had to remind herself Deborah was ill. No sane woman would consider what happened to Benjy as God's will.

"Where is he now?"

"Rachel took him to school."

"Deborah, Benjamin is too young to go to school, and he's too ill."

"Rachel insisted. She said since I'd be here all day with you, and she'd be at school, it would be best if he went with her."

Carly took a deep breath. She had a horrible suspicion she knew the answer before she asked, but she asked anyway. "Why will you be here all day?"

Deborah's eyes widened, making her look like an innocent child. "Why, to help you of course. I told you Luther can't spend all day alone with you now you're married. You might tempt him to sin."

"What?" Carly exploded. Deborah was not only insane, she was a fool.

"Weren't you listening when he explained I'd be your assistant from now on?"

Carly groaned. Much as she detested Luther, even feared him, she suspected working with Deborah might be worse. "He never mentioned it," she muttered from between clenched teeth.

"Lying is a sin, you know. My dear husband says even little lies are forbidden."

It was going to be a long day. Isaac didn't trust her, and after seeing the room below she understood why he kept a spy hanging around the infirmary, but spending ten or twelve hours each day with Deborah would test her own sanity.

Wolf glanced up from the gun he was assembling when Luther slammed the infirmary door. Seeing Luther's scowling face and the beginnings of a black eye, Wolf guessed the man had tangled with Carly and come off second best. Or maybe he'd only been interrupted. Isaac's empty-headed wife had entered the infirmary only minutes ago. Wolf's eyes narrowed and he rose slowly to his feet. Luther's face reflected rage as Wolf stepped toward him and his hand jerked toward his jacket, but Wolf's hand was there first. As Wolf's fingers closed around Luther's wrist with enough force to snap the bones of a smaller man, the gun Luther had been reaching for clattered to the plank floor. Without releasing his grip, Wolf twisted the man's arm up behind his back. The more Luther struggled the further up Wolf shoved his arm until Luther finally stood still, panting and swearing.

Wolf leaned forward until his mouth brushed his prisoner's ear. "Carly is *my* wife. If you lay a hand on her or even look at her wrong, I'll turn you into bear bait."

"You won't get away with this. Isaac will—"

"This doesn't concern Isaac. This is between you and me, but if you go to Isaac you be sure to tell him about the $600 in your wallet, and make sure he knows you're packing a government issue Smith & Wesson 4046. Because if you don't, I will."

Luther swore violently and pulled away, pausing only long

enough to snatch up the gun before storming across the compound. Wolf let him go, but watched him until he reached the gate. Luther was a sore loser, which could mean trouble further down the road. When Luther was out of sight, Wolf slipped quietly through the infirmary door. He had to assure himself Carly was all right.

He stood in the outer room and watched the two women for several minutes. Carly's coronet of braids was slightly askew, dark circles rimmed her eyes, and her blouse was bunched together where buttons should be.

Wolf's hands clenched into tight fists. He should have knocked Luther senseless. Even as he thought it, he admitted he'd already taken too great a chance. A personal feud between himself and Luther could only increase the risk of detection, and endanger Carly and her family further.

Carly lifted her head and her eyes met his. They seemed to welcome his intrusion. He stepped toward her and the corners of her lips turned up in a tentative smile. His own smile faltered when he saw a small bead of blood form where her bottom lip was split. He reached out with one hand to cup her shoulder while with the other he allowed one finger to gently blot the spot away.

"Are you all right?" He spoke softly, conscious that Deborah stood a few feet away.

"Yes." She nodded her head, but her eyes looked suspiciously as though if she said more she might cry.

He brushed her forehead with his lips. "I'll be right outside your door all day." He smiled encouragingly and his heart felt lighter when Carly answered his smile with one of her own. He nodded briefly toward Deborah before leaving.

Most of the day was spent on the front porch of the headquarters building tinkering with the guns Isaac had assigned him to assemble. Intermittent cloud bursts punctuated the day and fit Wolf's mood. Last night changed everything. Until he touched Carly's hair he'd convinced himself he could live with her and keep their options open, and that after they left the highly charged atmosphere of the cult they could sit down calmly and discuss whether they wanted to stay together or not. One time had been enough to convince him he couldn't sleep beside Carly night after night without making love with her.

The wrench he used to tighten a bolt slipped, pinching his finger, and he threw it down in disgust. His mind was already made up, he knew what he wanted. He wanted Carly, even if that meant giving up his career. He wanted her not for just the length of this case, or even for a lifetime. Ma talked about a kind of marriage that lasted forever and that was what he wanted. Forever with Carly.

When he became a lawman, he'd decided to never marry. He'd seen what his mother and sister-in-law had gone through when Pa and Jeb were killed. A lawman always faced the possibility of an early death, and he'd vowed he wouldn't leave a grieving widow behind. He'd always figured if he made it to retirement without catching a stray bullet, he'd retire to Uncle Ulysses' ranch in the Bitterroot, but not this soon. No matter, he'd go back to the ranch if Carly chose to stay with him. But that was the important point; he had to make certain she had a choice.

Contrary to his intentions, he was married, but he could still keep Carly from becoming a marshal's widow. He'd taken a lot of choices away from her, so if she wanted to stay married to him after this was over, the least he could do would be to offer her a stable life. The only way he could do that would be to give up the Service. And so, until they got away from Steeple Mountain he had a responsibility to avoid making Carly emotionally dependent on him. Ethically he couldn't push her to share a physical relationship either. He decided it might be wise to wait until Carly was asleep before joining her that night.

Dinner was an ordeal. He had no idea what he ate, he was too conscious of a crown of blond braids across the hall, and when the meal was finally over he trailed Carly outside. He stood on the porch to watch her until she was safely inside their cabin, only she didn't go there. She detoured past Josh's cabin and Wolf followed her, staying in the deep shadows early evening cast beside each cabin. From a distance he heard Carly laugh and listened to the excited chatter of Petra and Daniel. He found himself wishing it was his child she rushed to hold at the end of her day. He stayed out of sight and waited patiently.

From the black shadows of a neighboring cabin, he watched her return to the cabin they shared. He stuffed his hands in his pockets and watched until long after she extinguished the lamp.

A watery moon slid between wispy clouds and the night was far spent when Wolf lifted the latch and stepped inside the cabin. He listened for her breathing and relaxed slightly when he heard it slow and even. He eased off his boots and carried them in one hand to the end of the bed where he set them by his chest. His jacket followed, then he lifted his revolver from its holster and slid it under the mattress. Carly stirred softly and he held his breath until her breathing resumed its natural rhythm. Off came his shirt, followed by his pants. He stood hesitantly beside the bed until the cold encouraged him to climb under the quilt.

His weight settled on the narrow mattress, and Carly turned into his arms as naturally as though she'd been there many times instead of just once. She buried her face against his bare chest and her arms circled his neck. She clung to him with a quiet desperation.

"Carly, you don't have to do this." Wolf struggled to be fair.

She lay still for what seemed an endless time, then she spoke softly, hesitantly. "I'm sorry, I thought you wanted . . ." He could hear the hurt in her voice.

"Wanting isn't the issue. And there's no lack of wanting, you can be sure." He felt a fine film of perspiration dampen his skin. He had to say this right. "Physical intimacy isn't something I take lightly, and I don't believe you do either. You were railroaded into this marriage. It wasn't your choice. I told Daniel the day you arrived here that no one has a right to own another person, and I really meant that.

"I said some other things, too, about doing what you have to while keeping your own thoughts and feelings inside. Carly, I don't want you coming to me because you think you have no choice. Your choices are limited now, but someday you'll be free to determine your own life again. I don't want to restrict your future options. And I want no part of duty or gratitude either."

"And if I choose now?" She spoke in a whisper, soft as a caress.

"Then you better mean it for longer than time."

"I do."

He couldn't have denied her if he'd wanted to, and he certainly didn't want to. Slowly he threaded his fingers through her hair and drew her closer. Perhaps Ma was right when she said marriage was ordained of God because what he felt now went beyond right to something unearthly sweet.

Eleven

Carly looked up to see Wolf waiting for her on the porch. Each night he finished dinner before she did, then waited outside to walk her to Josh's cabin. Her eyes went to him the moment she emerged from the dining hall. A spark of awareness arced between them, lifting the gloom left behind by a day spent in Deborah's presence. He reached for her hand, drawing her to his side, and she sighed softly as his cheek touched hers. It was like coming home.

Over his shoulder she could see tarps spread over the gun pieces he'd been working on. The ugliness they represented was a painful reminder that she was still a prisoner.

"Did you get one finished?" she whispered as he took her arm. She hoped not. Marriage made life in the compound easier for her, though she couldn't attribute the peaceful lull entirely to her newly married state; Captain Isaac spent most of every day closeted in his office with his closest aides, and Luther had left the camp for a couple of weeklong assignments, both of which went a long way. At times during the past weeks, wrapped in her new-found love, she'd been able to almost forget her fear of Isaac and his cult. But the guns were a grim reminder of the underlying evil in the camp.

"They're starting to look like guns." Wolf's remark wasn't really an answer. She wished he'd answer straight out when she asked about his involvement with the cult. Her heart told her he wasn't one of them, yet the way he dodged real communication made her doubt her instincts. He frequently made her laugh with his tales of his and his brothers' escapades, and she'd learned a lot about his mother and the ranch where he'd grown up, but he never spoke of his reason for coming to Steeple Mountain.

When they reached Josh's door, Wolf lifted her chin with two fingers. He bent his head and kissed her nose. "See you."

"Aren't you coming inside? The children will want to see you."

"Not tonight." She watched him walk away and immediately doubt assailed her heart. At night in his arms, there were no doubts and their time together took on a splendor that left the shabby, hate-filled compound far behind, but at the back of her mind lurked a constant awareness that Wolf held something back.

She glanced toward Josh's door and frowned. Wolf seldom spent the evening with her and the children. The few times he did, the little cabin rang with laughter as he romped and played with her nephew and niece. They clearly adored him and he seemed to have as much fun as the children. Guiltily she wondered if he resented her going to Josh's cabin each evening to spend an hour with the children when the two of them had so little time together. No, it wasn't the time she spent with the children that formed a vague wall between Wolf and herself. It was all the unanswered questions.

She opened the door to be immediately assailed by conflicting emotions. Rachel sat on the bed between the children who were washed and dressed in clean pajamas. Carly felt a deep stab of jealousy. She didn't want Rachel to replace her in the children's affections, yet if Josh did marry the woman it would be better for the children if they could like their stepmother. If only Rachel weren't so solidly linked with the cult.

"Hi!" Rachel's voice always held a wary note when she spoke to Carly. "I was just leaving." She stood and quickly moved toward the door.

"Good night." Carly spoke politely. She berated herself for ignoring the pleading look in the other woman's eyes. She felt stiff and awkward. She knew her inability to unbend toward Rachel was widening the wedge between herself and Josh. She seldom saw him anymore. He spent every day inside the end cabin working on some secret project Isaac had assigned him. On the rare occasions she did see him, Rachel came between them.

"Aunt Carly!" Petra and Daniel ran to her. They were excited to see her, but their days started so early they were soon yawning. They were asleep minutes after tumbling into their beds in the loft they now shared. Carly stood at the foot of their beds watching them sleep. She'd mothered them so long, it was hard to think of another woman taking her place. If Rachel were anyone other than Isaac's daughter, would it be easier? She didn't know. Her arms felt heavy and she wondered if another child, a small replica of Wolf, could ease the ache. She smiled, envisioning a baby with dark curls snuggled against her breast. She brushed aside the whimsy. She couldn't bear the thought of a child born a prisoner of the compound.

Long after Carly returned to their own cabin, Wolf joined her. He seemed preoccupied and unwilling to talk. Yet he held her in his arms communicating a desperate tension that frightened her. Even the air around them felt intense. She sensed he was waiting for something. He seemed to be listening for some secret signal even when he was asleep. Did he know something she didn't? Sometimes she marveled at the closeness between Wolf and herself. Other times she was shocked to discover she didn't know him any better than she had the day he married her. She longed for time together, free of all the secrets and suspicions of their strange environment. She wished they could be a normal young couple in love, taking long walks in the woods, sharing a private dinner, even folding the laundry together.

Lying beside him in the dark, she faced the certainty that he was hiding something from her. When he made love to her, all the ugliness and fears melted away; then at moments like this, all the doubts and insecurities returned. Every look and action told her he loved her, but he never said the words.

How long she lay awake beside her sleeping husband, she couldn't begin to guess, but eventually she drifted into a light, restless slumber. When Wolf rolled away from her and quietly rose from their bed, she was instantly awake.

Carly lay still, pretending to be asleep. She didn't need the faint sliver of light coming through the muslin window cover to tell her Wolf was dressing, preparing to leave her. Again. Too many nights after Wolf thought she was asleep, he got out of bed, dressed, and left the cabin. Some nights he returned in an hour, other nights he barely made it back to bed before it was time to get up. An inner insecurity, fed by their aberrant environment, kept her from confronting him about his nighttime disappearances.

His secretive activities, she suspected, were part of the reason he'd married her, but she felt reluctant to face confirmation that their marriage was simply an expedient means of providing himself with more freedom of movement for whatever secret mission drew him out into the night.

She held her breath listening for the soft sweep of the door. When the sound came, she leaped from bed and pulled on her jeans and a black turtleneck sweater. She slid her feet into her Reeboks and left the cabin as soundlessly as Wolf had.

Carly didn't hesitate, wondering which way to go. She'd followed him once before, barefoot, as far as the chicken coop, but had to turn back there. Now she stopped in the deep shadow of the cabin to listen. Hearing nothing, she hurried to the wire enclosure. She released the gate, stepped inside, then hurried to the coop. Once inside the lopsided building, she paused again. Wolf wasn't inside the structure, but she hadn't expected he would be, though she felt certain he'd come this way. She didn't want to disturb the chickens, neither did she wish to alert Wolf that he was being followed. The interior of the building was dark, and she wouldn't have dared use a light even if she'd brought one.

There had to be another exit. Wolf wouldn't get up in the middle of the night to visit the chickens, she'd decided the first time she'd followed him. Remembering the secret door in the drug closet, she moved ahead unerringly. The back wall abutted the stockade wall; the door had to be there. She tugged against the nesting boxes until four swung inward on well-oiled hinges. The chickens roosting a few feet away made gentle squawking sounds, ruffled a few feathers, and settled back to sleep.

Crouching low, Carly crawled through the opening, then pulled the door behind her. Though not as dark as inside the hen house, it was too dark to see more than a few feet ahead. Fortunately, there weren't more than ten yards between the log wall and the edge of the forest. She moved toward the trees. She had no idea which way Wolf had gone, but surely he'd headed for the trees, too, once outside the compound.

In the shelter of the trees she considered the hopeless task she'd set herself. She'd been naive to think she could follow Wolf in the dark. She sat on a log and considered her next move. Somewhere in the distance she heard the scream of a night bird. She ought to go back, but being outside the walls of the compound was exhilarating. This was the first time she'd been outside in a month, and she didn't want to go back. Not right away.

She straightened her back and stood in one quick motion. She was wasting time. Even if she couldn't follow Wolf, she could enjoy her freedom for a short time, and she wouldn't get lost if she stayed near the river.

Half an hour later Carly sat on a boulder between two tall pines watching the moon rise, casting its silvery glow across the river. The water appeared black and mysterious. And free. It drew her like a magnet. Freedom was a quality she'd learned to appreciate. Life was hard in the compound, especially hard for the women and children from whom total obedience was expected. The work was endless and she'd noticed most of it was done by women while the men held their endless military drills. But worse than the hard work was the constant sense of being watched and the lack of choices in her life.

She scooted forward until her feet touched the ground, then step by step she worked her way down the incline until she stood beside the water. Stooping, she played her fingers in the icy stream. When she lifted her fingers to let the water drizzle back to the river, she saw a large, heavy shape moving toward her on the water. Freezing in place, she watched.

Clearly highlighted for brief seconds by the bright moon, a small canoe shot toward her, then disappeared in the deep blackness near the shore. Carly's heart pounded. Someone was coming downriver. She'd have to hide. She wished there was a way to warn Wolf, but she didn't have any idea whether he was near or miles away.

On trembling knees she crawled beneath the bows of a tree that grew near the water's edge and hunkered down in the hollow of its great roots. A black shadow floated by mere feet from her hiding place. It wasn't a canoe, but a one-man kayak headed toward the compound.

Crouching low, Carly decided to follow the small boat. This close to the water she didn't need to worry about sounds because the river made enough noise to cover any she might make. Taking advantage of the brush growing near the pebbly bank of the river, Carly moved downstream. The kayak soon disappeared from sight, but she followed doggedly.

Her journey ended sooner than she expected when she nearly stumbled onto the small, rocky beach where the craft had been pulled clear of the water. Twenty feet away she made out the shapes of two men with rifles in their hands standing together under the overhang of the higher bank. They were too far away for her to hear what they were saying, but some sixth sense told her the man facing her was Wolf. The other man was as tall as Wolf, but had a slighter build. Their stance betrayed both familiarity and a high level of tension. This was a planned rendezvous, one she suspected Isaac knew nothing about.

Shrinking into the willows bordering the small beach, Carly moved closer. She flattened herself to the ground to creep to within two feet of the overhang and took care to stay close to trees and shrubs where she wouldn't be silhouetted against the sky. Through the darkness she could make out two dark shapes and hear the murmur of voices, but she couldn't distinguish words. She stifled a twinge of guilt for her spying activities and wished she knew what they were saying to each other. She didn't dare move closer. Frustration kept her teeth clenched tightly together as she strained to hear words she sensed would bring answers to her many questions about Wolf. From her position above them she couldn't see either man's face, but the timbre of Wolf's voice was unmistakable.

Moonlight glittered across tall grass a few feet from where the two men stood and to her horror she saw the grass part. She prepared to shout a warning, but it wasn't necessary. Two fat raccoons waddled into sight and made their way to the water, oblivious to the intruders sharing their beach.

Carly turned her attention back to the men and swallowed an exclamation of fright at seeing them both with their rifles at the ready. She froze, unable to breathe.

Wolf relaxed his stance first. The other man took his time. They spoke a few minutes more, then Wolf handed something to the second man before he turned toward his kayak. Wolf moved deeper into the shadow at the foot of the bluff. Suddenly the retreating figure turned back toward Wolf. He, too, stepped into the darkness immediately below Carly and his softly spoken words carried to her ears.

"Don't worry. The Marshal wants this arrest badly, but he won't move until you're set."

Carly's mouth dropped open and she quickly placed one hand over it to stifle a gasp. Wolf and the other man were cops! She glanced toward the stranger, but he wore a billed cap pulled low and he stood in deep shadow.

A sense of jubilation swept through her. She remembered the star on Wolf's rifle. And the handgun he carried. Of course it was similar to the one she'd found in Isaac's hidden cellar because Wolf was a federal agent, too! Why hadn't she thought of that before? No wonder he was secretive. He was investigating Isaac and his cult! She'd been right; he wasn't one of them. She felt a moment's elation, a surge of hope.

She started to rise, anxious to go to Wolf, when a sudden cold chill stilled her action. There was a reason Wolf hadn't told her his identity. She bit her lip to hold back her cry. She clung to her hiding spot as the man guided the kayak into the water, lifted his paddle, and disappeared back the way he'd come. She turned her head back toward Wolf, but he was gone.

She stared at the spot where the two men had stood and remembered a disaster in Waco, Texas. It was a terrible story of children trapped in a burning inferno that erupted when law officers attempted to arrest a militaristic cult leader. And before that there had been another story of a young boy caught in the cross fire between a white separatist band and U.S. Marshals during a shootout not too far from here. In both cases children died.

Carly rocked back on her heels and tears streamed from her eyes. Was Isaac's compound about to become another Waco? What about the children? Would they die in a gun battle? With the amount of ammunition and dynamite Isaac had stored at the compound, they could all die in an explosion if the compound were attacked. How would Isaac react if the battle went against him? She shuddered, remembering the final hours of another cult in far-off Guyana, and a picture of the green punch Isaac sent the children each day swam before her eyes.

She had to get back to the compound. There was no time to waste. Her muscles protested as she rose to her feet to begin the long walk back. She wanted to run, but even though the moon was now high, she couldn't trust her footing. Several times she took a dead-end path and had to retrace her steps. Her mind raced with all she'd seen and surmised. Should she confront Wolf? She decided against it, fearing that if he knew what she'd guessed, it might precipitate the very action she feared. He might even prevent her from getting the children out lest their departure alert Isaac he was being investigated.

The closer she came to the stockade, the more her feet dragged. Wolf had used her. He'd seen her predicament and capitalized on it to gain entrance to the compound. Her eyes smarted from unshed tears. She'd been a fool. It had been so easy to pretend Wolf shared her feelings, to believe he loved her, even though he'd never said the words. Was their marriage a lie? But what had made her think a forced marriage could be anything other than a lie?

It shouldn't bother her that he was a spy since they were on the same side. But it did bother her; it frightened her. Because it endangered the children and because she loved him. Spying on Isaac placed Wolf in terrible danger. If anyone else discovered what she had learned, Wolf could die just like those other two agents had.

Carly reached the edge of the trees. Ahead of her stood the compound. Her teeth chattered and her hands were freezing and damp, whether from cold or fear she couldn't be sure. There was enough cloud cover now to make her way to the hidden door, but on the other side of that door she'd have to face Wolf. She estimated he'd returned at least half an hour ahead of her. He'd demand an explanation for her absence, but she couldn't tell him. She squared her shoulders and took a deep breath. There was only one thing she could do. She'd have to lie to him.

Wolf paced the floor. He'd sensed something wasn't right the moment he'd stepped inside the cabin. It took only seconds to discover Carly was missing. He lost no time covering the window with a blanket and lighting the lantern. Her nightshirt lay beside the bed and the jeans she'd worn earlier were gone. She must have awakened after he left, but where had she gone? She might not have left the cabin voluntarily. A cold sweat broke out on his skin when he considered the possibilities. If Isaac had discovered Wolf's identity, he might hold Carly hostage. Then there was Luther. If he'd discovered Carly was alone, he wouldn't hesitate to harm her. He'd do it to spite Wolf if for no other reason. Wolf hadn't missed the malevolent stare Luther directed Carly's way each time she entered the dining hall, and he suspected her former assistant blamed her because once again he'd lost a chance to snatch Rachel's fortune. Fresh anger boiled to the surface at the thought of Luther threatening Carly. Guilt mixed with the anger. He shouldn't have left her alone.

Wolf turned the lamp to its lowest setting before opening the door a crack, just enough to slip through. Stealthily, he crossed the dirt road to Josh's cabin. His ears strained to hear any sound. All was quiet. He decided not to wake Josh except as a last resort. He clung to the blackest shadows of the compound until he reached the infirmary. One look inside satisfied him Carly wasn't there. No lights shone in any of the cabins; that ruled out a medical house call.

Grasping his revolver in one hand, he moved toward the men's barracks. Flattening himself against the side of the building, he eased open the door. The first bed belonged to Luther and there was no mistaking he was in it. Wolf would recognize the racket he made in his sleep anywhere. Thank God Luther didn't have her!

Slowly Wolf made his way back to the cabin, checking the women's bathhouse on the way. Inside the cabin there was still no sign of Carly. Where could she be? Cold fear clutched the pit of his stomach. If Isaac were responsible, where would he take her? His shoulders shook with the intensity of his fear for her. Ma had taught him to pray when he was a little boy and scared at night after his father was killed, but he'd never been as scared as he was now. And he'd never prayed harder.

At the sound of the door opening slowly behind him, he turned so fast he nearly lost his balance.

"Carly!" He crossed the room and wrapped his arms around her. For several minutes he couldn't speak. She was alive and in his arms! Carly didn't respond, and gradually he became aware she was shaking and her face and hands were icy cold. Wherever she'd gone, she hadn't taken the time to grab her jacket. He stepped back and grasped her shoulders so he could see her face. "Where have you been?"

"I might ask you the same thing." There was a determined tilt to her jaw as she glared back at him. After several long seconds she continued, "A guard knocked on the door to tell me I was needed at the infirmary, and I awoke to find you were gone."

Wolf recognized her tactics; a good offense always made a good defense. "Who needed you at the infirmary?" He ignored her implied question.

"It wasn't important. One of the guards had a splinter imbedded in his hand from climbing the ladder to one of the towers." She turned her back and walked a few steps away.

She was lying and it was like taking a solid punch. She hadn't been at the infirmary, and from every indication he'd seen, the tower guards were asleep. A sense of desolation swept over him. Carly had never lied to him before. She'd covered for him, and he suspected there were things she'd omitted telling him, but it had never occurred to him that she would deliberately lie to him. Lying didn't come naturally to her, and this lie said she was scared and didn't trust him.

"What's wrong, Carly? Why can't you tell me where you've been?"

"I don't notice you answering my questions."

"Oh, honey, I would if I could." He clenched his jaw in frustration. He hated being less than honest with her.

"You have your answer then."

"That answer won't do. I'm your husband and I'm responsible for your safety. How can I protect you if I don't know where you are?" Anger was replacing the fear.

"I can take care of myself." Carly shrugged and in her eyes he saw pain and fatigue. She wouldn't back down and he couldn't. Yelling at her would accomplish nothing. "It's almost morning. Go back to bed and get what sleep you can." He felt flat and discouraged.

Carly moved away from him to pick up her nightshirt. She kept a wary eye on him as she moved to the far side of the bed to pull off her jeans. Turning her back, she quickly tugged the sweater over her head and jerked the nightshirt in its place.

Wolf felt an ache deep in his soul. Not many hours ago he'd held her in his arms. A cold chasm separated them now. He'd put his job first, but he was no closer to finding the evidence he needed than he'd been a month ago. And now he was losing Carly. It was all for nothing. He'd never disobeyed a direct order, but he'd never been as tempted before as he was now to tell Carly the truth.

She lay down and pulled the quilt to her chin before Wolf lifted the lamp chimney and blew out the flame, plunging the cabin into darkness. He removed his jacket and lay it and his holster on the floor beside the bed, then he lay down and reached for Carly. Her body stiffened, but he didn't let her go. Instead he held her and slowly stroked her back. He didn't speak, and neither did she. His fingers kneaded and smoothed their way from her tangled braids to her waist. Rhythmically, he erased the knots of tension and lulled her to sleep.

Long after she fell asleep, he lay beside her striving to make sense of the night. After the fright she'd given him he wanted to shake her, somehow force her to tell him where she'd gone, and what had happened. An even stronger desire urged him to hold her, shelter her, and make her world safe. He could only surmise she had awakened and been frightened by his absence. Guiltily he wondered if she'd gone hunting for him. But something had changed between them; she was afraid of him and he didn't know why. His absence alone didn't account for the fear.

The first glimmer of daylight crept into the room as he left the bed for the second time, but he couldn't lie beside her, listen to her breathe, and smell the sweetness of her skin any longer. He had to think, undistracted by her warm body lying next to his.

Pink streaks were lighting the sky as he made his way past the sentries and onto the dock. They rubbed their eyes and waved. He returned a brief salute and walked on. Reaching the end of the plank pier, he gazed across the lake. Puffs of hazy whiteness lay like clouds along the opposite shore. Close by, a trout seeking its breakfast broke the water. On the surface it looked as peaceful as his valley in the Bitterroot.

Lately he'd dreamed a lot of taking Carly to the Wolverton ranch; now he wondered if that dream had been foolish fancy. Would there ever come a time when he could put violence and terrorism behind him and know peace and love with Carly? Pain washed through him anew as his mind returned over and over to the cold fact that she had lied to him. He had no right to be upset—he'd been less than honest with her too—yet the pain persisted.

It was obvious that the confinement was getting to Carly, and she was deeply unhappy over her separation from the children. Josh and Rachel's approaching marriage only added to her worry. She hated everything Isaac and his cult stood for, which endeared her to him all the more, but did nothing to make her current situation more bearable. Carly had deep spiritual instincts and had known from the start that Isaac was a false prophet, seeking his own agenda of power. He admired the quiet faith she'd maintained in the face of the bombardment of pseudo-religion thrown in her face each day. She'd make a good Mormon.

Wolf started. Where had that thought come from? Was it because she shared so many of his mother's strong qualities? Or could it be because he'd been comparing Isaac's values to the compassion and justice of Ma's religion? Was it possible that the missionary lessons he took while still a boy and his mother's adherence to those teachings had taken deeper root in his own heart than he'd ever real-ized? He closed his eyes and with his back to the compound, he bowed his head and mouthed a plea to the God his mother testified lived. With all the fervency of a soul newly awakened to spiritual hope, he begged to be reconciled with Carly, to be given a chance for a future together.

He wished he knew whether she had gone hunting for him or if someone inside the camp had frightened her. It didn't seem likely she could have left the compound, not unless she'd chanced to slip through the gates while the guards were asleep.

He didn't like the picture he saw of Carly wandering around out there on the mountain in the dark. On the other hand he didn't like the risks any better when he thought of what could happen to her if Luther discovered her alone at night inside the compound. How could he make certain she didn't leave the cabin at night the next time he had to sneak out to meet Bradley? And how could he restore her trust in him? She was a strong, intelligent woman, but without the full facts how could she protect herself when he was away? He trusted her with his life, so why shouldn't he share his identity with her?

He couldn't shake the feeling she was in imminent danger, and if the information he held could make her more vigilant, he owed her that. If only he could forget Isaac and just take her away. But other lives were involved and Carly's commitment to her family ran deep. She wouldn't leave them, even to save herself.

Over the past month he'd kept careful tabs on the bombs Josh was building. They didn't look like bombs. They looked like ordinary briefcases, sack lunches, books, and shopping bags. A remote control detonator would set them off simultaneously, but where? Why hadn't he been able to discover Isaac's planned target? The project was nearly complete and Wolf had detected a suppressed excitement in Isaac's actions lately. Both were warnings to Wolf that he was out of time.

"Wolf?" He felt the brush of fingertips on his sleeve. Immediately he stiffened. He should have heard footsteps approaching, but he'd let personal problems dull his awareness. He turned to see Carly watching him. She appeared poised to run if he even raised his voice. Her chin quivered and she glanced from side to side as she waited for him to speak. She was obviously scared to the bone.

"What is it? What has happened, Carly?" He made a move to draw her into his embrace.

"No! Wait!" She took a step back and her voice dropped to a whisper. "I have to talk to you."

Wolf waited for her to continue. She swallowed a deep gulp of air, then straightened her shoulders.

"I lied to you about where I went. There wasn't a medical emergency. I followed you and I found out you're some kind of federal agent."

He felt only relief that she knew. Now was the time to tell her everything. Holding out his hand to her, he smiled.

"Deputy marshal. I'm glad you know; I'd just decided orders or not, it was time I told you."

Her stance didn't soften and he could still see the fear in her eyes. He couldn't believe she'd followed him and he'd been completely unaware. If she had followed him, who else may have?

"Does anyone else know?"

"No, I don't think so. Isaac will kill you if he finds out." He knew she didn't mean the words in a figurative way.

"Is that why you're afraid?"

"Yes."

But he could see she struggled with more than fear for his safety, or even fear for the children and herself. Something else troubled her.

"Why did you change your mind about telling me?" He phrased the question as gently as possible and for several minutes he thought she wouldn't answer.

"I'm so sick of the lies and deceit in this place. I lied because I was angry and hurt that you didn't trust me enough to tell me why you were here. Even more, I'm afraid of the consequences to the children if you try to arrest Isaac. I have to get them away from here, and to do that I need your help. How can I ask for your help if I can't trust you? When I woke up a few minutes ago, I could hear a voice inside my head repeating over and over, 'Terrorism is wrong. Tell him! End the lies.'" She sniffed and swiped the back of her hand across her cheek. "You've got to promise to get the children away from here before your people attack the compound."

"We'll do everything possible to ensure their safety if and when any arrests are made."

"I want them out before. If they stay here, they'll die!"

Her voice rose and Wolf looked around to make certain they hadn't drawn the guards' attention. He dropped his voice another notch and asked, "Why do you think they'll die?"

"You don't really care about me or my family." There was a world of hurt in her voice. "You're here to arrest Isaac. He has crates of explosives and if he's attacked he'll blow up this place before he'll surrender. Even an accidental bullet could detonate an explosion."

Wolf took a step closer to her. "You're wrong, not about Isaac, but about me. I do care about you."

"I don't think so. You knew all along that Isaac kills people, but

I had to discover for myself that he's a murderer. You stood by and let Josh get in deeper and deeper and endanger his children. I handed you a perfect cover to get in here, and you took it instead of warning us or helping Josh get away from Isaac. I thought you cared a little bit about me when you saved me from marrying Luther, but you were only using me!"

"You said murder. Tell me what you know about that." Wolf clasped the tops of her arms. There was no longer any reason to evade telling him.

"Isaac killed those poor old trappers and Daniel saw him. I'd hoped it was just a story until I found Two-Toe Johnny's silver medallion and two wallets belonging to the two agents Isaac said were snooping around here."

"Where, Carly? Where did you find those things?" Wolf spoke in a harsh whisper. The hard light in his eyes frightened her as his fingers tightened around her arms.

"There's a room under the infirmary," she stammered. "I found a hidden door in the drug closet. There's dynamite and gold and all kinds of things there. Guns too. On the wall is a big map of San Francisco and posters of rock groups. I think Isaac plans to have Josh blow up Candlestick Park, but Josh wouldn't do something like that. He only blows up old buildings that need to be demolished so new ones can be built. You've got to believe Josh wouldn't deliberately hurt innocent people." She used her hands to stem the tears she couldn't prevent falling.

Wolf stared at Carly incredulously. If she knew about the bombs, she couldn't be naive enough to think Josh didn't know their purpose. He felt an ache of pity for her, but he suspected she wouldn't accept words of compassion from him now. He turned his mind to the other things she'd said. He'd spent a month searching for the evidence Carly had just stumbled onto. A stab of remorse reminded him that if he'd followed his instincts to level with her weeks ago, this situation would be over by now.

Excitement began to mount. This was it. There was no longer any reason to stay. He could get a warrant now. He'd have to get the information to Bradley tonight, and set in motion plans to get Carly and the children out before the warrant was served.

"Wolf, please help me get the children away from here."

"I will," he promised. Seeing the tears shining in her eyes, he cupped her face between his hands and wiped away the tears with his thumbs. "You've been brave beyond belief, but it won't be much longer now."

"Will Josh be arrested?" Carly freed herself from his hold and watched him carefully, suspicion in every line of her body.

He didn't know how to answer, so much depended on what actually happened with those bombs, how much Josh knew of the reason for their construction, and whether or not coercion had been used to secure his cooperation.

"He'll be questioned. More than that I can't say." He tried to spare her further grief and still be honest. She shrugged off the consoling hand he offered and turned her face away. Her shoulders sagged, and Wolf felt a cold wind in the vicinity of his heart.

Twelve

Carly made her way back inside the compound. She didn't want Wolf's sympathy. She didn't know what she wanted from him, but it wasn't pity. He'd promised to help her get the children out, but could she trust him? She would have to; he was their only hope. If only Josh could see Isaac in his true light! Her heart twisted as she contemplated escaping the compound with Petra and Daniel while leaving Josh behind. A heavy weight settled in her chest and her stomach clenched with pain. She couldn't do it. She had to speak with Josh one more time.

Almost running, she darted across the common intent on reaching Josh's cabin. People were gathered near the main building and gradually she became conscious of hurrying steps as others left their cabins and barracks to join the growing crowd. She slipped past a knot of soldiers and threaded her way through scattered clusters of people. Focused on reaching Josh, she ignored those around her until she heard his name mentioned in a hushed tone. Then she heard Rachel's name and her steps slowed.

"Isaac says it's time." A whisper reached her ears.

"They'll marry this morning, then the great plan will begin."

Josh and Rachel were getting married this morning? No, Josh would have told her. Perhaps he'd been given no more notice than she'd had of her own rushed wedding, a bitter voice inside her head reminded her. Warning Josh that the compound was about to be raided by law officers took on added urgency. She had to reach him before he linked himself irrevocably with Isaac's army. Fear for her beloved brother sent her feet flying forward.

Without warning a hand grabbed her shoulder and spun her around. Luther loomed over her, hatred and venom distorting his features. His fingers dug into her skin as he shook her. He muttered a vile name, so low it only reached her ears.

"First Josh, then you. I'll enjoy hearing you beg and scream. I might even let Wolf watch." His lips stretched over his teeth in a macabre grin before he shoved her viciously aside. Unable to catch herself, she tumbled to the ground. Luther's boot grazed her ribs as he stepped over her body and strode away.

She sat dazed in the dirt for several minutes before pulling herself painfully to her feet just as Wolf reached her side. His strong arms enfolded her and drew her face against his shoulder.

"Josh! I've got to talk to Josh." Carly struggled to free herself. "Wolf, let me go." She squirmed against him.

"Sh-h, it's all right." He whispered words of reassurance. His hands smoothed away the dirt and weeds clinging to her clothing and hair.

"No! I've got to stop him before—" Wolf's hand pressed against her mouth cutting off her words.

"There's nothing you can do, sweetheart. It won't be so bad; they love each other and want to get married."

"You don't care; you don't care what happens to any of us."

"Carly, I do care. I know you don't trust me, but I'm telling you the truth. You have to walk over there and watch Josh marry Rachel without saying a word. Anything you do to draw attention to us will endanger us all. Now walk."

Carly caught back a sob as she watched Josh approach the steps where Isaac waited with Rachel beside him. Slumping weakly against Wolf, she felt him relax his tight hold on her. She took several deep gulps of air.

She took a hesitant step toward her brother, but before she could move far, Wolf circled her waist with one arm and began walking casually toward the crowd gathered for the wedding.

The sun had not yet taken the damp chill from the morning when Josh took Rachel's hand and the ceremony began. Wolf kept his arm around Carly's waist and felt her tremble. A sense of déjà vu reminded him of their own wedding. There was nothing he could do or say now to alleviate her pain.

Whether she would have objected to anyone Josh chose to marry or if it was Rachel herself Carly disliked, Wolf didn't know. There were the children to consider, too. Carly might be reluctant to have a stepmother take over her role in their lives. No, Carly's reason ran deeper than that. She blamed Rachel for her present situation and feared Josh's marriage to Isaac's daughter would link them all irrevocably to the cult. He wished he could reassure her on that score.

Wolf drew Carly closer and stroked her shoulder in a gesture of comfort and support. She stiffened and pulled as far away as his arm allowed. Wolf glanced down to see tears streaming down her pale, set face. A cold fist of fear clutched his heart; Carly might never forgive him for all he'd failed to tell her.

Carly struggled to gain control of her emotions. Wolf had been evasive when she'd asked about her brother. Whether he was trying to spare her feelings or had another motive she didn't know, but being married to Rachel, Josh would appear totally involved with the cult and that would make Wolf's case against him even stronger.

It was too late to stop the wedding, but she still had to warn Josh. Her mind was too busy devising a plan to listen to the words. She was only vaguely conscious of an air of excitement and exultation in Isaac's voice. Josh appeared stiff and severe, and Rachel, pale and subdued. Missing was the joy and self-conscious smiles Carly remembered from Josh's first wedding. As soon as the ceremony was over, she'd follow Josh back to his cabin and insist on talking to him alone. Once he knew about the secret room and Wolf's real identity, he'd find a way to defuse the explosives and get the children to safety. She knew in her heart Josh was too smart and caring to be deceived any longer by Isaac. She'd seen cracks in his defense of Isaac and suspected he'd believe her at last.

The rambling ceremony ended and Isaac raised his voice to announce, "The newlyweds will leave immediately for Josh's cabin down the river. When they return tomorrow, I'll fly them and their children to Seattle for a combined honeymoon and business trip. When our business trip is finished, I'll bring my new grandchildren back here and let Josh and Rachel stay there for a few days."

The unusual note of excitement in Isaac's voice disturbed Carly.

If having Petra and Daniel become his grandchildren pleased him so much, why weren't they at their father's wedding? Suddenly she realized Isaac was leading the newlyweds toward the dock. They weren't returning to Josh's cabin.

Panic tore through Carly. Josh couldn't leave before she talked to him. Something was horribly wrong. Wolf's grip on her relaxed and Carly, taking advantage of his brief lapse, slipped away. Anxiously she elbowed her way through the crowd. She had to get to Josh. She lost sight of him in the crush, but pushed on toward the boat dock.

By the time she reached the compound gate, the crowd had thinned and she could see Josh and Rachel on the dock. Isaac walked with them. Breaking into a run she screamed, "Josh!" Isaac turned toward her with a frown.

Josh turned as she catapulted into his arms. "I have to talk to you," she whispered in his ear. "It's urgent." He gave her a quick hug, then held her at arm's length.

"Watch Petra and Daniel until we get back. They can stay with you tonight." He squeezed her fingers, then released them.

"The children stay with me tonight," Isaac interrupted.

"They stay with Carly." Josh rose to his full height and turned to face his new father-in-law. His words were laced with a hint of steel, and something black stirred in the back of Isaac's eyes. Then Isaac shrugged as though the matter was of no consequence. Josh's stance didn't waver for several long minutes, then he turned to Carly. Speaking more gently, he said, "Go with Wolf now."

"Wait!" She felt Wolf's hands settle on her shoulders. Josh helped Rachel into the canoe, then leaped in himself. With a wave they were off. When Carly would have taken a step toward them, Wolf held her back. She turned her head frantically seeking help. Isaac still stood on the dock, a smugly satisfied expression on his face. It was gone in an instant, and he brushed by her as though she weren't there.

"Carly, come on back to the cabin," Wolf coaxed, his voice soft and full of compassion. Carly shook off his hands and marched ahead of him. She didn't want to return to the cabin. She thought of grabbing a canoe and following Josh, but she dismissed the idea as quickly as it came. Wolf would stop her. If he didn't, Isaac would.

"Carly!" Wolf took her arm insistently.

"Go away! Leave me alone." She struggled to free herself.

"No, Carly. We have to talk." Quickly he propelled her toward their cabin.

Once inside, she paced the floor restlessly while Wolf leaned against the wall watching in silence. Would it do any good to appeal to him? Or would it be better to wait until Josh returned? Heaven help her, she didn't know what was best.

Wolf stood with his arms folded across his chest and a closed expression on his face. Finally he spoke. "Is it so terrible for Josh to remarry? I think you'll like Rachel once you get to know her."

Carly shuddered before she turned angrily on Wolf. "No, I don't mind Josh remarrying. I always expected he would. But married to Rachel, he and the children won't have a chance of living a normal life, and you know it. If they get out of here alive, they'll still always be tied to this madness!"

"When we have more time, I'll tell you all about Rachel. Believe me, she has less reason to love Isaac than you do. But right now, we'd both better go back to work and give no one any reason to consider either of us a problem." He held out his hand to her. "Will you be all right?"

"What about the kids? Josh asked me to watch them."

"They're both in school. I checked on them earlier. I'll be on the front porch all afternoon with the gun I'm supposed to be assembling. From there I can keep an eye on the school and watch who enters or leaves the infirmary."

"There's another door to the cellar room from Isaac's office."

That explained a lot. "I'll watch Isaac, too, and if there's any trouble, I'll skin my knuckles and come visit you for a little first aid." He grinned and took her hand. In spite of their precarious position, Wolf felt lighter. Carly hadn't lost all trust in him, and from now on they'd be working together.

They'd passed Josh's house when Wolf noticed something was happening at the end cabin, the one where Josh spent most of his time. Taking care to shield Carly's view, he kept walking. Once Carly was inside the infirmary, he returned to his position on the porch where as unobtrusively as possible he watched the activity occurring between the far cabin and Isaac's plane. Isaac was directing a small group of men who were rushing about in a near-frenzied state of excitement.

With a sinking heart, Wolf understood the bombs were being moved. Most likely they would travel with Josh and his family to Seattle. If Candlestick Park was their intended destination, then from Seattle they would most likely be trucked in order to avoid airport security. He'd have to get to Bradley tonight, so he could warn the authorities to be on the lookout. Carly wouldn't like it, but at least she'd have the children with her, and this time he'd tell her before he left. That should help.

Instead of returning to the compound when the plane was loaded, Isaac, Luther, and two other men climbed aboard. Isaac turned back at the last moment to speak to Reuben. Then Wolf watched the small plane taxi out onto the lake, before lifting gracefully into the sky. In minutes it disappeared from sight.

He supposed he should feel relief the bombs wouldn't be traveling on the same flight as Josh's family, but he couldn't help suspecting this was a sudden change of plans. The morning had been unreal; too much had happened too fast. Isaac had been planning something for months, but the hurried loading and departure of Isaac's plane didn't feel like the result of careful planning. Something nagged at the back of Wolf's mind. He couldn't help thinking he was missing some vital point.

Wolf surveyed the compound then rose unobtrusively to his feet. With Isaac and Luther gone, there was something he needed to do. He feigned a casualness he was far from feeling as he reached for the doorknob and entered the building. No one was in the hall. In seconds he was inside Isaac's office.

He avoided crossing in front of the window as he made his way to the closet. He knew what to look for and marveled that he hadn't found it before, especially with his knowledge of Reuben's secret door in the chicken coop. He pressed against the panel behind the file cabinet and watched a section of the wall swing away from his touch.

Light was no problem. Like the rest of the building, power was provided by the generator. The stairway was just as Carly had described it. Wolf moved cautiously; he didn't care to make any noise that might frighten Carly or alert Deborah that someone was in the room beneath them. Slowly he walked the length of the room, taking care not to touch anything.

He silently whistled at the extent of Isaac's arsenal. It was far more extensive than even Josh knew. When he reached the end of the room, he lifted his eyes. From Carly's description, he'd expected the map of San Francisco. It was the location marked in red that drew his attention. Carly was right. Candlestick Park was the target.

Turning to the poster, he sucked in his breath. Deep slashes crisscrossed the faces of four young black men. A heavy hunting knife lay imbedded in the paper figure of the single woman singer in the group.

Moving around the corner of the table, Wolf spotted a page torn from a recent teen magazine. It sent tremors of shock ripping through him. In his hand was an amended itinerary for the black rock group, the Dreadnaughts' concert tour. Bold headlines stated the Labor Day concert had been moved up. On August 23, just three days from now the group would join with several other rock, rap, and reggae groups in San Francisco's Candlestick Park for a massive concert. Thousands of screaming, excited adolescents would pack the huge arena.

Barely controlled anger suffused him. Isaac planned to blow up thousands of kids, representing every ethnic group in the country, as they sang and danced to the music they loved! To Isaac all those kids were just a political statement. Nausea almost overwhelmed him, then a deadly calm took its place.

He couldn't wait until nightfall; he had to get this information to Stewart immediately. A terrorist strike of Oklahoma City proportions must not be allowed to happen again.

Carly glanced up from wrapping Reuben's palm. He'd come to her minutes ago with blood dripping from his hand and a story about falling while carrying a gas can. She practically had to hold her breath to escape the fumes while she picked out several small rocks. Her eyes widened when she saw Wolf standing in the doorway. She glanced at his hand, then saw him shake his head.

"Best be goin', ma'am." Reuben stood. "Thanks for fixin' me up, and I want you to know I consider it a downright honor to look after your chickens. I've got quite attached to them red birds." He nodded his head when he passed Wolf. Wolf drew back slightly as the strong odor of gasoline hit him. Reuben reached the door, then turned around to clomp back to Wolf in his heavy high-top work shoes.

"I'd sure appreciate a pair of them mocs like you been wearin' if'n I was to make a long trip." He gave Wolf's tall laced moccasins an approving nod, then looking Wolf full in the face, he said, "An old sow from up on the high ridge moved her cubs down closer to the river a couple of nights ago. She most got me before I could get these clodhoppers of mine movin'." He started for the door again.

"Reuben."

The older man paused.

"There's an extra pair in the chest you built for me. Help yourself." Something about the look that passed between the two men set off a small alarm in the back of Carly's mind. Evidently she wasn't the only one who knew about Wolf's nighttime prowling. She peered anxiously after Reuben as he disappeared out the door.

"Where's Deborah?" Wolf surveyed the clinic room.

"She's gone to pick up our lunch."

"I'll talk fast then." Keeping his voice low he told her he'd been in the cellar room. "Isaac and Luther both left in the plane a short time ago, so you don't have to worry about either of them for a while. I have information that must get to the Justice Department immediately. I hate to leave you alone, but if I leave right now, I'll be back by midnight. Have the children ready; we might have to leave in a hurry."

Her heart gave a fierce jolt. He really did intend to get the children away. "Won't you be seen if you leave now?"

"I'll make it." He leaned over and kissed her, then was gone before she could recollect herself enough to caution him to be careful.

Carly rushed through dinner. She was anxious to be with the children. School let out half an hour before the adult dinner hour, and Rachel, of course, wasn't with them today. During the days when the children were being drugged, half an hour was just enough time to get them tucked in bed before their parents left them alone. With the vigorous program Rachel had enacted, some of the younger children were still ready to be put to bed as soon as they returned from school. A few of the older children had been assigned chores to keep them busy, but they didn't always do them. As the days passed, they'd become more mischievous. Carly knew Isaac had to be aware the children were no longer docile and quiet, and she worried he would order them drugged again.

With Isaac and Luther gone, she closed the infirmary early. She found Petra and Daniel in their cabin, sitting alone in the dark. When she came closer she could see Petra's cheeks were streaked with tears and Daniel's shirt was torn and dirty.

"What happened?" She dropped to her knees to pull both children into her arms.

Petra spoke first. "Matthew said Daddy went away and he's not coming back."

"He said Captain Isaac is our grandpa now, and we belong to him. I told him what Uncle Wolf said about how people can't own other people, but he just laughed, so I hit him."

"Oh, Daniel." She hugged him, then hugged Petra too. She didn't know if the children had even been told about their father's marriage. "Your daddy will be back, but not tonight. Lots of things happened today and we'll talk about them in just a little while. Let's find you both a change of clothes, and I'll take you to my cabin. You can stay with me tonight."

She searched through their clothes until she found sweat suits and sturdy overalls, hiking boots, and warm jackets. The children gathered up their quilts. Once they reached Carly's cabin, she poured a pan of water for them to wash in, and told them to change into their sweat suits.

"Are we going to sleep in our sweat suits?" Petra asked dubiously. "It isn't winter."

"I know, but this cabin gets colder than yours does." She didn't want to tell the children they might be leaving in the middle of the night, but she wanted to be certain they were dressed warmly just in case.

"Your cabin smells funny." Daniel sniffed. Carly caught the faint odor of gasoline too and smiled. Reuben must have gotten his moccasins.

"I wish we were back at our own cabin." Petra's voice was wistful and she didn't seem to be the same exuberant child she'd been a month ago.

"Me too." Daniel chimed in. "I want to go fishing and climb trees. It isn't fun here, and if I say something bad, I get whacked."

"Daniel! Who whacked you?"

"Sister Hampton whacked my hand the first day I went to school 'cause I spilled my punch."

"She made him sit in the corner on a tree stump every day cause he made up words instead of saying Bible words. One time he told her he'd rather go fishing, so she boxed his ears." Daniel giggled, but Petra looked sad and bewildered.

"Does Rachel hit you?" Carly asked the awful question.

"Sister Rachel doesn't whack anybody," Daniel said in his new teacher's defense. "I missed her today. We didn't get to run or do anything 'cept listen to Sister Hampton read that old Bible. She got real mad too when Michael threw his biscuit at me. Will Sister Rachel be back tomorrow?" Daniel pulled down his pants and reached for his sweats. As he bent over, Carly caught a glimpse of a large angry bruise on his thigh. She turned him around slowly. There were more black smudges on his back and down his legs. Were these the normal bruises of an active six-year-old? She wasn't sure. She closed her eyes and begged a higher authority to protect Wolf and bring him quickly back to help her get Petra and Daniel away from this place.

"I thought you said Rachel never hit you." Carly's voice trembled as she confronted her nephew over the bruises. It was too horrible to contemplate turning the children over to Rachel if she did this.

"Rachel never hit me, just Luke and Matthew."

"Luke and Matthew? But they're a lot bigger than you."

"They pulled Petra's hair, so I had to stop them. I almost

whupped them."

"They're bigger than you so you're the one that got whupped," Petra said sadly. "They tore your shirt, too."

Carly didn't like what she was hearing. The children were being teased by the other children, and Daniel was responding with violence. Why hadn't Josh done something?

Once both children were scrubbed and had their sweats on, they sat in the middle of Carly's bed. Daniel craned his neck back to look up at the unfinished loft. "Where's Wolf going to sleep? This bed isn't big enough for all of us."

"It isn't, is it?" Carly laughed. "Wolf won't get here until really late, so he doesn't need a bed yet."

"There are enough beds at our old cabin. We could go there." He ended on a hopeful note.

"No, Daniel, but your daddy is sleeping there tonight." The time had come to tell them.

"Why didn't he take us?" Petra was clearly hurt.

Carly sat down beside them. "Captain Isaac only allowed your daddy to take Rachel there. This morning your daddy and Rachel got married."

"Is Rachel my new mama now? Daddy said she was going to be my mama pretty soon." Daniel seemed quite pleased with the idea.

"I don't want a new mama," Petra whispered. "I want my very own mama."

"Oh, darling," Carly cradled the little girl in her arms. After tonight she didn't know if Josh and Rachel would be free to make a home for them, but some instinct prompted her to prepare them to accept their stepmother. "You loved your mama so much and she loved you, too. But you understand why she can't be with you any more. She didn't want to go away, she couldn't help it, but she wouldn't want you to grow up without a mother. It can't be her, so I know she would want your daddy to pick the very nicest lady he could find to love you and teach you all the things a girl needs to know about growing up."

"Couldn't you do that, Aunt Carly?"

Carly thought her heart would break. It was like giving away her own children, but for their sake the sooner they accepted Rachel as their mother, the better.

"No, sweetheart. I'm married to Wolf now and I live where he lives, just like Rachel will live with you and your daddy. You won't ever forget your mama and you'll always love her, but you can love more than one mother. After a while you'll love Rachel, and she told me she already loves you two."

"Really?"

"Yes, now snuggle down in bed. It's time you got some sleep." She kissed them both, then turned down the lamp and moved it closer to a chair where she sat unmoving for a long time. She had so much to think about.

Her heart felt lighter knowing Wolf intended to see that the children got away from the compound. A moment's guilt assailed her as she remembered her earlier doubts. She should have trusted her heart. Perhaps she could persuade Wolf to stop at Josh's cabin and give him and Rachel a chance to leave with them.

A little before midnight she arose and changed into warmer clothing, blew out the lantern, then sat back down to wait. At first every little sound caught her attention, but gradually the long day caught up to her and she drifted asleep.

She jerked awake with a start. She stared around in confusion, seeing little in the darkened room. Then a sound brought her bolt upright. It was the drone of an engine. Isaac was returning. He'd never before flown at night that she was aware of. Why was he returning now? And where was Wolf? She glanced at the illuminated dial of her watch. One o'clock! He should have been back an hour ago.

The rhythm of the engine changed and she knew the plane was taxiing toward the compound. Working her way quietly across the dark room, Carly lifted one corner of the muslin window covering and peered outside. The full moon made the outdoors lighter than inside. She watched, catching glimpses in the spaces left between the front row of cabins, as several running shadows hurried toward the dock. There was a suppressed excitement in the air as the group of men moved back toward the headquarters building with Isaac in the lead.

She debated following them to see if she could discover what was going on, but Wolf might come any minute. Besides she couldn't take risks while responsible for the children. She sat back down and shifted nervously as she waited. A soft tap on the door startled her. Wolf wouldn't knock.

Easing the door open a crack she peered outside. Reuben stood there in bib overalls and a pair of Wolf's moccasins. He shuffled back and forth from heel to toe several times before he finally spoke, "Where's Wolf?"

Carly swallowed nervously. She didn't know whether to admit he wasn't there. "Do you need him, or is someone else asking?"

Reuben slanted his head and watched her for several interminable seconds. "Captain Isaac said to peek in your window and see if he's asleep, but I cain't see nothing through that muslin stuff, so I thought I'd just ask."

"He's asleep." It was a lie and Carly suspected the man standing before her knew it was a lie, but she didn't waver.

"Ma'am," Reuben held out his hand toward her. "Tell Wolf they're some right ornery cusses comin' after you'n' him in a little while an' he better git them babies up to the high country." Carly gasped and reached out to meet Reuben's hand. He took it, placed something inside, and gently closed her fingers. Then he was gone.

Carly closed the door and leaned her back against it. There was no mistaking Reuben's warning. She had to get the children out tonight; Isaac was threatening them in some way and his suspicion had turned on Wolf. It was two in the morning and Wolf wasn't back yet, which meant he might not make it back. That possibility was too horrible to consider. She had to believe he was coming. But if she waited any longer, she might lose her chance to get the children out of the compound. There was no way to pass on Reuben's warning to Wolf. And no way she could wait around for Isaac to come after her and the children.

Reuben's message filled her with a sense of urgency. With one shaking hand she opened the trunk at the foot of the bed and reached for a tiny pen light. She shone it on the contents of her other hand. Feathers! Reuben had given her a handful of red feathers. Reuben might be a crazy old man, but she knew the feathers were a warning for Wolf to get them out through the secret door. Time had run out and Wolf wasn't here; she'd have to get the children out by herself.

Carly pulled her jeans on over her sweats; with the amount of weight she'd lost the past month they slid on easily. She found her Reeboks and stuffed the small flashlight into the pocket of her parka, then dug quickly in her chest until she found a box of rifle shells. Then she turned to the children.

"Petra! Daniel!" She shook them gently while cautioning them to be quiet. "You have to wake up."

"What's the matter, Aunt Carly?" A soft whimper came from Daniel.

"We're leaving. Be very quiet and I'll help you dress."

"Are we running away?" Petra whispered sounding more awake than Daniel.

"Sort of. We're going to sneak out of here, but we have to be careful or Isaac will find out, and he won't let us go." Her hands worked in the dark, dressing the children in overalls over their fleecy sweats. She tied their hiking boots and began stuffing small arms into down jackets.

"Where are we going?" Daniel moved sluggishly.

"Back to our old cabin to find your daddy."

"Right now?" Daniel was suddenly alert and eager to go.

"Yes, but you must be very quiet and do everything I tell you."

"Is Wolf going too?" Petra barely breathed the words.

"Wolf isn't back yet." The uncertainty of his whereabouts tore at her heart.

"How will he find us?" Petra persisted.

"He'll know we've gone to find your daddy. All right, Daniel, when we get outside, hold onto my hand. Petra, take his other hand and don't either of you speak or make a sound. Okay?" She could barely see them bob their heads.

Carly picked up her rifle, then stealthily pulled open the door. She looked from side to side until she felt certain no one was watching. Daniel's hand gripped hers as they rounded the corner of the cabin and crept toward the hen house. Seconds later they huddled in the small shelter.

"Where did the chickens go?" Daniel spoke softly, but Petra

immediately clapped her hand across his mouth. Amazed, Carly realized the chickens really were gone, but there wasn't time to puzzle it out. She opened the small door and pulled the children through behind her, then headed for the deepest shadow. Thankfully a bank of clouds drifted toward the moon providing cover for their dash to the trees.

Reaching the trees was only the beginning. They weren't out of danger yet. They would have to work their way around the compound until they reached the downriver side. She glanced back once and a sharp longing for Wolf sliced through the wall she'd erected around her emotions. Was he safe? And if he made his way back to the cabin, would he understand what the little pile of red feathers she'd left on his pillow meant?

She chafed at the time it took to reach the river on the opposite side of the camp. Leading two small children in the dark without the benefit of a trail and keeping in mind the need to keep silent wore at her nerves, but a gleam through the trees told her they'd finally reached their goal.

Estimating that the compound was a quarter of a mile behind her, Carly began searching for a secure hiding spot for the children. Finally she spotted what she was looking for. Two tall pines grew close together, and in the place where their roots humped above the shallow soil, a black pocket was formed. She ushered the children into the dark recess.

"You'll have to stay here while I go get a canoe. It will seem like I'm gone a long time, but it really won't be very long. Don't talk, and don't answer if anyone calls your names. Do you understand?"

"Yes," Petra's voice quavered. Carly hated to leave them alone, but she had to get a canoe. Taking them back toward the compound would only increase the risk of being found out.

It took only ten minutes to reach the narrow beach below the compound. She flattened herself against the ground and watched for several minutes. Guards filled the tower overlooking the dock and half a dozen men stood in an excited cluster near the gate. Lights were on inside the compound. Terror filled her heart. Had they already missed her and the children? Had they caught Wolf?

She'd better grab a canoe quickly. She searched the small beach with her eyes. With the large number of canoes usually beached on the narrow spit of sand, there should have been several in the deep shade at the outside curve of the strip. Tonight there were none. Only a handful of canoes remained on the beach and they were fully exposed by the bright moonlight. She couldn't possibly reach one, she'd have to return to the children on foot, and then what would they do? They couldn't go back, and between them and Josh were five miles of steep mountainside, dangerous crevices, swift mountain streams, and an untold number of wild animals.

Thirteen

Wolf felt uneasy. Too much didn't measure up. Why had Isaac let Josh and Rachel leave the compound overnight? That privilege certainly hadn't been extended to Carly and himself when they got married. Thinking of Carly brought a twinge of pain. He'd never expected to meet a woman who would matter more to him than his career. But Carly did. He'd married her and he wanted to stay married to her. He just hoped she'd give him a second chance once Jerome Isaac and his stinking cult were behind them.

A dark object moved at the corner of his vision. Readying his rifle, Wolf left the game trail. Hidden by foliage, he watched two bear cubs chase across the path. The lead cub stopped to swat his brother, and the two tumbled in the dirt. Sweat trickled between Wolf's shoulder blades. The cubs didn't worry him, but their mama did. He should've paid closer attention to Reuben's warning. The old man had made a point of telling him an old sow had moved into this area. He wondered fleetingly how much the old man knew about his nocturnal wanderings, but at the moment bears were uppermost in his mind. The last thing he wanted to do was tangle with another bear.

Of all the rotten luck! He'd have to leave the trail, backtrack to the mouth of the canyon, and take the upper route. The detour would cost him an hour. That is, if he were lucky enough not to run into the sow. She was probably behind the cubs, but Wolf wasn't taking chances.

Cautiously he backed away, thankful the wind was in his favor as he retraced his steps with precise care. He didn't breathe easy again until he'd put a mile between the bears and himself. Half an hour later from high above, he spotted the bear fishing in the stream, her cubs frolicking around her.

Dusk came early to the high country and shadows lengthened to long black streaks. A chill bit through his jacket by the time he slipped over the ledge to make his way down the tree. He'd hoped to be starting his return trip by this time. He paused over the mouth of the cave to whistle two short notes. He waited a minute, then whistled again. One long blast answered and Wolf swung into the cave.

He wasted no time filling Bradley in, and in minutes they were both scrambling back up the tree with the radio equipment. There was no time to hike around the mountain. They would have to use code and risk interception. With Isaac away, the radio at the compound would be set on the plane's channel, improving the odds their own signal would go undetected.

It seemed to Wolf to take forever to make the connection. While his partner repeated details, he glanced at the dials on his watch. He'd never make it back in the time he'd allotted. Carly would be worried, then she'd think he wasn't coming back for her.

When Bradley finally finished the message, he removed his earphones and grinned broadly at Wolf. "Boss says it's time to get your lady out of there; the posse's coming in. We should figure forty-eight hours. He says it's too dangerous to go downriver because Isaac will look there the minute he knows they're gone, and with a power-boat and a plane, he's holding the aces."

"He's right, so where do we meet?"

"Stewart said we've got to get them up this canyon, then follow the first deep creek going south. When we run out of water, we climb the wall and walk. A chopper will meet us in a flat meadow south of here in two days. As soon as we reach the meadow, orders will go out to take Isaac into custody."

"Okay, let's get the gear back to the cave and pack up, then I'll take the canoe to the compound for Carly and the kids. You'll have to use the kayak to reach the canyon mouth where we'll meet."

They worked with a practiced economy of motion. Wolf was ready to leave when he remembered to warn Bradley about the bear. "Keep to the center of the current until you reach the sandbar where

Deep Creek empties into the river. There's an old grizzly sow with two cubs just about where Stewart told us to head south on our way out. I nearly ran into them on my way in. A strange old guy at the compound mentioned them to me, but I wasn't paying close attention. He smelled so bad, I . . . Smelled!" Wolf knew with a sick certainty that Reuben had been warning him about more than bears. "He made sure I smelled the gasoline!"

"Gasoline, what was he doing with gas, refueling the plane?"

"No, Isaac doesn't let him anywhere near that plane. He considers the old man a doddering fool. But now I understand why Isaac let Josh and Rachel go back to the Peterson cabin. He plans to burn it! I've got to get there first." He gripped his pack and swung toward the tree.

"No," Bradley spoke calmly. "You go after Carly. I'll warn Rachel and Josh."

"It could be dangerous. Josh was with that party that came hunting for you a few weeks ago."

"I'll have to risk it."

"All right, get going, but be careful." He helped Bradley lace himself into the one-man kayak, then shoved the smaller craft ahead.

Minutes later he watched from behind as Bradley headed for the white water churning between two boulders. The longer route along the shore was safer, but with the bears roaming the shallow area and speed paramount, Bradley opted for shooting the rapids. The small craft picked up speed, lifted high, then disappeared for a heartbeat.

Wolf stroked toward the curl of water, felt the lift, then plunged through a wall of spray. Almost clear of the rocks, he felt a drag against the bottom of the canoe. His heart sank knowing the heavier canoe had snagged against a rock the light kayak had skimmed over. Almost immediately he felt cold water seeping in where he knelt. He glanced up to see Bradley watching him. He motioned him closer.

Knowing there was little chance he could be heard above the roar of the rapids, Wolf called out, "I hit something. I'm taking on water. Head for that cove." He pointed across the river to a small inlet. "We're too exposed here."

Bradley nodded his head and dug in his paddle. By the time Wolf reached the secluded spot, he was breathing hard and the canoe was half submerged. He leaped from the craft and rolled it to its side to check the extent of the damage. The tear was small, and he was grateful for that. He could plug the hole, but a temporary patch wouldn't hold long.

"You'd better go ahead," he advised Bradley. "Stay on this side of the river until you reach the lake. Don't cross back until you're past Josh's cabin. Hide the kayak a little way up the little creek by the poacher's camp where we left their other canoe, and head back to the cabin on foot. Use Josh's canoe to return and come back the same way. We'll meet you here before dawn. If you can't get out before daylight, find a place to hole up well away from the cabin until it's dark again and we'll meet up at Stewart's meadow."

Suddenly Wolf stood still, listening. There it came again. The unmistakable drone of a plane flying low! Wolf lunged for the canoe. Bradley followed his lead, and in seconds both the canoe and kayak were out of sight in the deep shadow of the cliff. The sound of the engine changed, alerting Wolf that the plane was landing. It had to be Isaac, and that could only mean time was running short for Josh and Rachel. Would Isaac go after Carly now, too? No, Wolf would get to Carly first! He had to!

The moment Wolf heard the plane's engine cut back, he grabbed the canoe again. At the water's edge he laced Bradley back into the kayak before giving it a shove, then waded out of the water to dig into his pack for a strip of leather to tamp into the jagged tear in the canoe. Bradley was already out of sight by the time Wolf launched. At the first smooth stretch of water, he crossed back to the north side of the river.

Once free of the canyon, Wolf guided the canoe closer to shore to take advantage of the shadows. The water flowed slowly now and he used his paddle more to steer clear of rocks and submerged logs than to increase speed. He kept one eye open for floaters, trees, and branches, which, broken free of their moorings upstream, floated along partially submerged waiting to sabotage the unwary. The canoe was taking on water slowly and Wolf despaired of reaching his goal in time.

When a familiar small cove came into sight, he heaved a sigh and paddled for shore. He stepped into water halfway to his knees and shoved his paddle back into the canoe. He considered sinking the canoe, then decided against it. In less than two minutes he had it well hidden in a copse of willows.

With long strides he covered the ground. He envisioned Carly waiting in the dark, wondering if he'd let her down. She'd be frightened knowing Isaac's plane had returned. Thinking of Carly lent urgency to his feet.

More than an hour had passed since Isaac's plane had landed. He topped a rise and stared. Lights were burning in the headquarters building and a fire blazed before the front gate. Dark figures warmed their hands in its heat. Spotlights swept the ground from both towers. A cold sweat beaded Wolf's face. Getting to Carly was going to be tough. He just hoped he wasn't too late. Finding a hollow log, he stashed his pack and hid his rifle. He checked his pistol to make certain it was secure, then moved forward.

Wolf surveyed the terrain carefully. He knew Reuben managed to come and go in broad daylight out here so there had to be a way in without exposing himself to the tower guards. Half an hour's careful maneuvering placed him inside the chicken coop. No soft grumble from sleeping hens reached his ears. The chickens were gone. What did that mean? Had someone left the gate open, or was he walking into a trap?

He opened the door a crack. It looked okay. He raced from the chicken run to the back of the cabin he and Carly shared. Almost there. He made a quick scan of the dusty track in front of the cabin and reached for the door latch.

"There he is! I found him!" A youthful voice shouted as the beam of a powerful torch held him silhouetted against the door. Heavy boots pounded toward him.

"Hold it right there, or I'll shoot." A second voice shouted.

Wolf froze. He couldn't risk gunfire slamming into the cabin, maybe hitting Carly or one of the kids. Keeping his hands spread before him, he turned slowly. "What's this all about?" He faced a circle of excited faces, most of them were young and idealistic. None were the real sharpshooters or hotheads in Isaac's army.

"Everybody's out looking for you, but we got you," someone crowed.

"Where's Doc?" someone else called out and Wolf's ears perked up.

"Why doesn't someone tell me what's going on and maybe I can answer your questions." Wolf folded his arms and leaned in pseudo nonchalance against the door frame.

"Captain Isaac called a meeting. He sent Reuben to get you, but the old fool never came back, so Luther went after you. He came running back, said you and Doc were gone, the kids too."

"Isaac said to shoot you and the Doc, but he wants those kids alive."

Another voice cut in. "We going to shoot him?"

"Now wait a minute." Wolf stood up, the image of wounded dignity. "Are you going to shoot a man for chasing after his wife's chickens?"

A snicker reached his ears from the back of the crowd, and someone called out, "Are you claiming you were chasing chickens all this time?"

"Ever try to catch a chicken if you don't dare shoot it?"

"He's telling the truth; the chickens are gone!" The cook pushed her way through the crowd. She was panting and wringing her hands. "Somebody find them! The Lord blessed us with those chickens. He'll be powerful displeased if the foxes get them."

"Shut up," a deep voice growled. "We've got more important business than chickens to take care of."

"Where are the others?" A tough-looking young man with a shaved head pushed his way to the front.

Wolf straightened abruptly, dropping his relaxed pose. "Is Carly missing? What're we standing around for; let's start looking for her." He moved as though making a dash for the gate.

"Not so fast." The young neo-Nazi barred the way. "Isaac's got most of his army out looking. They'll find her. You're staying right here until Captain Isaac gets back."

"I can't sit around doing nothing if my wife is missing," Wolf protested. "I've got to find her."

"Inside the cabin." The young tough prodded Wolf with the tip of his gun. "I'll be right outside this door, so don't try anything."

The door closed and Wolf found himself a prisoner. From outside he heard the cook continue to wail and plead for someone to find the chickens.

"Why didn't you shoot him?" Wolf heard an older voice join the fracas. Wolf drew the Blackhawk. He knew Schmidt, Luther's buddy. "Isaac said to kill him."

The younger man answered smoothly. "In time, but I have a hunch Isaac's going to want to question him first. The captain needs those brats, and someone might get trigger happy and kill that fool woman before she tells him where she's stashed them."

"You get his rifle?"

"He didn't have it with him. It's not in the cabin either. He probably left it with the woman."

"All right, I'll go after Isaac, but you and Murdoch stay right here. If he sets one foot through that door, shoot."

"Yes, sir!"

Wolf took a step and felt something crunch beneath his foot. Suspecting the cabin had been trashed, he felt his way across the room in the direction the lamp should be. At last his fingers encountered something he could use. With his thumbnail he struck a flame to the wooden match. Chaos met his eyes. The lamp had been smashed and matches and glass were scattered around the overturned bookcase. An ugly slash down the length of the mattress spilled cotton batting across the room.

Before the tiny flame reached his fingers, Wolf retrieved a handful of matches from the floor. With the third match he found a flashlight. With it, he examined the debris more carefully. Her rifle was gone. He hoped that meant she had it with her. Her parka was gone too, but he couldn't tell what else she might have taken with her. He found the children's quilts.

A tiny object caught his eye, a single red feather. He looked around and saw several more, then he smiled. A small tug of hope that Carly's departure had been deliberate arose in his heart. Whether Reuben had told her or she'd found it herself, Carly knew about the secret door. He hoped she had used it.

His smile disappeared and fear took its place. Carly had been clever enough to get the children out of the compound, but once on the outside, she'd head straight for Josh, and Isaac would be waiting there for her. His eyes slowly scanned the room. He had to get out of here. He had to get to Carly before Isaac did.

Carly melted back into the trees. Already her mind was struggling to formulate a new plan. Going back wasn't an option. Everything depended on getting to Josh before he and Rachel returned to the compound tomorrow—today actually. Dragging two small children across five miles of raw wilderness would be daunting, but it was the only way. They couldn't even follow the smooth river plain where the river had receded from earlier high water. With a couple dozen canoes out there somewhere on the water, she couldn't risk someone spotting her and the children.

Petra turned tear-streaked cheeks to her when she pulled the little girl from her hiding place. Daniel clung to her leg, but neither child spoke until they'd placed half a mile between them and the river. Pulling them into the shelter of an overhanging rock face, Carly explained they would have to walk.

"Petra was scared," Daniel whispered.

"You were too," Petra defended herself. "Aunt Carly, we peeked through the trees at the back and we saw lights coming, so we got way down in the hole and almost didn't breathe."

"When the light got close we heard Luther. He was really mad. He called you a bad name, and he said he was going to peel your hide off an inch at a time."

"Isaac told him to just shoot you and Wolf and be done with it, but to save the brats for him. He meant Daniel and me, didn't he?" Petra's eyes were round as saucers.

"I didn't move and I was really quiet." Daniel was scared enough to keep his voice down.

Carly's heart slammed into her throat. They'd been missed already. "You did the right thing and you were awfully brave, both of you. But now we've got to keep moving. Follow me closely, and if you see anyone or need to stop for any reason, give a tug on my pants, but don't talk. We can't make any noise."

"If Isaac catches us, will he really shoot us?"

Carly didn't want to answer that question. "I don't know, but I'm sure he'll hurt us. We just have to make sure he doesn't catch us."

"I think he'll shoot us dead just like Mama." Petra's voice carried a weight of fatalism far beyond what a seven-year-old should understand.

"Uncle Wolf won't let him." Daniel sounded so positive. Carly wished Wolf were there beside her. If anyone could get the children over this mountain to their father, he could, but she didn't have any idea what had happened to him. If Isaac had discovered his real identity, he might already be dead. He could have drowned in the river or fallen from a cliff or run into a wild animal . . . No, she couldn't think about it. She had to believe he'd only been delayed and that he would follow them.

They made better time after they discovered a faint track. Carly considered following it, but she knew they couldn't continue to pick their way through brush and hope to reach the cabin by morning. When the trail petered out in a thicket at the top of a cliff, Carly motioned for the children to sit down. They dropped gratefully to the grass while she picked her way over rocks to the edge of the precipice. She peered over the rim and caught her breath in a gasp. The bright moonlight didn't reach to the bottom of the chasm, but from far below she caught the roar of water spilling over rocks in a frenzied rush to the river.

Despair licked at the edges of her strength. They couldn't go forward and they certainly couldn't go back.

Slowly she moved back to sit beside the children. "I don't know which way to go," she admitted in a whisper. "We can't cross here. If we go up the mountain we'll eventually find a place to cross, but it may make us too late to get to the cabin before your daddy goes back to the compound in the morning. It might take days, and we didn't bring any food."

"If we go the other way, will Isaac catch us?" Daniel pondered the problem with adult somberness.

"He might. We'd have to go all the way to the river and look for a place where we can climb down to the river's flood plain. Anyone on the river could see us until we cross the creek and find a place to climb back up to the trees."

"Aunt Carly," Petra's voice was barely audible. "Mama said if I don't know which way to go, I should say a prayer. Will you help me?"

Tears sprang to Carly's eyes. Yes, Anna would have prayed, and Carly was relieved that Petra still clung to her mother's sweet faith instead of succumbing to Isaac's fanaticism. Rachel's presence in the classroom instead of Mrs. Hampton's had surely protected more than the children's physical well-being. She felt regret for all the overtures of friendship the other woman had made and she had rejected.

"All right, Petra." Carly bowed her head and reached for the children's hands. After she said amen, Daniel spoke up. "And God, help Uncle Wolf catch up to us. We need him a whole lot. Thank you. Amen." Carly's heart echoed the sentiment. She opened her eyes and surveyed the clearing.

"I think we should go that way." Carly pointed toward the river, then bit her lip. She wasn't sure why she'd said that, but it felt right. Dawn couldn't be far away and the moon would disappear behind the mountain peaks soon. If they made it to the river about the time the moon set, they could take advantage of that brief bit of time when the night was darkest before the sun sent tentative forerunners of the day. But would it be enough time, and could they find their way in the blackness? She squeezed through the brush and began the trek toward the river.

"Wow!" Daniel clapped his hands over his mouth and looked apologetically at Carly.

"What is it, Daniel?" Carly tightened her grip on the child's hand.

"See that?" He pointed toward the chasm. "There's a bridge."

Carly's eyes followed the direction of his pointing finger. It did look like a bridge. As they drew closer she could see a huge tree trunk spanned the gap in the earth. Daniel broke free of her grasp and ran toward the log.

"No, Daniel." She caught up to him as he jumped onto it. "It's too dangerous."

"No, see." He jumped, demonstrating the log was securely anchored. Near where Daniel stood, Carly could see the tree tip had splintered when it crashed to the ground. To her eyes the break had the sharp new look of having recently occurred.

"We prayed it here," Daniel crowed.

Carly eyed the log speculatively. Would she actually consider letting the children cross that black chasm on a fallen tree? What if it broke? Or they slipped?

"Daddy showed us how to cross log bridges." Petra was on the log before Carly could stop her. She sat down, her thin legs straddling the log, and began to scoot forward. Carly held her breath. She couldn't watch, but she couldn't not watch. She had to restrain Daniel to keep him from following right behind his sister. Petra reached the other side and turned to wave her arms; Carly lifted her hand from Daniel's shoulder.

"Go slowly," she warned. In spite of her warning Daniel crossed more rapidly than Petra had.

Carly took a deep breath. She wasn't as confident as the children. Across that log was the only way to get to Josh, and the children needed her help. She sat down and pushed herself forward, keeping her eyes on the children who were dancing around the gigantic tangle of roots at the end of the uprooted tree. She didn't like heights. Fear froze her muscles, making movement impossible. But she had to go on! She closed her eyes and took a deep breath, a fervent prayer whispering from her heart. As she opened her eyes, a feeling of comfort enfolded her. A sudden calmness came over her, and she felt the warm strength of Wolf's arms surrounding her, urging her on. She moved a few inches, a few more, then kept moving steadily, secure in Wolf's grasp. Her feet touched solid ground and she heaved a sigh of relief.

Wolf's intangible presence slipped away as she rushed to gather the children to her. She longed to stop and call him back, to savor the feel of him, but she knew there was no time to indulge in even a comforting fantasy.

The terrain was rougher on this side of the cleft, forcing them to move closer to the cliffs overlooking the river. When the moon no longer lit their way, Carly estimated they had covered more than two thirds of the distance to the cabin. Without light, movement became more dangerous and the children's steps lagged with fatigue. When Daniel tripped, skinning his knee, Carly decided to stop and wait for the gray light of predawn. A sprained ankle or a fracture would doom their escape.

Carefully she eased their way off the narrow trail. Feeling a carpet of thick pine needles beneath her feet, she dropped to the ground and leaned her back against a tree. Petra scrambled onto her lap and Daniel curled in a ball, his head resting against her thigh. They were both asleep in seconds.

Wind soughed through the tops of the trees, and now that they had stopped moving a deep chill began to soak through Carly's clothes. Wrapping her arms around the children, she pulled them closer to protect them from the cold. The quiet gave her time to think and her thoughts went immediately to Wolf. Had he returned for them? Had he been captured—or killed? Pain tore at her heart, a pain she could only equate with the desolation she glimpsed on her brother's face when he held Anna's lifeless body in his arms. She wasn't sure she could go on living without Wolf. But she must; the children were not safe yet.

A sound reached her ears. Footsteps. No, something heavy crashed through the brush. On the trail sounded the pounding of hooves. Carly clutched the children tighter and froze against the tree. Several small animals she couldn't identify in the dark skittered past ahead of the approaching heavier beasts. She sensed a dozen or more heavy animals moving rapidly past where she huddled with the children. Probably elk. Something had frightened them, and Carly hoped it hadn't been a bear or someone from the compound. After that the woods seemed filled with ominous sounds, and some unnamed fear took residence in the pit of her stomach.

As soon as the deep black around her dissolved to gray, she awakened the children. They didn't complain, but moved obediently back to the trail. Carly nervously glanced at the sky as it grew lighter and dark shadows turned into rocks and trees. The forest was too quiet.

At last they topped a rise and found a small valley spread before them. In the distance she saw something familiar. Highlighted by the first streaks of sun touching the opposite side of the valley, a crooked pine tree caught her attention. She knew its twisted shape. It stood sentinel over Josh's cabin. They only had to cross the small valley where she'd first found Wolf, climb the hill, and they would be with Josh. Perhaps Wolf was there, too. Her heart lifted.

She felt a sharp, unexpected tug on her pants. Glancing down she saw Daniel pointing toward the river. Glimpses of the river could be seen through the trees and on the river were moving shapes. Canoes! Dozens of them. Carly gasped. Slowly anger and determination replaced her initial fear. They'd come too far to be stopped now.

She pulled the children into the thick brush bordering the valley and crouched with them, waiting for the canoes to disappear from sight.

"I smell something, Aunt Carly." She turned toward Petra's pale face. "I think it's a forest fire."

"Me too. Are we going to burn up?"

Carly sniffed the air. A soft wind blew from the east carrying the distinctive odor of burning wood. "Hurry, this way." As she led the way down into the valley and angled toward the river, her mind searched frantically for a hiding place. A heaviness filled her chest and warning bells clamored in her brain. She glanced up to see thick black smoke billowing behind the sentinel pine. Over that rise was no forest fire.

Halfway up the hill, she darted off the path and into the rocks where she'd once hid Wolf's rifle.

"Crawl into the rocks and get as far under the bushes as you can," she whispered tersely.

"But Carly, our house is—"

"I know, honey, but I have to make sure Captain Isaac isn't there."

"Is our house burning up? I'm going to help Daddy carry water." Daniel made a dash for the path. Carly grabbed the back of his jacket.

"Listen, both of you. Something is wrong. I have to find out what, and you have to stay here. Understand?" When she had both their agreement, she moved up the hill parallel to the trail, using the thick brush for cover.

Flat on her stomach, she peered over the hill and fought the screams rising in her throat. Nothing remained of Josh's cabin but the stone chimney pointing toward heaven like an accusing finger. A pile of smoldering rubble continued to send black smoke into the air, and a blackened trail led across Josh's garden to where hungry flames licked at the old hen house.

"Josh! Oh, Josh." She buried her face in her hands and bit back tears. Instinct warred with reality. Love for her brother urged her to run forward to try to save him, but common sense warned that it was too late. No one could still be alive in that smoldering heap.

A movement caught her eye and she looked toward the dock. Four men stood on the wide planks. Two more emerged from the ice house carrying burlap bags as she watched. Isaac's men!

Rage consumed her. Those men were stealing the supplies she'd counted on to get the children as far as the reservation. It took all the control she could summon to prevent herself from running down the hill to confront them.

She knew as surely as if she'd seen them strike the matches that they'd deliberately burned the cabin. Isaac had murdered Josh—and Rachel. Agony tore through her. How could she bear losing Josh? And was Wolf dead, too? How could she possibly continue on?

A shout reached her ears and she saw the motorboat pull up to the dock. A man leaped out and splashed his way to the shore. He was too far away to identify, but she had no trouble identifying the two men who stepped out of the trees to meet him. Isaac and Luther! The man gesticulated with his hands and pointed back toward the compound. Isaac and Luther sprinted toward the motorboat, shouting orders Carly couldn't quite make out. A dozen more men came running from the trees.

Isaac turned back toward his men. His voice, but not his words, carried to Carly giving her the gist of his message. He and Luther were returning to the compound to attend to some emergency while the other men were ordered back into the trees to keep watch around the burned cabin. Cold chills crept up her spine as she realized they were waiting for her and the children. Her back stiffened. Their wait would be for nothing; she wouldn't let Isaac lay a hand on either child. She'd protect them somehow.

She slid carefully backward until she reached the children. From their scared faces, she knew they'd recognized Isaac's voice. She had no doubt Josh and Rachel had died in that fire, but she couldn't think about them. She had to focus on the children. They were two days by river from the reservation, and who knew how long it would take on foot! And they were without supplies. She lifted her eyes heavenward.

"What should I do? How can I save them?" she wanted to scream, but instead she prayed.

"Aunt Carly." Petra tugged on her pants. "What are we going to do?"

Carly took a deep breath. What could she say? How could she answer? Something flickered at the back of her mind, and suddenly she knew what to do. "Remember, your daddy said if our cabin ever caught on fire, we should go to the river cave and we'd be safe there. Don't you think we should get started?"

Both children nodded solemnly.

Wolf prowled his way across the room. He paused to eye the one lone window and dismissed it immediately. It wasn't more than two feet from the door. Fat lot of good it would do him, even if he could squeeze through it. He might as well rush the door. He clicked off his flashlight, reached once more for the Blackhawk, and flattened himself against the panel next to the door. He stopped with his hand on the latch. He wouldn't be any good to Carly if he got himself killed.

Clenching his teeth, Wolf gazed upward. He wished old Reuben'd had a hand in building this cabin. The man had a genius for building escape hatches. Wait a minute. A picture of Reuben patching a hole in the roof the day he and Carly moved in and grumbling about back doors came to his mind. If he could remove the patch, he'd have his back door!

It was easier than he expected, almost as though the old man knew Wolf might need an emergency exit one day. Wolf tugged on the patch until he pulled it free. Through the hole he could see the sky had lightened considerably. He grasped the sides of the hole and pulled himself through. Flattening himself against the roof, he stayed on the back slope, then dropped silently to the ground. Weighing each step before he moved, Wolf worked his way to the chicken coop. Deep shadow still hid the entry as he slipped inside.

He reached for the bank of nesting boxes and pried the door open a crack. Too light, but he couldn't wait for a better moment. With the first faint streaks of morning wiping away the blackness of night, time had run out. He retraced the route he'd followed earlier that night to gain entrance to the compound.

Within two feet of the protection of a thicket of chokecherry bushes, a shot rang out and Wolf felt a sharp burn whip through his side. Throwing himself forward to roll beneath the bushes, he clasped his hand to his side and felt blood spread between his fingers. He couldn't stay here, not long enough to assess the damage. Isaac's soldiers would be on him in minutes.

Stifling a groan, he plowed into the heart of the shrubs and kept moving. He angled to pick up his pack and rifle and loped for a quarter of a mile up the trail he'd come in on, then swung toward the river. He could feel wetness spreading across his chest, and numbness reached from his armpit to his belt. He'd have to stop soon, before he passed out from loss of blood.

It wouldn't take long for his neo-Nazi guard or tough old Schmidt to find the trail and come after him. Golden tendrils of light were racing down the mountain peaks, seeking out the hidden valleys and crevices. Carefully keeping to the rocks, he left the trail and slipped silently into the river; the cold water should check the bleeding. He held his pack and rifle clear as he searched the bank. At last he found what he sought. Icy and swift, high water had undermined the roots of a sturdy pine, then receded to leave a deep, narrow cleft in the river bank, just large enough to hold his guns, jacket, and pack.

Leaving the cache, Wolf moved upstream to where the river's current swung close to shore. He waded beneath the bank's overhang and waited in water up to his shoulders. The icy water soothed and deadened the pain as it stemmed the flow of blood. He slipped a hand inside his shirt and felt where the bullet had shredded his hide about four inches below his armpit. It was a flesh wound, but it had torn up some muscle. At least he wasn't packing around the bullet.

Someone shouted. His pursuers had to be close for the sound to carry above the roar of the river. He waited, his eyes never leaving the water until an uprooted tree drifted into sight. He thought longingly of the canoe he'd left less than a half mile further upstream. It might as well be ten miles.

Beneath the surface of the water, he swam out to meet the swift current. As the floater drifted toward him, he dived deep, praying he could pass under any dragging limbs. He surfaced with the log between himself and the shore. Bracing one arm against the jagged stump where a limb had recently been, Wolf leaned his forehead against the rough bark and drifted.

Carly leaned against the back wall of the cave and drew in deep gulps of air. They'd made it, but she wasn't sure how. At least they were safe for now. The children were so tired they'd fallen asleep sprawled on the soft, sandy floor the moment they'd tumbled inside the cave, but when they awakened, they would be hungry and she had nothing to feed them. If it weren't for Isaac's men, she could find something in the ice house or dig up Josh's garden. But if it weren't for Isaac and his army, they wouldn't be in this predicament!

She needed rest. Without a few hours sleep she wouldn't be able to guide the children through the next phase of their journey.

If only Wolf were with them. Never far from her thoughts, she dreamed of how it might have been if she'd met Wolf some other place. Might he have fallen in love with her if he'd met her in her starchy uniform, her hair washed, and a smile on her face? The wide corridor of Central Hospital stretched before her. She smiled and saw him reach for her hand.

Carly awoke abruptly. Daniel was tugging at her pants.

"Isaac's still hunting for us. Come look." Abruptly shaking off the sleepiness, she followed Daniel to the mouth of the cave. A lip of rock hung low over the front of the cave leaving an opening no more than eighteen inches high. The cave was only a few feet higher than the river bank, but the opening was concealed completely by a thick stand of birch and a tangle of wild rose bushes. It had been formed by centuries of high spring runoff biting into granite, before the current of the river had shifted and left behind a hole in the rock, nearly oval in shape. At its deepest point it was ten feet from mouth to back wall and almost that wide. Carly could stand if she hunched over a bit.

Only one person could negotiate the narrow opening at a time, and then only if he crawled on his belly. Daniel had found the cave one day last summer when he'd followed a rabbit into the brush.

Lying flat on the cave floor beside Daniel, Carly strained to see through the trees. By the slant of the sun she could tell she'd been asleep for several hours and it was now late in the afternoon. She caught an occasional glimpse of a canoe, then heard the roar of an engine as the plane swooped low following the flow of the river. She shuddered and pulled Daniel deeper inside the cave. They'd have to travel by night and sleep in the daytime well away from the river.

Petra shifted and opened her eyes. "I'm hungry," she announced.

"I know."

"After Captain Isaac goes to sleep, I'll catch a fish like the bears do." Carly smiled as she watched Daniel in the dim light confidently demonstrate how the bears scoop fish out of the water with their paws.

If only it were that easy, Carly thought, then nearly stumbled as Petra jerked at her pant leg and pointed to the mouth of the cave.

A man knelt at the opening. Only his hips and legs were visible. Carly's hand found her rifle without taking her eyes from the figure. Her hands trembled; she didn't want to shoot anyone, but she would if she had to. All that mattered was keeping the children safe. The intruder stooped lower and an arm appeared. She released the safety catch and lifted the gun to her shoulder.

Carly concentrated on the arm, holding her breath. Waiting. An alarm went off inside her head. The arm! It was black! And so was the face that slowly appeared under the overhang. A tremble shook her frame, and she stifled an hysterical urge to laugh. The eyes looking back at the rifle aimed at his chest mirrored her shock.

"Don't shoot. I want to help you."

Carly had no idea who the intruder might be, but he definitely wasn't a friend of Isaac's. No black man would ever be part of Isaac's army. If spotted, he would die, just as she would. A man who would burn a cabin where his own daughter slept and whose racial hatred was a tenet of the philosophy he preached wouldn't hesitate to kill a black stranger. Carly stared unmoving for several seconds, then slowly lowered the tip of her rifle and beckoned him inside the cave.

The man visibly relaxed before crawling inside. Once through the narrow opening, he rose to a half crouch and looked around curiously.

"Good," he nodded in appreciation. "You've chosen a good hiding place, much better than mine. No one will find you here."

"You did." Carly spoke bluntly. She nervously clutched her rifle, taking care to stay between the stranger and the children.

"Extreme luck. I was hiding up Short Creek near the falls this morning when I caught a glimpse of the three of you through the brush making for the ridge above here. I tried to follow you, but you disappeared."

"Why did you follow us?" Carly lifted the barrel of her gun a fraction.

"That's what I'm trying to tell you. I couldn't find you, and I was afraid one of Isaac's trigger-happy soldiers might spot me, so I crawled up a tree by the falls until Wolf showed up."

"Wolf!" A tremor of shock laced with hope ripped through her tough facade.

"Is Wolf here?" Daniel's voice held a note of excitement.

The man merely nodded without taking his eyes off Carly. "He said the kids told him about a river cave once, so I sneaked back up here looking for it. When Isaac's plane flew over, I ducked into the bushes a few feet from here—and I got lucky when Daniel poked his head out."

"Daniel!" Carly turned anguished eyes toward the child. "I told you not to leave this cave for anything."

"I didn't leave, I just looked."

"Don't do it again! Is that understood?"

"Mrs. Wolverton, he wasn't seen by anyone but me. I know where every one of Isaac's men are stationed. None of them were close enough to see him."

"How do you know my name?"

"Wolf told me about you."

"Where is he? Is he safe?" She had to ask. For twenty-four hours she'd struggled to block the worry for the man she loved from her thoughts. Anxiously she strained to see Bradley's face in the dusky light of the cave.

"He got back to the compound right after you left. He ran into a little trouble, but he got out and came after you. He was afraid you might have been in the cabin when . . ." He stopped and looked helplessly toward the children. "I've got to let him know you're safe. Stay right here while I go get him."

"Mr.—?"

"Bradley. I'm sorry, I should have introduced myself right away. Wolf and I have been partners for three years and friends for longer than that."

"You're a deputy marshal, too?"

"Yes, ma'am." He smiled widely, then dropped to his stomach to crawl out of sight.

Bradley had been gone a long time. Wolf shifted uncomfortably, trying to ease the ache in his side. He should have been the one to go. Carly was his responsibility and though his partner wasn't exactly a novice, he didn't have the mountain experience Wolf had. Besides if any of Isaac's people spotted the black man, they'd shoot him on sight. He shuddered and pulled the foil blanket Bradley had wrapped him in closer.

He'd have never made it to shore this morning without Bradley's help. He'd been in the icy water so long his muscles wouldn't obey. Much of the trip down the river was a blur, though he did remember passing by canoes full of Isaac's men a couple of times, and he had a vague recollection of begging God to look after Carly. He'd seen Josh's burning cabin and the shock had revived him briefly. At the mouth of Short Creek his sluggish mind told him to let go of the tree, but once he did, he'd found himself unable to swim to shore.

Bradley had pulled him out of the water, got him out of his wet clothes, dressed his wound, and set about getting him warm. Wolf had been determined to search for Carly, but Bradley insisted she was safe for the time being. Isaac had been concentrating his search on the compound side of the burned cabin at that time, and since Bradley had seen her earlier on this side of the cabin, Wolf had agreed to rest for a short time. Bradley had gone searching for Carly and the kids while Wolf remained behind, wrapped in a blanket and struggling to regain his strength.

Wolf strained his ears to hear the sound. There. It came again. Two softly whistled notes, then Bradley eased his way into the thicket. His smile told all Wolf longed to hear.

"You found them? They're safe?" He needed to hear Bradley confirm it.

"Safe and snug. They're in a cave down by the river just as you suspected. I can't believe she traveled all that way in the dark with two little kids right past fifty or more of Isaac's soldiers. That's some woman you found."

She was safe! Wolf couldn't speak. A lump formed in his throat and tears smarted at the back of his eyes. She'd gotten this far and he vowed nothing would stop her from getting those kids the rest of the way. He ducked his head, not wanting Bradley to see how the news affected him.

"Are you okay? I told her I'd collect you and be right back. Do you think you can make it?"

"Sure." But his movements were slow as he flexed his shoulder and rose to his feet. "You didn't tell Carly I've been shot, did you?"

"No, I was kind of busy making sure she didn't shoot me. Soon as we get back will be soon enough. She can check you over and make sure you're ready to travel."

"I don't want her to know."

"But, man, she's a nurse and you were half dead when I fished you out of the river this morning."

"You bandaged me just fine. There's nothing she can do but worry, and I don't want her attention diverted from those kids."

"If you say so." He looked a little dubious before he turned to pick up his pack and start the arduous climb up the ridge.

Carly watched the mouth of the cave as the minutes crawled slowly by. Would Wolf and Bradley be caught making their way to the cave? Or followed? She shuddered. She didn't have to wait more than a half hour, but it seemed like an interminable length of time. When the two men finally wriggled their way beneath the rock over-hang, tears burned her eyes.

"Wolf!" At last he was here. Emotion choked her voice. She longed to fly to him and throw her arms around him. The children had no reservations about doing just that. Over their heads, he smiled at her and she hurried to his side. She felt a twinge of disap-pointment when he didn't reach out to embrace or even touch her. Of course Daniel and Petra were still clinging to him, but after a moment he freed himself and moved a couple of feet away to lower himself to a sitting position. He leaned his head back against the rock wall, his eyes closed. He mumbled something she couldn't under-stand, and she knelt beside him.

"Are you all right?"

"I'm fine. Just tired."

"What happened?" she asked, but already a cold rime of ice formed around the edge of her heart. He was moving away from her.

She'd saved him from bleeding to death from the wound the bear gave him, he'd protected her from Luther; they were even. Married to her, he'd been able to leave the barracks and enjoy greater freedom to search the compound at night or meet with Bradley, but he no longer needed to pretend he cared. He hadn't denied using her and he'd never claimed to love her, but her heart refused to accept that was all there had been between them.

He opened his eyes briefly. "We'll talk later." He settled back against the rock wall and closed his eyes again. Reaching out, she placed her hand on his chest and felt heavy, even breathing. He turned away from her, leaving her hand to fall idly to her side.

"Mrs.—"

"Carly, just Carly." She continued to watch Wolf in disbelief. He'd rejected her when she'd reached for him. Without answering any of her questions, he'd fallen asleep. Had she imagined out of fear and loneliness that he'd come to love her, that there was more between them than being trapped together in an ugly situation? Didn't he feel any tender emotion at being reunited?

"Carly, he's exhausted." Bradley's voice held gentle under-standing. "He hasn't slept for two days. He must sleep now because in a few hours we have to move, and he's the only one who can get us past Isaac and off this mountain. A helicopter is being sent to pick us up in twenty-four hours. The problem is it's a two-day hike to where we're supposed to meet it."

Nodding her head, Carly turned away; she couldn't speak past the lump in her throat. She found a place to sit with her back against the stone wall of the cave where she could think and wait for dark-ness. She slid to the ground and blinked back tears. She wouldn't cry. Later, she promised herself. Later she would mourn for Josh. Later she would cry for the man she would love forever, but who had only needed her for a little while.

Numbness took over until she couldn't feel embarrassment when Daniel asked Bradley why his hands were two colors and if he were one of the black devils Sister Hampton said would get them if they didn't memorize all the Bible verses she assigned them. She couldn't muster the strength to explain to Daniel that all races are God's children. She was vaguely aware of Bradley giving each of the children a small pull-tab can of peaches and a foil packet of trail mix. When he insisted she eat some, too, she didn't resist. She would need strength for the ordeal ahead. Even with the help of the two men, her endurance would be taxed to the limit to get the children to safety.

"I don't understand," she said. "If Isaac has men posted further downriver, why don't we just follow Short Creek to the upper lake? It's a shorter distance to where a plane can land to pick us up." Going back up the river, right past the compound, sounded dangerous to Carly.

"It's also a highly exposed route and one with which Isaac is familiar. He's obviously keeping it under surveillance and can land his own plane on the lake." Wolf clearly didn't like his judgment questioned. He'd been giving orders and sounding cross ever since he awakened. It seemed to her he was also going to great lengths to avoid touching her.

After sleeping until dusk, he'd left the cave for about an hour, then came back to tell them they had to cross the river before the moon came up. Once on the other side, they'd head upstream toward a narrow canyon above the compound. It was too dark in the cave to see his face now, but Carly didn't have to see to know Wolf wouldn't accept any argument.

"Come on, kids." She urged the children to their feet.

"I want to wait for Daddy." Petra's voice trembled.

"Your daddy can't go with us right now." Carly hugged the child to her. Had she been wrong not to tell the children?

"Did Daddy and Rachel get burned up in our house?" Daniel had put his observations together. She'd told them they couldn't go to the cabin because Isaac had burned it. Only now was the little boy connecting the fire with his father.

Petra began to sob and Carly dropped to her knees to comfort both children.

"Is Daddy dead?" Daniel's eyes were round and scared. Petra gulped noisily as she cried.

"Stop that!" Wolf pulled the children from her arms. "I told you that no matter what, you mustn't make any noise."

"But, Wolf, Josh is their father. They can't help crying. Just give them a minute to get their grief under control."

"Not for any reason. Understand Petra? Daniel?" Both children whispered a subdued yes, but tears continued to stream down their cheeks.

Carly wanted to protest. Wolf needn't be so harsh with them. They couldn't be expected to not react at all to their father's death. She bit back her own grief for the children's sake. Wiping their eyes, she whispered words of encouragement and reminded them to be brave. She didn't contradict Wolf's stricture. Their lives might depend on their silence—and their obedience.

"Carly, the cabin was already in flames when I got there," Bradley whispered. His voice revealed real anguish. "It was too late to do anything, but they might have gotten out before I arrived."

Carly could tell he didn't believe they had, but was only trying to give her hope and comfort.

Deep blackness offered concealment as they emerged from the cave. It wasn't far to a hidden canoe. She was glad it was one of old Frank's handcrafted canoes rather than one of Isaac's aluminum ones. Sensing Daniel was about to ask if the canoe belonged to the old trapper, she clapped her hand over his mouth until he nodded his head, signaling he'd remembered he mustn't speak.

Three adults and two children were a heavy load for the small craft, decreasing its speed and flexibility. Wolf knelt at the front and Bradley at the back with Carly seated in the middle and both children, one in front of the other, between her legs. She held her breath as the canoe began to glide into the pull of the river's current. She could only pray that if they were spotted from shore, the inky darkness would hinder a sniper's aim.

The current tugged at the overloaded canoe, pulling them into a diagonal crossing. In the deep channel on the south side, the river was quite tame in August except for the increased risk of exposed boulders. The roar of water rushing over and around rocks warned of the channel not far away. Only the straining muscles of the two men kept the canoe from succumbing to the powerful draw of the current that coaxed them relentlessly down-stream.

When the shore finally loomed ahead, Carly glanced nervously toward the sky. The blackness surrounding them was growing lighter. If the moon arose before they were off the water, it would expose their flight. Overhead she saw a faint sprinkling of stars. Soon the water would be bathed in a silvery sheen of stars and moonlight.

As soon as the canoe bumped against the gravely shore, Wolf leaped over the side to pull it up the bank. Bradley reached for Petra. Carly grasped Daniel, and jumped. She splashed through shallow water at the men's sides. Wolf hustled them into the security of the trees, then returned to hide the canoe.

"If the children can't keep up, carry them. Isaac has a patrol on the south side of the lake, so we'll go high to skirt them." Wolf whispered then set off at a blistering pace. He led them away from the shoreline and deep into the trees.

They climbed steep ridges and waded shallow streams. When Daniel's steps began to lag, Carly carried him. His sturdy body was heavy and several times she staggered. She glanced over her shoulder to see Petra on Bradley's back, her arms clasped around his neck. When her burden became too much, she placed Daniel back on his feet, but soon had to carry him again. Bradley never seemed to tire carrying Petra, and Carly wished Wolf would take Daniel for a little while, but he never offered. Perhaps scouting ahead as Wolf did would expose the child to more danger. If that were the case, she certainly wouldn't complain or let her aching muscles slow them down. Fear drove every thought save escape from her mind.

Carly's numb arms were beyond pain and her knees threatened to buckle with each step long before Wolf halted, but she never once asked him to slow the pace. He reached out an arm to stop her when she would have walked into him.

"We've passed the lake, and the river is about fifty feet down this slope." Wolf's voice was barely audible. "Bradley, keep going until you reach the cove where we stopped last night. I'll catch up to you there." His fingers brushed Carly's cheek so lightly she wasn't certain whether she'd only imagined his touch. Like a wraith, he faded into the trees and was gone.

She stared at the place where he had stood. One part of her mind screamed for him to come back, but her practical side kept her silent. She trusted Wolf. Looking back, her earlier doubts and suspicions seemed another lifetime. He would do whatever was necessary to get them to safety. He might not love her, but he would protect her and the children with his life.

Daniel squirmed to get down and Carly set him on his feet. The pace was slower now, but they continued to move steadily upstream. She had no idea what time it might be, but the moon had traversed more than two-thirds of its path across the sky by the time Bradley led them into the enveloping blackness beneath a slanting rock face.

"We'll wait here." Bradley lowered Petra to the ground.

Carly sank down beside her and leaned gratefully against the granite cliff. The children sprawled in the sandy earth and fell asleep with their heads on her lap. She smoothed a lock of hair beneath the hood of Petra's parka. Her love for them and the pride she felt for their steadfast courage brought tears to her eyes.

"Get some sleep if you can. I'll watch," Bradley urged, but Carly knew she wouldn't sleep until Wolf returned and they were miles away from Steeple Mountain.

She turned anxiously toward the water and peered into the darkness. Her arms ached and muscles twitched in her calves. The soles of her feet felt scalded. Now that they were no longer moving, she felt the deep chill of the night.

She wondered where Wolf had gone, but she didn't ask Bradley. Surely Wolf hadn't returned to the compound. *Please, God,* she prayed, *don't let him be caught.*

She never heard him arrive. He was just suddenly there beside them. He motioned toward the children, and without hesitation she picked up Daniel while Bradley scooped up Petra. At the water's edge she saw the dark outline of a canoe. Wolf held it steady while the rest of them boarded, then gave it a shove before leaping into the bow. Instead of returning to the river, Wolf guided the canoe up a side stream.

Kneeling in the bottom of the canoe, dampness seeped into the knees of her jeans. Searching around with her hand for the source of the moisture, she encountered a thick chunk of wadding. She glanced forward. Where had Wolf gotten this canoe? Did he know the bottom was torn and clumsily patched?

Again the men paddled while she held the children. With smooth, even strokes they moved soundlessly into the night. Overhead Carly could see a thin ribbon of star-studded sky. On either side loomed only darkness. Petra whimpered once and Carly pulled both children closer for warmth. Exhaustion teamed with the stillness of the night, and she shook her head to clear away creeping drowsiness.

It happened so gradually she wasn't aware of the blackness around her turning to gray until a faint, familiar sound alerted her senses. Already Wolf was pointing the canoe toward a cliff she could barely see. In moments, he ordered them to duck as the canoe slid beneath a tangle of bushes along the shore. The children awoke as leaves brushed their faces and branches poked their skin. Their small bodies shivered in the cold while an airplane swooped low above the canyon. The roar of its engines receded, then minutes later sounded again as the plane reversed its route.

For long minutes no one moved, then Wolf spoke tersely. "Daylight is almost here. We only need ten minutes more on the water. Let's go." Branches snapped and Carly bent over the children to protect their faces as Wolf dug in his oar. The canoe moved faster and a cold wind brought tears to Carly's eyes. Tendrils of hair pulled free from her braid and whipped about her face. The water in the bottom of the canoe seemed to be getting deeper, and there was nothing but her hands to scoop it out.

A muted roar reached Carly's ears, and she strained to see if Isaac's plane was returning. The narrow canyon was rapidly growing lighter, and they would be sitting ducks if a plane flew over now. But it didn't sound quite like Isaac's plane. Surely they weren't approaching rapids. Her eyes moved automatically to Wolf. She could only see the back of his head and watch the motion of his back and shoulders as he dug the oar into the water, pulled, lifted, and dug in again. He showed no sign of altering their course.

The canyon veered sharply to the right and once they rounded the bend, the roar became deafening. A cascade of water spilled from the cliff at the blind end of the canyon. A deep, clear pool, ringed by boulders and a few straggling bushes filled the pocket between towering cliffs.

Carly's heart sank. They were trapped in a dead-end canyon without even trees or shrubs to protect them from Isaac's relentless search. Wolf headed straight for the most jagged cliff. As they drew closer she could see it wasn't quite as perpendicular as she'd first thought, but it looked impossible to scale and offered nothing in the way of a hiding place.

There was no possibility of speaking over the roar of the waterfall. Wolf used his hands to give directions, and Carly soon found herself huddled behind a boulder with the children while Wolf slashed deep gashes in the canoe and Bradley heaped rocks in it to sink it to the bottom of the pool. For the first time Carly realized Wolf's pack lay beside Bradley's, and there were two rifles beside them. Carly kept her own rifle clasped tightly in her hand.

Sometime during the night Wolf had changed clothes, put on his leather jacket, and collected his personal effects. She scanned his face as he hurried toward her, seeing deep furrows around his mouth and white lines radiating from the corners of his eyes. He looked exhausted and she longed to go to him, but his eyes never met hers and her heart plunged deeper into a pool of pain.

Bradley touched her shoulder and she turned to see him holding a coil of narrow nylon rope. Several loops crossed one shoulder and circled his waist. He looped the rope around Petra to form a harness, then did the same to Carly and Daniel before passing the loose end to Wolf. They were going to scale the cliff.

Petra and Daniel would be fine, she assured herself. They were as agile as mountain goats, but she didn't like heights herself. Crossing that chasm on a log in the dark last night had been a nightmare. Only the strange illusion that somehow Wolf was beside her had made it possible. Well, he was with her now and somehow she would do the impossible.

Wolf watched Carly gaze up at the cliff and knew it frightened her. He also knew she'd climb it anyway. He felt a surge of pride. She was tired and bedraggled with her loose braid straggling down her back and bright red scratches crisscrossing her face and hands, but she'd never looked more beautiful. After trekking across the mountain two nights in a row, she was still doing what had to be done to protect her young nephew and niece. Her loyalty and devotion to her family endeared her more firmly in his heart. He wished he could help her more. He should have been the one lugging Daniel around the lake. He glanced down at his side in disgust.

"Wolf," Bradley tapped his shoulder. "If you haven't already ripped open your wound again, going up that mountain will. The patch job I gave you won't hold after all you've gone through tonight. Let Carly dress it again before we start up."

"No, there isn't time." Wolf spoke sharply. He didn't want Carly to know. He didn't want anything to distract her from looking after the kids or protecting herself. Besides, what would she use for dressing? She and the kids had no spare clothing and he'd used Bradley's change of clothing when he'd crawled out of the river on the verge of hypothermia yesterday morning. He'd had to swim the river again a few hours ago to retrieve his pack and the canoe so he was wearing his own change of clothes now and the few first-aid supplies in his pack wouldn't cover the hole ripped in his side.

Carly glanced over at the two men who stood close together for several precious seconds and appeared to argue. Suddenly Bradley stepped back, picked up his pack, and started up the mountain. Wolf fell in behind her, and she wondered if it was her imagination or had he stumbled, then quickly righted himself?

Carly had never felt so exposed and vulnerable in her life as she struggled up the steep precipice. She expected Isaac to fly by at any moment and swat them like flies on a wall.

"Here," she saw Bradley mouth the word as he held out his hand to clasp Petra's small hand and swing her to the ledge where he clung. He tightened the line around a large rock to give Carly a better purchase as she followed them up. She turned to pull Daniel up behind her, and Wolf thrust the little boy into her arms. Wolf grasped the taut line in his right hand and literally walked up the rock.

They were almost to the top when they ran out of narrow ledges and protrusions. Almost ten feet of perpendicular, slick rock separated them from the top. Carly glanced back the way they'd come. It was a mistake. Nausea churned in her stomach. They couldn't go back, but she couldn't see any way to go on.

Her eyes lit on Petra. The little girl huddled against the hard rock and her eyes were round and pleading. When she began to vomit, Carly forgot her own fear. She reached instinctively for her niece to keep her from falling. There wasn't room enough to hold the child. All Carly could do was steady her, then wipe her chalky face.

Over and over she glanced at the sky expecting Isaac's plane to reappear. There wouldn't be much warning. Though the roar of falling water had lessened as they climbed, it would still mask the sound of the plane until it was almost overhead. Well, she wasn't going to sit here waiting for Isaac to spot them. They could at least boost the children to safety. She turned to urge Wolf to assist her and saw him lift Daniel toward Bradley.

After Wolf released himself and Daniel from the rope, he shouted instructions in the kid's ear before passing him up to Bradley. He could see Petra was sick and Carly was occupied trying to help her, but he'd have to get the ropes off them.

Over Carly's head the two men's eyes met. Wolf could read the concern in Bradley's. He tried to assure his friend that he was okay, that he'd make it, but Bradley wasn't convinced. The wound in his side was bleeding again. He could feel wetness spreading down his side and he feared it would soak through his jacket and Carly would notice before they reached the meadow.

While Bradley retied the rope around Daniel, Wolf tossed the end to Carly and indicated she should untie herself and Petra. Her hands shook, but she did as he instructed. Bradley pulled on the rope until it lay coiled at his feet before picking up Daniel and setting him on his shoulders. Wolf eased forward to bolster Carly and Petra. Together they watched Daniel grasp Bradley's hair and slowly rise to a standing position. He stiffened his legs and Bradley boosted him higher. In seconds he scrambled over the edge and disappeared, trailing the rope behind him.

When Daniel reappeared, Wolf heaved a sigh of relief. He hoped the boy had anchored the rope around a big enough tree. He urged Petra forward, keeping a grasp on her jacket until Bradley's hand closed around hers. She followed the same route Daniel had, up to Bradley's shoulders, and over the cliff lip. Wolf signaled for both children to move back, then he reached for one end of the rope. His strength was too far spent to act as counterweight; he'd have to go first.

The cliff face wasn't too bad for someone accustomed to climbing. He tested his weight against the rope, then fingers and toes found cracks and fissures. One last pull placed him over the top and he felt a sharp stab in his side. He could feel wetness pooling under his jacket, but he couldn't stop.

After checking that the rope was secure around a sturdy tree trunk, he signaled for Bradley to send up Carly. He pulled from above and with the tree acting as a pulley, Bradley pulled from below. If he'd had the strength, he would have whooped for joy when Carly's blond head appeared. Minutes later she stood beside him. Their eyes met and she smiled. He was too tired to let go of the rope and wrap his arms around her the way he'd like, but no matter what happened, when they got back to civilization he'd do everything in his power to persuade her to stay with him. She dropped her eyes and ran toward the children.

Shaking off a wave of dizziness, Wolf approached the edge of the cliff to drop the rope down to his partner. Bradley stood with his feet planted on the narrow ledge, his face turned up to them. Wolf lifted the rope and far in the distance a slight movement caught his eyes. A motorboat was negotiating the narrow canyon passage. In less than a minute it would enter the deep pool below and Bradley would be discovered.

"Bradley! Hurry!" he yelled as the rope dropped over the side. "Carly, help me!" He was unsure whether his words would reach either of them. His panic seemed to communicate to Bradley, who instantaneously scrambled upward as Wolf threw his weight against the other end of the rope.

The rope burned his hands and he felt it begin to slip, then Carly was beside him, pulling hand over hand. One of Bradley's hands reached for a clump of weeds just as the first shot rang out. He lunged forward and rolled onto flat ground. An angry curse reached Wolf's ears over the roar of the falls. Luther!

The soft thwack of a bullet hitting a tree, followed by a volley of shots ricocheting off rocks lent strength to his muscles. Reaching deep inside himself, he found the stamina to go on. Luther would show them no mercy and he wouldn't hesitate to kill. He had to get Carly back, away from the cliff. He grasped her around the waist and rolled into the brush with her body locked against his.

When Wolf stopped rolling, Carly lay sprawled atop him, gasping for breath. She was too scared to draw a breath for several seconds.

"Are you okay?" Bradley was upon them, rapidly coiling the rope as he walked.

"Yes," Carly gasped as she struggled to her feet. They had to run. It wouldn't take as long for Isaac's soldiers to scale the cliff as it had for Wolf and Bradley to help the children and herself make it to the top.

"Let's get out of here." Wolf sounded winded and his movements appeared sluggish. She must have knocked the breath from him when he pulled her clear of the gunfire.

"Where are the children?" She followed Wolf deeper into the trees.

"Right here." Daniel and Petra charged from their hiding place.

"We heard shooting." The fear was back in Petra's eyes.

Wolf set off due south in long, smooth strides. Petra jogged behind him, followed by Daniel. Several times Carly twisted her neck to check behind and thanked God each time she saw only Bradley bringing up the rear. Wolf paused and Carly heard crashing in the distance. Their pursuers were following through the brush. She urged the children to greater speed.

They topped a small rise and Petra squealed. Tears burned Carly's eyes. They'd made it. There before them in a wide meadow squatted the helicopter.

"Are we going to ride in that?" Daniel's eyes gleamed with excitement.

"Run for it!" Wolf shouted as he motioned to her to go ahead. "Get the children aboard!" He and Bradley stepped off the trail, rifles at the ready. Carly tossed her own rifle toward Wolf, grabbed the children's hands, and began to run. The moment they left the trees, two men with rifles leaped out of the chopper to take up a protective stance on either side of the door and the craft's rotors began to turn. Less than a dozen steps into the open, she felt a heavy pull on her arm as Daniel catapulted to the ground.

"Keep running, Petra!" She released her niece's hand and dropped beside Daniel. His leg was twisted at a frightening angle, but before she could lift him, Bradley was beside her. He scooped up the child in one swift motion and sprinted for the chopper with Carly at his heels. He passed Petra halfway across the open space. Carly grasped the girl's hand and together they ran the remaining distance. One of the agents helped them aboard while the other continued to scan the trees. Carly glanced behind her once. There was no sign of Wolf.

Daniel whimpered and immediately Carly knelt beside him. His face was pinched and white, but he grinned heroically back at her. Someone offered her a first-aid kit and she reached for a pair of scissors to split his pant leg. The unmistakable sound of rifle fire stilled her hands.

Wolf! Wolf was out there alone! Agony tore at her soul. She rose to her feet. Blindly she turned toward the open door. Through the dust stirred by the whirling chopper blades, three figures emerged, bent nearly double. A fourth trailed behind. Two agents helped the third man board. His face was caked with dirt and blood-shot eyes stared back at her from black holes. Wolf! Had he been hit? She started toward him.

"Look after Daniel," he spoke harshly and turned away from her to take the seat beside the pilot.

Stunned, she stared after him. Once again, he'd pushed her away. She closed her eyes and tried to block out the pain she'd felt at his rebuff. She'd have to be content that he was still alive. Gathering her strength, she turned back to Daniel and caught a glimpse of Bradley ducking under the rotors. She hadn't even realized he'd gone back for Wolf. Her eyes stung. She would love Bradley forever for his devoted friendship to Wolf. The agents turned to help him aboard, and before they could even secure the door, the pilot began his ascent.

A burst of gunfire sounded in the distance, but it was smoth-ered by the steady beat of the chopper blades. Carly's hands shook and tears choked her throat. It was over; the children were safe. She longed to go to Wolf, lay her head against his strong chest, and feel the comfort of his arms. But she didn't dare.

She made Daniel as comfortable as possible and prayed the flight would be short. She was distantly aware of Bradley strapping Petra into a seat and talking softly to her. The engine vibrated and she was aware of the sensation of motion, but her heart felt like a block of wood. She questioned whether her own exhaustion and the traumatic events of the past forty-eight hours were making her unreasonable. Was she overreacting? She didn't think so. Wolf had had his hands full all night and he was exhausted. He'd saved their lives and she was grateful. But something else was wrong. Wolf was deliberately distancing himself from her, and he'd been doing it since the moment he'd crawled inside the river cave.

She immobilized Daniel's leg and assured him he was the bravest boy in the whole world, her heart aching for Wolf the entire time. They hadn't really talked about the night she'd followed him; had her fear and anger that night convinced him it would be best if they separated? Had her fear and lack of faith destroyed the love they might have shared? She needed the touch of his hand, one kind word, one little sign that he considered her more than part of his job. But she knew he wouldn't give it.

Fifteen

The big military-style chopper landed to a flurry of wailing sirens and a rush of attention. Two orderlies clambered aboard. They lifted Daniel from Carly's arms and carefully moved him to a stretcher. Grabbing Petra's hand, she hurried after them. As she stepped onto the tarmac someone tried to shove her into a wheelchair, but she resisted.

Once inside the small hospital, she and Petra refused to leave Daniel's side until a doctor had examined him. Carly paced the floor outside X-ray, then held Daniel's hand while the doctor set his leg. Petra slumped on a chair, but refused to go anywhere with the nurse who wanted to clean her up and give her something to eat. They stayed beside Daniel until his gurney was wheeled into a small room, and he was transferred to a hospital bed where he promptly fell asleep.

At a small sound Carly looked toward the door, hoping Wolf had come looking for her. She was disappointed to see the doctor standing there.

"All right, ladies, who's next?" He turned to Carly and Petra with a warm smile. "I'm the only doctor available, so you'll have to take turns."

"I didn't fall down." Petra announced primly while her hand reached for Carly's.

"It looks to me like you might have tangled with a bush." The doctor smiled as he reached for the little girl. Petra stuck her hand behind her back and glared suspiciously back. Carly smiled apologetically and took her niece's hand. Petra clung to Carly as the doctor walked them down the hall and swung her up to sit on the examining table. He reached in a drawer and handed Petra a mirror. She gazed into it solemnly for several minutes then a smile tilted one corner of her mouth.

"I look funny," she giggled.

Her matted braids sprouted twigs and grass, and her dirt-smudged face had a long, blood-caked scratch running down her cheek. Carly's heart contracted. Petra didn't look funny. She looked brave and tired, and oh so precious.

"I think you need a bath." Carly put her arm around Petra and gave her a hug.

"I think I need a hamburger."

The doctor laughed. "As soon as the nurses get you cleaned up and tucked in bed, you can have two hamburgers, french fries, and the whole works! And that goes for you too," the doctor turned to Carly.

"I'd like to find Wolf—Mr. Wolverton, then I'll get a motel room for the night."

"No way, lady. I've got orders to see that you receive everything you need right here, and that includes food, a bed, and an examination."

"But Wolf—"

"Not until morning."

No amount of persuasion would change his mind. Besides, if Wolf had wanted to see her, he would've come to her by now. It was a small hospital, not more than forty beds. Wolf could have found her.

After the examination she was assigned a room across the hall from the one the children shared. A nurse brought her a tray and Carly picked at her food. She couldn't eat. Too many thoughts crowded into her head. Finally she set down her fork. She'd lived with fear so long, she couldn't accept the reality of being off Steeple Mountain. Petra and Daniel were safe. But what about the other children?

She screwed her eyes shut, but the pictures came anyway. Before her she could see the cabin in the little clearing, now a smoldering pile of rubble. A sob escaped her throat. Josh, oh Josh, why had he been drawn to Isaac's world of hate? Was it because there had been a flaw inside him that allowed him to hate a whole race of people because of a few drug-crazed adolescents? She believed he had begun to change and that he had begun to regret his involvement with the cult. But now she'd never know if he was really the concerned, self-sacrificing brother she'd loved all her life, or the harsh, hate-filled man she'd known the past few months. Tears streamed down her face.

She wished Wolf would come. Perhaps he wouldn't come. She tried to chase away the doubt, but it persisted in sneaking into her mind. He probably had to report to his superiors. She'd heard police work was more than half paper work. Perhaps he didn't want to come. He'd married her to ensure a place for himself inside the compound and to gain the privacy and greater freedom of living in a cabin. He cared about her; she knew he did. But did he care enough to want to continue their marriage in the real world? She didn't know.

He wouldn't be deliberately cruel. Perhaps he thought quietly walking away would be the kindest way to let her know he wanted to return to his old life and that she was free to get on with hers.

The peace and quiet of the small hospital, the drawn shades, and intense exhaustion finally won. Her eyes closed against her will. Resisting sleep became impossible for her exhausted body. Her last thought as sleep claimed her was of Wolf. She remembered the shots fired before Wolf boarded the helicopter and his haggard appearance. Her heart felt like lead as she faced the possibility he couldn't come to her. She willed herself to climb out of bed to go search for him, but her weary limbs wouldn't obey.

When she awoke, it was morning and she could feel a wet spot on her pillow beneath her cheek. She told herself she should get up and check on the children. She'd have to talk to them about Josh and help them deal with their grief. Fresh tears spilled down her cheek. They were safe now from Isaac, and Wolf had all the evidence he needed to close the compound and send Isaac to prison, but how was she going to face life without Josh? Or Wolf? *Especially Wolf,* her heart added with a painful twist.

"May we come in?"

Carly's heart lurched. She was hearing things. The voice

coming from the doorway sounded like . . . Her eyes widened. "Josh!" He stood in the doorway holding Petra. Beside him was Rachel.

"Look, Aunt Carly. I got crutches." Daniel lurched toward her.

"But how . . . ?" She leaped out of bed and ran across the room to throw herself in her brother's arms. "Oh, Josh," she sobbed. "I thought you were dead."

"I know, Carly." He hugged her tightly. "I've spent the past two days worried sick about you and the children and hating myself for placing you in danger. We didn't know until this morning whether you were still in the compound or if Wolf had been able to get you out. I tried to bribe Reuben to take Rachel to safety and let me go back for you, but he said you'd gone. I'll never forgive myself for placing you in jeopardy."

"I'm just glad you're not involved with the cult anymore. You're not, are you?" She glanced nervously toward Rachel.

Josh took Carly's face between his hands. Gently his thumb brushed away a lingering tear. "No, Carly. I've been foolish and stupid, but I no longer have any connection with Isaac's group. Rachel never did. She's the one who made me see him for what he really is, and I realize now that violence knows no racial boundaries. Isaac has held her against her will with threats against Benjy for two years. Since the day she agreed to be my wife, I've searched for a way to get her free of her father, but I never realized the extent of his madness until he held you and my own children ransom to ensure my cooperation in building his bombs."

"How did you escape the fire?" Her head was spinning.

"We would have been trapped if it hadn't been for old Reuben."

"Reuben?"

Josh reached out an arm to Rachel and pulled her into their embrace. "We knew some time ago that Isaac wanted us out of the way so he could control Rachel's money through Petra and Daniel, but we thought he would wait until we got to San Francisco to try to get rid of us. Rachel managed to get a message out to her attorney once, and we got our hopes up when we heard two federal agents had been seen on the mountain. When nothing came of it, we made our own plans to escape once we got to Seattle.

"When Reuben appeared at the cabin in the middle of the night and insisted we leave at once, we thought he was crazy. He told us Isaac had told him to load gasoline in a canoe earlier that day and that men would be at the cabin before dawn to burn it down. The stench of gasoline on his clothing was so strong we couldn't doubt him."

Carly hugged them both. "But how did you get away?"

"Reuben had a couple of canoes. We were miles down the river before daybreak. You should have seen us," Rachel laughed, "Reuben, Josh, me, and fourteen red chickens in one canoe, towing the second canoe heaped with supplies."

"He took the chickens with him?"

Behind her Josh roared with laughter. "He made it clear, he wasn't stealing your chickens. He said you'd put him in charge of them, and he'd become quite partial to 'em."

"When we met a squadron of reservation police headed up the river, he offered them two of the chickens to take us off the mountain." Rachel picked up the story again. "They accepted us, but refused the chickens, and the last we saw of Reuben, he and the chickens were headed up a side creek into another wilderness area."

"We need to go now, Carly." Josh smiled happily. "We've got a motel room nearby. I've got a lot of explaining to do to Petra and Daniel, and we all need to rest. We'll see you again in a few hours. As soon as Daniel can travel, Rachel and I are buying a little farm in Wisconsin. We'd like you to come with us if you'd like to, but if you decide to stay with Wolf, we'll understand." He wrapped his arms around her and hugged her tight again. The old Josh was back.

"I'll think about it," she promised.

She sat back down on the bed and watched Josh and Rachel walk away arm in arm down the hall. When they reached the outside door, Josh picked up Daniel and Petra took Rachel's hand. No matter what happened she couldn't go with them. She'd always love them, she'd write and call them, but she couldn't live with them. It wouldn't be fair to Rachel, and in the long run it wouldn't be best for the children. Rachel was their mother now. But Carly couldn't stop the tears that rolled down her cheeks or the sobs that shook her shoulders.

She thought longingly of Wolf. She needed him. Giving up the children would be unbearably hard, but she could do it because it was best for them. What she couldn't do was give up Wolf. She felt disgusted with herself. Why was she sitting around weeping when she should be going after him? She reached for a tissue to wipe her nose. If Wolf thought he could just walk away, he had another think coming. She'd go after him, and when she found him she'd tell him she loved him. He might not care, but he was going to know! She wiped away the last of her tears.

"What's this?" A matronly nurse bustled into the room. "We can't have tears on a morning like this. Your man's out of surgery and doing just fine. You should—"

"Surgery! Wolf was in surgery?" Carly leaped to her feet. "Why?"

The nurse staggered backward as Carly stalked toward her. "Why, he . . . uh, he was shot," she stammered. "The bullet went right through his side, but he did quite a bit of damage to the wound running and swimming and climbing mountains. He lost a lot of blood, too."

"Where is he?" Carly demanded.

"Room 216." The nurse pointed vaguely. "But you can't—" Carly didn't wait for her to finish. If she passed anyone in the hall, she didn't notice.

At the door to room 216, she stopped, suddenly shy. From inside the room she could hear voices. She peeked inside to see Wolf half-sitting in a hospital bed. He reclined against the elevated head talking to Bradley, who sat in a chair at his side. An IV drip was attached to one arm. She drank in the sight of him. He needed a haircut, but his mustache looked freshly trimmed. Her eyes dropped to the wide bandage circling his chest, and she felt a stab of pain.

"Come on in." Bradley motioned to her. Wolf turned toward her and echoed his partner's words. Even with a bandage across his chest he looked wonderful. Too afraid of what she might see there, she couldn't quite meet his eyes.

Belatedly she became aware of her bare feet and the heavy mass of her unbrushed hair hanging in tangles to her waist. She wore a faded, shapeless hospital gown that could come untied at any moment. But when Wolf held out his hand, she forgot everything as she rushed across the room.

"Why didn't you tell me you were hurt?" she cried as his arm circled her waist. And when he pulled her unresisting body onto the bed beside him, she buried her face in his neck and shook with sobs.

"Don't cry, sweetheart, don't cry," he whispered into her hair. "I'm fine."

"Why didn't you tell me? I could have helped you." Her tears increased as she wailed softly, "I'm a nurse, I should have known without being told."

"There wasn't anything you could do. Bradley wrapped the wound before he found the cave. I'm just sorry I wasn't able to help you more with the kids."

Carly turned a tearstained face toward Bradley. "Thank you," she whispered. "I'm not sure we could have made it without you. You were wonderful with Daniel and Petra."

"They're great kids." He smiled warmly, but appeared slightly embarrassed at her praise.

Carly was quiet for several minutes, then she had to ask. "What about the other children? The ones in the compound. Do you know if they are safe? And did your men catch Isaac?"

Wolf looked at Bradley. "You might as well tell her."

"Marshal Stewart arrived at the compound just as Isaac was preparing to board his plane. Isaac opened fire and the agents returned it. He was wounded, but managed to get the plane in the air, though he wasn't able to clear the trees. He and one other man died in the crash. Most of Isaac's men were scattered looking for you, so the officers met little resistance at the compound."

"What about the children?" Carly urged him to continue.

"They're all safe. They and their families are being transported to Boise. It will take a few weeks to sort out all of the details, but charges will only be brought against those who were involved in weapon smuggling or in the conspiracy to blow up Candlestick Park."

"Deborah has lost all touch with reality," Wolf added quietly. "Stewart is recommending that charges against her be dropped on condition she receive custodial psychiatric care. If Rachel is willing,

Benjy will be turned over to her and she can file for legal guardianship."

"I don't doubt she'll want him, and I know Daniel and Petra will love having a little brother." Carly smiled in relief. "What about the others? The ones hunting for us?"

"The reservation police rounded up about thirty of them, mostly around the cabin," Bradley said. "Luther and the two men who followed us to the meadow made their way back to the compound where they were arrested. There's enough evidence in addition to Josh's testimony to put Luther away for a long time."

Carly grimaced at the mention of Luther's name.

"The Washington state police intercepted the bombs," Bradley continued, "and as far as Wolf and I are concerned, we've been told to consider the case closed and go home. As anyone else from the compound makes their way out of the mountains over the next few weeks, they'll be taken in for questioning."

Wolf pulled Carly closer and his mustache brushed her cheek. It felt right to snuggle against him.

"Guess I'd better be going." Bradley rose to his feet. He gave them a jaunty grin and left, closing the door behind him. For several minutes neither Wolf nor Carly moved. Carly hesitated to risk shattering the warmth and closeness of the moment. Finally gathering her courage, she spoke.

"Wolf, there's something I have to say even if you don't want to hear it." She took a deep breath then let the words rush out. "I love you. I thought I would die when I thought you'd gone away, and I wouldn't see you again."

"I wasn't sure you'd want to see me again, but I wouldn't have left without trying to convince you to go with me." He smiled into her eyes and pulled her closer. "You didn't have any say about marrying me, but I couldn't let the woman I love marry someone else. And for all my good intentions to give you a choice once you were free of the compound, I hope you want to stay with me, because I can't let you go."

"Do you love me?"

"Need you ask?" Wolf lifted her face. His thumb brushed the side of her mouth, then his lips settled on hers. When he lifted his head several minutes later, he whispered, "Now do you believe I love you?"

"Yes." Carly snuggled happily against Wolf's uninjured side.

"Now where was I?" Wolf smiled. "Oh, I know. I was just getting ready to tell you about the family ranch. If you think you'd like to spend the rest of your life with me, we could go there to live. It's in a peaceful little valley in Montana."

Carly turned so she could see his face. "I thought you were a dedicated lawman."

"I plan to leave the Service." Something in his voice told her the decision was breaking his heart.

"But you love being a deputy marshal."

"I love you more." Like sunrise over the mountain, Carly's heart filled with streamers of joy. She knew he spoke the truth.

"You don't have to give up being a marshal to have me." She leaned forward until her lips brushed his. She left little butterfly kisses across his mustache.

"I think I do." He held her away from him so he could see her clearly. Carly's heart ached at the sadness in his eyes. Wolf's voice was gruff. "My pa was head of mine security and my brother, Jeb, a county sheriff, both lawmen. They both died in the line of duty, leaving young widows to struggle alone to raise their kids. I swore I'd never put a woman through the suffering Ma and Katie have gone through."

"I'm sorry." She brushed her fingertips against his cheek. "But did you ever ask your mother or sister-in-law if they regretted that their husbands were lawmen?" She rushed on without waiting for an answer. "Wolf, you said I was a lot like your mother and maybe I am. There's something you don't know about women like us. We'd rather spend a short time with a man who is happy with his work, than forty years with a man who hates his job. I love you, all of you, and being a marshal is part of who you are. It's peace officers like you who make all of our dreams of a better life, free of violence and bigotry, possible. I'd be insulted if you didn't think me strong enough to be a peace officer's wife."

Wolf's arms tightened around her; she thought she detected a touch of moisture on his cheek, but there was no mistaking the tenderness with which he held her against him. There would be time when they were old and gray for his peaceful mountain valley.

"Are you sure that's what you want?" Wolf whispered as his hands caressed her cheeks.

"There's one other thing I want."

"What else do you want?" His mustache tickled her lips.

"I'd like to get married again. This time by a preacher who teaches love and tolerance."

"I think that can be arranged, but first there's something you should know. About fifteen years ago Ma became a Mormon. She wanted all four of us boys to join, too, but we weren't interested. Well, I'm interested now. There were times out there on that mountain that I felt the only thing that got us through was God. I discovered my faith runs much deeper than I realized."

She was quiet so long, Wolf began to wonder if her ordeal had left her with an abhorrence to religion. Or maybe she'd heard that nonsense about Mormons being another radical cult and was afraid to associate with them.

When she finally spoke, her voice was husky with emotion. "I felt it, too. In spite of all the fear and worry, there were moments when I felt a spiritual awareness unlike anything I've ever known before. I don't want to lose that feeling. I don't know anything about being a Mormon, and after Steeple Mountain, I won't affiliate with any religious group until I study it thoroughly and know with all my heart that love and truth are basic tenets of that religion."

"Fair enough." Wolf smiled. "I don't think you'll be disappointed. Is there anything else you'd like?"

"I'd like a son." Her voice almost disappeared as she ran a finger lightly across the top edge of his bandage.

"That can be arranged, too, but we'd better postpone the technicalities until I get out of here." His mouth quirked upward at one corner.

"And let's name him Colin Powell Wolverton," Carly went on. She pressed a kiss to the scar on his shoulder.

"Something tells me you're going to get along just fine with Ma."

"I'm going to get along just fine with you, too." She lifted her head until her mouth met his.

Wolf released her reluctantly. "Then let's get moving. We've got a wedding to plan so we're checking out of here today. And I might as well warn you—Mormons don't believe in 'till death do us part.' They plan on the long haul, this life and the next one, too."

ABOUT THE AUTHOR

Jennie Hansen attended Ricks College and graduated from Westminster College in Salt Lake City, Utah. She has been a newspaper reporter, editor, and librarian, and is presently a technical services specialist for the Salt Lake City library system.

Her church service has included teaching in all auxiliaries and serving in stake and ward Primary presidencies. She has also served as a stake public affairs coordinator and ward chorister. Currently she is the education counselor in her ward Relief Society.

Jennie and her husband, Boyd, live in Salt Lake City. They are the parents of four daughters and a son.

Jennie has written three previous best-selling novels, *Run Away Home, When Tomorrow Comes,* and *Macady.* She is currently working on a sequel to *Run Away Home.*